BADGE
and
BLADE

BADGE
and
BLADE

B. R. VINEYARD

authorHOUSE®

AuthorHouse™
1663 Liberty Drive
Bloomington, IN 47403
www.authorhouse.com
Phone: 1-800-839-8640

Published by AuthorHouse   07/25/2012

ISBN: 978-1-4685-3989-9 (sc)
ISBN: 978-1-4685-3990-5 (e)

Library of Congress Control Number: 2012900100

Chapter 1

The man wore a black ski mask and carried a five-inch blade knife that gleamed in the moonlight. He crept closer to the bedroom window at the back of the red brick house and carefully peered inside. The young girl was sleeping soundly on her right side, turned away from him. There was a small nightlight that added a golden glow to the white walls. This was the teenager he had seen dashing up the front walk yesterday while he was staking out the house. The man in black took the knife and carefully pried up the window. When he placed the knife between his teeth, he carelessly nicked a spot on his lip. He wiped the blood with his gloved hand, sheathed the knife and proceeded to crawl through the window and quietly enter the bedroom. All he wanted was the money, jewelry, and, the best part—blood. A cruel sneer crossed his scarred face. His drug and sexual habits needed to be satisfied on a regular basis and it was apparent that his appetites were at their peak.

Suddenly, the young blond girl turned over toward the intruder and slowly opened her eyes. She blinked. When she saw the masked man standing over her, fear flashed across her pale face. As she opened her mouth to scream, a rubber-gloved hand was placed over it. She bit down hard, while the intruder fumbled for the knife. The next sound that came forth was the gurgling where the knife struck her throat and sliced through the carotid artery. She struggled briefly, made a gasping noise and then lay still. The man hesitated for a second, fascinated by the crimson liquid as it pumped from her lifeless body and pooled in the bedding. He wore an expression of excitement and pleasure.

That is her life oozing out of her body. I can let her live or let her die! I choose to let you die, bitch. He listened for any noises, hoping he hadn't disturbed her family then he turned to look around the untidy room. He heard a sound from the next room.

I'd better get out of here. He scanned the table and chest for anything of value. His adrenaline peaked. Excitement did that to him. Maybe he didn't need any drugs after all. He quickly grabbed a piece of jewelry lying on the nightstand, jumped out of the window and disappeared.

The next morning Sheriff Maxie D. O'Bryan was at the office double-checking murder cases that were pending when she received the call about the death of a teenage girl out in the country. For a few moments she indulged in her own selfish thoughts. *Another killing! That makes the third one in two years. Sometimes, I am not sure why I took this job. I hate seeing anyone murdered. Especially, young children. I have a 13 year-old daughter of my own. Darn that Matt for getting himself shot anyway! I could sure use your help right now. I need you, Matt.*

Matt O'Bryan had been the sheriff of Duncan Creek County fourteen years ago when he was shot and killed in the line of duty. They had been married for twelve years.

It all began when a gang of punks had penned Maxie down just outside the city limits near an old abandoned warehouse. She had called for backup. Matt wasn't on duty but heard the dispatch from their home and had answered the call

His life ended when a gang member came up behind Matt and shot him in the back. Just like that, he was gone! Maxie suffered from guilt, grief and her loss for a long time. If the truth were known, she was still struggling with these emotions. The loneliness was the worst part. She often thanked God for her daughter. For their sakes, she had to make a life without Matt. That was tough, but it was the real world and not very pretty at times.

Maxie O'Donough had been a curious child, with red hair, green eyes and a smile as big as Texas. That was what her dad often told her. She was blessed with three brothers, and considered a tomboy. However, they were crazy about "little sister," as she hated to be called. During the teen years, they teased, protected, scared off all the boys who showed an interest in dating her and fiercely loved her.

Maxie was born in the southern part of Texas, near the Gulf Coast. She was the third child of a family of four children. Her dad, John, was a policeman. Her mother, Alice, worked at City Hall.

The older two boys had entered law enforcement, following in their father's footsteps. After all, that is what they knew best. When she was growing up, she remembered the nights that her dad came home late, or not at all, because he was working on a case that he just couldn't leave. She knew her mother worried a lot and waited up or fitfully slept in a chair on those nights . . . wondering if he was dead or alive. Maxie was hesitant to make that worry a part of her own life. Instead, she decided to attend college with an open mind and perhaps she would discover another roadmap for her future.

Finally, Maxie made her career decision after her dad, John, was killed in a high-speed chase one dark, rainy night on his way home. His vehicle had collided with a cement bridge railing. She thought her world had ended but tried to stay strong for her mother.

Alice was an independent woman, with soft brown hair, a gentle voice and a quick smile. Perhaps all those late nights and worries had helped prepare her for the moment of her husband's death. Certainly, she had imagined it many times, although she pictured her John being shot, not mangled in a tragic automobile accident.

Maxie, too, understood that policing was a risky job. Upon the death of her dad, she realized she had always feared that some hoodlum would shoot him. It was a wake up call for Maxie. Life has no guarantee that one will live to old age whether one wears a badge or not. She felt compelled to continue the work of her father. He was a good man. She prayed she could be half the officer he had been.

Maxie attended the police academy after college graduation. She got a job on a beat in Houston. She was a good officer and her work was her life. Because she was a small-town girl, she was never content to live in a big city. To Maxie, Houston was a big city. Therefore, when her brother, Bobby, called her about an opening for a deputy sheriff in a small central Texas town, she eagerly applied and was accepted for the position.

Two years later, Matt O'Bryan came aboard. He was appointed sheriff when the current one retired. Matt was smart and aggressive. Although he was only four years older than Maxie, she looked up to him and had respect for his ability as an officer. Maxie was honored to be his deputy. By then, she had developed other, stronger feelings, for this man. When he entered a room, his eyes searched for her, then he would smile and make his way to her side. This made Maxie feel very special. One day, she realized she was as important to Matt as he was to her. A romance blossomed when they came together. Soul mates. That is how Maxie and Matt felt about their relationship. They were truly meant for one another.

Happily and in love, they were married at the local church in a quiet ceremony with a few friends and family present. Maxie got pregnant, immediately, which surprised both of them. They hadn't expected to have a baby at this time. It appeared that God had other plans.

However, Matt was ecstatic. "Just think, I will finally have that little boy that I've always wanted. I can teach him to hunt and fish with me. Wow!"

"Mister, what makes you think it will be a boy?" Maxie teasingly joked.

Matt looked surprised, and then he grinned. "Yeah, a little red-haired girl would be great! She would look just like her mother, who is the prettiest woman in eleven counties! Just think, I can take her on camp outs and teach her to hunt and fish!" he exclaimed excitedly. Maxie just shook her head in amazement. *Men!*

After Matt's death, the county commissioners came to her and offered her Matt's job as sheriff. She was ready to refuse but told them she would think about it. Maxie and Megan, her daughter, sat down that night and discussed the pros and cons of the job. *We could sure use the extra money a sheriff's salary would bring in.*

Megan encouraged her mother to do it. "That would be neat for Duncan Creek County to have a real lady for sheriff, Mom. Go for it! You know Dad would have approved.

"Yes, I suppose he would. It's such a responsibility and I don't want you to feel neglected either. I love you, Punkin, so will you promise to come tell me if I'm not spending enough time with you or when you have a problem of any kind?"

Megan nodded her head in agreement. "Sure, Mom, I promise."

"Okay, I'll tell the commissioners tomorrow that I'll accept the position." She stooped to plant a big kiss on Megan's freckled cheek and whispered, "Goodnight, Baby, I love you."

"I love you too, Mom . . . And, Mom, you'll make the best sheriff ever!"

God, help me, Maxie prayed, but she only smiled at Megan and left the frilly bedroom saying, "Thank you, sweetheart."

Chapter

Maxie sat silent and thoughtful for a moment. She couldn't imagine how she would feel if it were Megan who had been murdered. She shivered at the very thought.

I've got to get my deputies on this investigation. Poor Betty Meyers. What must she be going through . . . losing her only daughter so horribly.

She turned toward the door and called to Jack Rankin whose office was down the hall.

"Hey, Jack, we have another murder! Can you and Charlee run out and secure the scene? I have to make a few calls but I'll be out at the Meyers' place as soon as possible."

"Boss, you can bet on it. Another one killed, huh?" Jack had sensed from his boss' tone of voice that Maxie was upset. He walked up to the desk and glanced at the message lying there. "Suzanne Meyers? Oh, my gosh! She's a friend of my son, Jason. Lord, she is only seventeen!"

"I know." Maxie said as she looked at the concerned deputy.

"Charlee, let's go get that SOB!" He yelled as he quickly walked to the county vehicle with Charlee, his partner, hurrying along behind him. Breaking all the speed limits, they headed out to secure the murder scene ouside the edge of town.

Maxie just shook her head as the deputies left. *I hope they don't kill themselves going out there.*

Picking up the phone, she dialed the number of the Texas Ranger Bill Sullivan. He was the person to assist in investigating the crimes occurring in Duncan Creek County.

She smiled when he asked how she was doing. "I'm doing fine," she lied.

Bill was a good officer. She liked him. He was professional, thorough with his investigations and he was a bulldog after the criminal. She admired that about the man. Recently, they had worked closely on a case. Maxie had really gotten to know the ranger. He was kind. She wouldn't have thought that about Bill because he was a blunt, opinionated bastard at times and very good looking.

She sighed. *Forget that, I don't need a man to complicate my life right now.*

With a grim determination to get this killer behind bars and quickly, Maxie drove to the site of the crime, which was located about two miles outside of the city limits. She hated that the last two murders had not been resolved. Now, she had another one to worry about.

At five-feet, two inches tall, Maxie O'Bryan was a petite package of dynamite with green eyes, red hair, and a temper to match. She was thirty-nine and had hardened somewhat the past five years. She believed in her abilities as an officer and in herself, and projected a confident air wherever she was and whatever she was doing. Most folks admired the lady sheriff. However, some had the opinion that law enforcement was no place for a lady. Maxie shrugged it off as total bull shit. One thing for sure, she would not put up with a lot of that today . . . or, for that matter, anytime!

The four-door, Ram truck pulled up to the Meyer's residence where Maxie was greeted by a group of newspaper and television reporters waiting for a story. Tim Allen stood by the van from KOTV broadcasting station, leaning back with one ankle crossed over the other, looking very relaxed. Maxie wasn't fooled. He was an eager snoop and wanted a scoop.

Well, the gang is all here! That's no surprise, thought Maxie. *Stay cool, Sheriff, you know that you have to deal with the news media at every turn.* Maxie got out of the truck, put on a pleasant smile and approached the reporters, "Good morning, y'all," she drawled.

All of them began speaking at once, "Do you have any clues as to who did this? Any suspects, Sheriff?"

"This is the third murder we've had in two years. What is going on with our county? Don't we have enough law enforcement to work these murders and catch the killer? What's the deal?"

"Can you catch the killer this time, Sheriff?"

Maxie took a deep breath and said rather loudly, "Hey, back off. I just got here. I promise you that when I get the facts, I'll give what I can to you. I **will** catch the killer. Now, why don't you good folks step aside so I can do my job, and, please, give the family a little time in private for their grief. They've lost a daughter, for heaven's sake!"

Maxie pushed her way through the crowd and entered the home. The first thing she noticed was the strong odor of blood. *I never get use to the smell of death,* she thought. As she glanced around the living room, she noted how neat and clean everything appeared. Over in the west corner, her young deputy, Charlee Barnes, was bending over Betty Meyers, the mother, who was quietly weeping. Charlee was trying to console her as best she could under the circumstances. Maxie could see tears in the young woman's eyes as well.

Charlee was a young deputy just out of the police academy, and at the ripe age of 25, she was doing a good job. The big blond female had a lot to learn but she was steady, level-headed and had common sense. In Maxie's opinion, that balanced out her lack of experience.

This business is tough on her. Charlee has yet to learn not to get too involved with the victims. I guess, if I admitted it to myself, I'm not immune to the pain of grief either. She walked toward them. Maxie stiffened her back, bracing herself for the scene in the next room. She knew she had to stick to business to control her own emotions.

As Maxie walked passed Betty Meyers, she gently patted her shoulder, whispered a few words of consolation and hurried to find Jack at the murder scene.

Jack Rankin, a seasoned law enforcement officer, had been with the sheriff's department for approximately twenty-five years. Although he was nearing the age of fifty-five, he had no gray in his dark brown hair. Jack stayed physically fit with diet and exercise but still displayed a bit of a belly on him. He still had a "get to it" attitude, and there wasn't a lazy bone in his body. Maxie often wondered where he got his energy. He would spend late hours on a case and still be up bright and early, raring to go the next morning. She was fortunate to have Jack. He was a good deputy and seemed to harbor no resentment in having to answer to a lady sheriff. He had the experience Maxie needed and she appreciated him.

As Maxie approached the bedroom, she saw Jack standing in the doorway with a pensive look on his face and she greeted him coridally, placing a hand on his arm, "Well, Jack, what do you think?"

"Brutal! Plain and simple, Sheriff," he said as he shook his head in disbelief. "He slit that poor kid's throat! Apparently, the killer came through the bedroom window, knifed her and left. Can you figure that? Looks like the SOB gets his jollies from watching his victims bleed to death. Go figure! It probably happened so quickly that the poor girl never knew what hit her. I guess we can be thankful for that. She apparently bled out very soon after the knife hit the artery." Jack was visibly upset about it.

"Has the Justice of the Peace been by?" asked Maxie.

"Yeah, Johnny came right away. Of course, there was no doubt about his ruling. Dead is dead, just as murder is murder. The difference is we have to prove it."

"I know, Jack, that's just a matter of record," Maxie said as she turned away from the scene. She felt guilty when she looked at the blond, dead girl and in her heart of hearts she was relieved that it wasn't Megan, her own daughter. She held back the tears that quickly surfaced.

At that moment, Maxie heard the voice of Texas Ranger Bill Sullivan, as he purposefully waded through the group of reporters in the yard, threatening to send them home without a story in his booming voice of authority, if they didn't let him through. She smiled and went to greet him.

"Bill Sullivan, as usual, you're out here ordering my people around. Can't you behave yourself for a few minutes?" she stated as she smiled and stuck out her hand to greet him. "Seriously, Bill, I appreciate your coming so quickly to help."

"You know I wouldn't miss a chance to work with you, Max." he said, smiling down at her from his six-foot-five frame. *She is a beauty,* he thought, *and doesn't even know it.*

Most Texas Rangers could be spotted a mile away. Except for a few attorneys, they were the only ones wearing suits and ties. Bill Sullivan was a different breed. He blew into town wearing his faded Wrangler jeans; white western shirt, with out a tie and topped it off with his gray Silverbelly Stetson hat. His feet were shod in his best buffalo-hide cowboy boots. He drove a black, Silverado 1500, Chevrolet pickup truck with super cab, He was a Texan all the way through and proud of it!

As he gazed at Maxie, he was thinking. "*She is one nice little bundle. Sullivan, old boy, you better concentrate on the job you're here to do and not let this little stick of dynamite distract you. Time for that later.*

Even before Maxie's husband was killed, Bill had a full appreciation for the red head. He liked her nicely rounded hips and the perky breasts, not too big, but definitely a hand full or so he imagined. Not that he had tried to do anything about it, except to admire her from a distance. He had too much respect for Matt to do more than look. Matt had been a good man and a fine officer of the law.

After Matt had been gone for a year or so, Bill had tried to approach Max in a more personal way. That lady was cold . . . . no doubt about it. However, he was not a man to easily give up trying.

Maxie was very much aware of Bill, as a man, gazing down at her with those charming ocean blue eyes. They made her feel very uncomfortable. Thoughts traveled quickly though her mind, *What is there about this guy that makes me really think of myself as a woman, not as the sheriff? Whatever it is, I have to shake it off. This is a time for professionalism.*

Anyway, there's no place in my heart for a man and probably never will be. Hell, I won't ever consider getting involved with another officer! She quickly turned and led the ranger down the hall to the crime scene.

"Hello, Jack, haven't seen you in a while." Bill greeted Jack with a handshake, plus a friendly slap on his shoulder.

"Well, I've been around, working my butt off for her." He grinned and winked at Maxie as he stepped aside to let Bill come in to get a good look at the crime scene.

Bill always took his time checking out a murder, step by step. Some of his working partners called him Eagle Eye. The forty-two-year old ranger was one-eighth Shawnee Indian so perhaps the name fit him. He walked to the open window first and stuck his head out to check the ground for prints or clothing or thread snags. He was very careful not to touch anything that might reveal the fingerprints or other evidence of the killer.

He studied the ground below for several seconds, turned back to the Sheriff and stated, "There's a good half-footprint down there. Can you take care of that, Jack? Guess you may as well get somebody from CSI to come out?"

"Bill, I've call and they are on the way here as we speak." Jack replied.

Bill asked, "Nothing else was disturbed?" He continued to roam around the room checking for evidence.

Maxie couldn't tell if he was speaking to her or just talking to himself, as he was prone to do.

"Looks like the SOB entered the window, cut the girl's throat with a knife and left the way he came in. We can try to dust for prints on the window. That is our best bet. At least we have a place to start, with the partial prints outside on the ground. Not much to go on though . . . Max, what do you think? Got any suspects in mind? I'm, curious if the

MO on this case similar to those other murders. Do you think the killer in both cases is the same man?"

"Well, there are some similarities. In the other cases, the murderer usually came through the window, but took something as he left. Betty says, as far as she can tell, there isn't anything missing. The small safe in their office is intact. So, it's possible the killer gathered up some things, the victim woke up and he murdered her to keep her quiet. I think poor little Suzanne woke up and saw him just as he got into her bedroom. He had to kill her and maybe he got scared and left without stealing anything. Or, she tried to yell and that scared him. There doesn't appear to have been a struggle."

"None to speak of, but the eyes show fear, don't you think?" Bill questioned.

"Definitely! Bless her heart."

"Well, let's go over those other two unsolved cases that you are working on and see if we can make any connections."

Voices out front were evidence that the news media had confronted another visitor. "I believe the CSI crew has just arrived and they will want us out of here while they do their job. We better get going, Max," suggested the ranger.

He turned to Max and commented, "Hey, I haven't had any breakfast" Without waiting for a reply, he motioned, "Come on, Max, you can at least have a cup of coffee and keep me company while I have breakfast." The two officers walked out to the front room, extended condolences to Betty Meyers and her husband, Bob, and walked out together to greet the CSI agents.

Bill and Maxie talked to the two agents, briefly, then Maxie turned to Jack and instructed him to assist CSI in anyway he could. Charlee would stay and help Mr. and Mrs. Meyers make some phone calls or run errands for them. "Just keep the reporters out of here for now." Maxie stated.

As she stepped into the yard, she addressed the newspaper and television media, "Okay, you fellows. This is what I can tell you right now. It appears that Suzanne Meyers was murdered last night. The perpetrator climbed through the bedroom window and slashed her throat. At this time, we have no suspects. Now, please, go back to your office while CSI gathers the evidence. You'll be hearing from me at a later time. The family will give you a brief statement soon. Thank you for your concern in this case."

Maxie walked through the crowd, ignoring all the questions, got into her four-year old Ram truck, yelled at Bill to meet her at Jake and Minnie's Café, and spun out, kicking up gravel and dust in the faces of those left behind.

Damn, she is a feisty redhead! Bill thought as he observed Max leaving the driveway. *Nice!*

Bill smiled as he headed in the direction of a popular café in town.

There was the usual morning crowd gathered for a cup of coffee and some for breakfast. As Maxie and Bill entered, the waitress, and several of the patrons, warmly greeted them. In a small town, there are few strangers. Even if the locals don't know you when you come in, by the time you leave they will. Friendly and nosey was a good description of these customers, as well as the majority of the town.

Hank, an oversized trucker, was perched on a barstool at the counter. When he glanced into the mirror behind the bar, he slowly swiveled around on the stool and yelled,

"Hey, Red, got any suspects in the murder that happened this morning?" Hank was just passing through. In a small town, news travels fast, especially bad news.

Maxie slid into a booth near the front window. Bill managed to scoot in on the opposite side. He was sitting there watching Maxie.

Maxie turned toward Hank and replied, "We're working on it right now, and, thus far have no clues. If anyone of you knows anything about this case, I certainly would appreciate any help you can give us. Just call the sheriff's office, won't you?" Maxie pleaded.

When the waitress approached their booth, Maxie greeted her cordially, "Morning, Fran."

Fran worked hard and was part owner of this establishment. She had dark circles under her eyes this morning and looked tired, but the big smile on her face overruled the other.

Bill placed his order for ham and eggs, a couple of pancakes and some hash browns. "You eating today?" he asked as he glanced at Maxie.

She just smiled and said, "Fran, just bring me a cup of coffee and a glass of orange juice, please."

"Don't you ever eat anything?" asked Bill, sounding a little concerned.

Maxie laughed, "If I had your framework, I could probably put away twice as much as you do, Bill. You know I have to watch my figure or I'd get as big as a barrel."

"Never mind that, Max, I'll be glad to watch it for you." He teased as he stirred the sugar into the cup of hot liquid. He glanced up and saw a frown cross Maxie's face so he quickly changed the subject.

"How is your beautiful little girl, Megan, doing? Has she now gotten past missing her daddy so much and settled down in school?" He spoke sincerely and with concern. Bill knew that Megan went through a tough time trying to adjust after Matt was taken from them. This evidence showed up in the drop in Megan's grades and her temperament. She had always done well in school and was an obedient child. For a time she was angry and sometimes verbally hurtful to her mother. At times she lashed out at everyone and seemed to blame herself for the death of her father. At other times, she heaped guilt on Maxie and blamed her for Matt's death. *Poor kid.*

Bill Sullivan had never married. Once he had had a serious relationship with a girl he grew up with. Even though she was a year older than he was, they were good friends, and made plans to attend the same college. Bill had always felt that they would someday fall in love, get married and have a family. The two of them had often discussed their future together. That hadn't happened. After college, while he was in patrol school, Annie had fallen in love with his best friend, married and moved away. Right then he made a decision to keep his heart out of any future relationships. So far, he had done a good job of doing just that.

Maxie looked down into her half-empty coffee cup and was thoughtful, "Thanks for asking, Bill. Actually, Megan is doing very well. She's finally gotten past the guilt and hurt enough to get on with her life. In fact, I think she is doing better than I am." She glanced up to see Bill watching her closely and she continued, "Sometimes, when I slow down enough, I get so damn lonely. I miss the companionship, the teasing, sharing life with someone . . . " She suddenly shook her head and added, "I shouldn't be telling you this! Really, we're doing just fine."

Bill reached across the table and took her hand. "Max, you don't have to be ashamed of missing your mate. You both planned to spend your life together. Listen to me, I don't want you blaming yourself, you hear? There was nothing you could have done. Matt was just in the wrong place at the wrong time. That's all. It's time to let it all go and get on with your life. Sure, everything has changed but you're still a beautiful, desirable woman. Yes, you have Megan but you won't always have her around, you know. She'll soon be grown and gone to college, then before you know it, getting married and having babies. Don't you want to share that part of your life with someone else?"

Maxie felt a tear stealing down her cheek and quickly wiped it away . . . She sat with her head bowed to get control of her emotions. Bill sat watching as he raked his hand carelessly through his blue-black hair and wished he had kept his big mouth shut.

"Thanks for your concerns and I guess you're right. I just don't know where to start! How do you stop loving one person and start loving another, Bill?" As her bottom lip quivered slightly, she bite down on it to hide the sadness that enveloped her.

"Maxie, you don't need to stop loving Matt. You'll never do that. You're not expected to. You didn't stop loving your mom and dad when you started loving Matt, did you? You didn't stop loving your favorite pooch just because he got himself run over, did you? When you had Megan, you didn't stop loving Matt, did you? Of course not. Max, you have to put those special feeling in a memory box and put it on a shelf and move on. You need to be making room in your heart and life for someone else. Oh, you may want to take the box down and look inside once in a while. That's all right. You may feel your grief all over when you do. That's all right, too. Matt would want you to be happy. He'd want to see you make peace with yourself, with God, and then get on with living. However, he would never want to be forgotten. And, he won't be. You have Megan to remind you everyday of her father. That's the treasure Matt gave you—Megan. You know, Max, he would want you to move on, not just for Megan, but for yourself." The food arrived at just that moment and Bill figured he had said enough and he dove into breakfast like he plowed into life, at full speed, devouring all on his plate.

"You don't know what it is like! You have no idea. How dare you sit there, Bill Sullivan, giving me advice. You don't know what I'm feeling. I hope you never will!"

When Maxie raised her voice a little too loudly, all eyes turned on the couple. They wondered what the big cowboy said to get the lady sheriff all riled up. With those green eyes flashing, she scooted herself out of the seat and marched out of the café, banging the door behind her.

Dang, what did I say to get that little gal upset? He had no idea. *Why do I always open my big mouth and put my boot in it knowing I can't take it back?* He was not exactly gifted with patience. *Hell, I didn't mean any harm.* Bill dug in his pocket for money for the food, left a generous tip and hurried out the door.

As he rushed out to try and stop her, Maxie was driving away without a second glance. She didn't slow down and was out of sight before he could drawn a breath.

Damn it! It seems that I have just set back our relationship by a few years.

Bill crawled into his truck and sped out into the lane of traffic. He knew he needed to give Max some time to think and cool down, so he but on the brakes and slowly drove back to the scene of the murder giving himself some time to think things through.

When he arrived at the Meyers' home, the reporters were gone. A couple of the CSI vehicles were still parked out front. Maxie's Ram was nowhere in sight. Bill exited his truck and entered the house. Charlee was on the phone. Bob and Betty were on the sofa comforting one another. Both had swollen, red eyes from crying over the loss of their only daughter.

Bill just nodded his head and went through to the bedroom. The CSI team cordially greeted him.

"Ranger! We're finished here. The guy wore gloves so we didn't get much evidence. We did find a blond hair on the bed and got a partial shoe print outside under the window." You'll have the results as soon as we can get back to the lab and get the testing completed, Bill."

The agent turned and began gathering his equipment. "Sure sorry that we couldn't find more evidence. I don't think the killer tarried long after he slit her throat." He removed his gloves, shield goggles and picked up his kit and headed for the door.

"Thanks. I'll see you later." Bill cordially dismissed the agents and turned to Jack, who stood quietly in the corner, awaiting any further instructions.

"The medical examiner is outside and ready to pick up the body, Bill. Do you want them to come in?" Jack asked.

"Jack, can you give the family a few minutes alone with their daughter? Just cover up the blood and gore. I know they have already seen it, but they just need to concentrate on their loss right now, don't you think?" Bill said as he headed toward the living room. Bill spoke softly to the parents, telling them they could be alone with Suzanne for a few minutes before the body was taken away for the autopsy.

Must be really hard to lose a kid. Bill thought as he left the house and got into his vehicle. He was going to the sheriff's office to study the other unsolved murder cases and see if he could run across any similarities that might indicate the perpetrator was the same party. After that, he needed to check with the neighbors to determine if there were any witnesses, and, if so, take statements. He would do a thorough investigation as he always did. He especially wanted to help solve this case because the victim was a young teenager. *This isn't right. Her life ended just as it was beginning,* he thought.

The school—her teachers and friends are a good place to start. I wonder, did she have enemies? Was there a special boyfriend? Many thoughts were running through his mind as he entered the sheriff's office and walked up to the desk of the receptionist Mary Bell Long.

"Hey, Mary B., how are those two grandkids of yours doing?" Mary Bell had been with Maxie the past two years and although her hair was silver, she was active, a good organizer and very protective of the sheriff. She beamed at the mere mention of her grandchildren.

Mary Bell smiled and answered, "Well, what do your think, Bill? They are teenagers and know it all! Gran is too derned old fashioned and just doesn't understand these modern times, you know? Seriously, Bill, it bothers me that they live in a 'me' mind set. Life is all about them and what they want. They aren't as courteous or as thoughtful as I would like. But, hey, I love them to pieces and pray for them everyday."

"Well, of course you do." said Bill. "That's what grandparents do, isn't it? I'm sure you had a hand in spoiling them, Mary. Be honest now."

Mary Bell laughed and agreed.

"Now what can I do for you today?" Mary asked.

"I would like to see those two murder case files that are still pending. I'm looking for something that might tell me if the murderers are the same in both."

"Max hasn't gotten back yet?" he asked casually.

"You and Maxie had another argument, huh?" she inquired, remembering the last time they had worked on a case together and had a few strong differences of opinion. "Bill, it is a mystery to me how you and the sheriff can get crossways so soon after you come together on a case. Your relationship is what I would describe as explosive. What is it this time?" asked Mary Bell.

"The usual! I opened my big mouth giving her advice—like I know it all—and, that just went over like a ton of bricks. Well, you know that redheaded sheriff, she just took offense and flew out the café door, jumped in her truck and was gone . . . just like that!" He snapped his fingers and had a guilty look on his face. Suddenly claiming a real interest in the boots he wore, he stooped and brushed off a little grass stem.

"So, what else is new? I swear you two beat all I ever saw! I keep hoping you'll someday discover you really like each other." Mary chuckled as he went into the office next to Maxie's and plugged in the coffeemaker.

"I'll be back with the files in the shake of a donkey's tail. Have a seat and help yourself to the coffee. There's clean cups and sugar over there. I just washed eight dirty cups." She laughed as she left the room. Shortly, Mary Bell returned with the file folders clasped in her hands.

"Here they are. Now, you get to work." Mary Bell said. She patted him affectionately on the shoulder and went back into her own office to answer the ringing phone.

Bill sat back in the desk chair and placed his booted feet on the desk. He stirred two packets of sugar in his coffee, opened the file and began to read.

For thirty minutes, Bill was deeply involved in the case. His thoughts were interrupted when he heard footsteps coming down the hall. He looked up over the file just as Maxie walked by. He heard her stop briefly by the doorway. She didn't say anything. Bill looked down at the file in his hands and acted as though he didn't know anyone was there. Maxie just marched to her office next door without saying a word.

Dang, she is still mad at me! Have to be careful to not make matters worse. Bill got up, refilled his cup and took his time stirring in the sugar. Then, on impulse, he poured another cup, went to confront the redhead and to apologize, if she would let him.

He walked into her office and found that Maxie was talking on the phone. He quietly set her cup of coffee on the corner of her desk, took a seat and sipped his own. He could tell from the one-sided conversation that Maxie was still in a foul mood. He opened the Solomon case and reviewed a part of the evidence, which was miniscule. *This new case isn't much different*, Bill thought, *the murderer was quick, brutal and deadly.*

Sheriff O'Bryan hung up the phone and turned to find Bill waiting patiently to speak with her. "Well?" she coldly asked.

"Well, what?" Bill innocently replied.

"What have you got on the murder? I see you have helped yourself to the files on the Solomon case." Maxie took the file from Bill and tossed it on her desk. She saw the cup of coffee and picked it up and took a sip.

"I don't care for cold coffee."

"A girl after my own heart. Want a warm up?" Bill rose to add hot coffee to Max's cup.

"Sheriff, there isn't enough evidence to determine if these murders might be committed by the same scumbag or not. There are a couple of things that I noticed but until we get the results of forensics . . . well, I just don't know." She didn't say anything so he continued.

"Max, I am going to go out and question some of the neighbors. Maybe someone saw something or heard something that could help. Do you want to come along?" Bill politely asked.

"No, not this time. I have some things I have to attend to. Then, at three I have to pick Meg up from school"

"Max, I'd be glad I pick her up for you, if that's all right with you. I'm going to go right past the junior high."

She paused, considering his offer. "Would you mind? I'll call the principal and give my permission for you to do that Just bring her to the office." Maxie said softly and added a polite, "Thank you." The lady sheriff turned back to her work. He was dismissed.

"Sure thing." Bill walked out of the office, waved at Mary B. Who was still on the phone, and left the building. Bill pulled his long legs under the steering wheel of his truck and drove down the street. His mind was not on his job. It was on Max. *So much for trying to apologize to her. Just didn't seem like the time to be doing that right now. I'll do it later. Maybe send her some flowers or something.* At that moment he noticed a florist just ahead, pulled in, set the brake and got out of the truck. *Women loved flowers. They can work magic!* He hoped for a miracle because it was his opinion that it would take a big one before he was forgiven.

When he came out of the shop, he smiled to himself, climbed into the cab and started down the street. *That lady sheriff better protect her heart because I'm fixing to lasso it!* Bill Sullivan was a very determined man, much like his grandfather.

Bill Sullivan's mother and father had been killed in a fire in East Texas when he was six years old. He was visiting his grandfather in Oklahoma at the time. Buffalo Hunter raised the boy, teaching him all the Indian ways on the reservation. Little Eagle was the Indian name given him by his grandfather, who often told the boy he had eagle eyes that seldom missed anything. Grandfather taught him the skill of tracking and trapping animals for food. He became a good tracker. Little Eagle learned to be tough, self-sufficient and in control of his emotions. As a child, everything he was taught came from living on the reservation. Boys don't cry was one of the things he learned, also.

Bill's father was a big Irishman with sandy-colored hair and bright blue eyes. He raised and trained horses. Irish, a name given Bill's father by the Indians, stuck with him.

After his horse had stepped in a gopher hole, Irish, as a young boy, had come into the Indian camp hobbling on a broken leg. The medicine man had splinted it and patched him up.

Buffalo Hunter, was an important leader in his tribe. He had a young daughter, Sunshine, who took care of Irish while he healed. He was instantly attracted to Sunshine. She was a small, quiet, beautiful girl with jet-black hair and expressive eyes. Irish was sure that the moment she stepped inside a room, the sun rose.

By the time Irish was able to leave camp, the tall Irishman and the lovely Indian maiden had fallen in love. Reluctantly, grandfather had blessed them and saw them married in an Indian ceremony. They moved into East Texas. Shortly after that, Irish built them a large log-cabin-style ranch house and within a year a son was born.

As a result of a forrest fire, his parents and his home went up in flames. Bill was six-years of age. He felt guilty and blamed himself for not being there. However, as an adult, he realized there wasn't any way he could have saved them. Since he was visiting his grandfather when it happened, Bill felt God had other plans for his life.

Bill remembered his dad, and, in fact, was named after the giant of a man. With his striking blue eyes and his six foot six height, he towered over others. Bill inherited his father's good looks. However, his mother certainly had marked him with her shimmering black hair.

Bill Sullivan was a striking presence. He wore his hair a little longer than most Rangers and didn't quiet fit the traditional stereotype. He was a good ranger, and credited that to his childhood training. For his size, Bill carried himself with a grace and a confidence that most big men did not possess. He was unaware that women gravitated to him.

Chapter 3

When Bill arrived at the farmhouse, which was in need of a coat of paint, it appeared to be vacant. The house was located about two miles down County Road 105, next to the Meyers' place. There was a beat up, red tricycle in the front yard and a swing set at the rear of the house.

Guess they have young children. He speculated as he knocked on the door of the framed house. He listened and waited.

Well, nobody's home. I'll check back in a little while. They've probably gone to town to pick up groceries or something. For now, I'll head over to Hooch's place and see if he has seen anything unusual. Not that he can see worth a hoot!

Smiling as he remembered a few times he had run into Hooch in the past two years. One thing he remembered was that Hooch was a character. For an old man, his mind was sharp. Although he had no formal education, life had taught him many lessons. There wasn't much that was going on in his neighborhood, or even in the whole town that Hooch missed.

Bill drove down the road and parked in the driveway of an old unpainted farmhouse, where a mama dog with seven pups ran out to greet him. She barked at him several times. This was more of a greeting than a warning. Bill smiled as he climbed out of his vehicle and looked around.

The place looks like a junkyard or a garage sale in progress. Suddenly, seven slobbering, black lab pups jumped up on his legs, clawing his boots.

Those little devils have scratched my boots! He rubbed his finger across the toe and said out loud, "You are cute little devils though, aren't you?"

I swear the tails wag the dogs. The puppies succeeded in licking his face as he attempted to pet them. Bill chuckled to himself.

"Okay, fellas, that's enough." Just then, the front door opened and a white-haired, elderly man hobbled out to welcome him with a big toothless grin spread across his wrinkled face.

"Well, howdy, Ranger! We ain't seen you in quite a spell. Come on in. The coffee is hot," Hooch invited.

Bill shook hands with Hooch and they entered the house. He was a strange one. Never been married, didn't want to, and Bill had heard the rumor that Hooch, in his younger day, worked an illegal still where he made a beverage for himself and others. Evidently, that is how he had acquired his nickname. Funny thing was, and one thing Bill noticed, his house was spotless inside. Not a speck of dust, dishes all done, and everything put away. The old man was 93 years old and crippled up at that!

How does he do it?

They sat down at the kitchen table. Hooch poured out two cups of syrupy black coffee and placed one in front of Bill.

"Ye take sugar?" Hooch asked.

"Yep, I sure do. Sugar is a great invention, Hooch." Bill commented as he stirred it in and took a sip.

"Dang! This is hot!" Bill went to the sink for a little water to cool the beverage and take a little of its punch out. *And strong!* He thought. As he poured a little water into his cup, he looked at Hooch.

"Ranger, you're jest ruinin' a good cup of coffee." Hooch complained.

Bill chuckled as he stirred the thick black stuff and took another sip.

"Hooch, this stuff is strong enough to walk across the room by itself."

"Shucks. I shore thank ye for the compliment." Hooch teased.

"Hooch, I guess you know why I'm here. There has been another murder and this time just down the road at the Meyers' place. Their seventeen-year old daughter was knifed in the throat. Not a pretty sight, I can tell you."

"I heared that! Reckon what this world is a'comin' to?" Hooch asked. "Got any clues, Bill?"

"Not really. Thought you might help. Have you seen anything unusual going on around the neighborhood? Any strangers driving down this road lately? Can you give me any information that might help me solve this crime? I'm asking for your help, Hooch."

"Well now, I have to say that there man who visited across the road at Margaret Jeffer's house was a stranger. Didn't like his looks none. Scum, I'd say. He ain't there now. I ain't seen him of late. Didn't know the feller and didn't want to! Trashy lookin' guy. I can't say fer sure, 'cause he wore a cap, but I think he had brownish-colored hair, kinda long. He weren't too tall. Course, I never seen him up close. He drove an old black, beat up, rusty-lookin' Ford pickup truck. Seen him pass the house a few times. In fact, drove like a bat out of hell. Ye can't do that on these gravel county roads. Well, most folks have got more sense not to. Not him!" Hooch hesitated long enough to take another sip of his thick beverage.

"Ranger, any of that gonna help you?" he asked.

"You bet, Hooch! Thanks for the info. I just stopped at the . . . . what did you say the lady's name was?" asked Bill.

"Margaret Jeffers."

"Yeah, I need to write that down." Bill took out a little black book from his shirt pocket and scribbled down a few notes before he continued.

"Do you know anything about Mrs. Jeffers? I saw toys and a swing in the yard so I'm guessing that she has young children. Does she have a husband or a man in her life at the moment?"

"Nah. Jest lives alone with them two youngin's. I heared tell that she lost her old man a few years ago. She's been here 'bout two or three years, I reckon. Just rents that old house. She works in town at Harts Real Estate; jest answers the phone and stuff. Seems nice enough. Not very friendly though."

"Why would she want to be friends with an old coot like you, Hooch?" Bill joked.

"Well, sir, you never know. There may be snow on the roof but there is a chance there is still fire in the furnace! Ain't that so?" Hooch grinned his toothless smile and winked at the ranger.

Why that old rascal? Sex? At his age? And I would bet he has a lady friend, who cleans house, as well as doing a few other favors for him.

"Hooch, I hate to leave such good company. I really appreciate all the information you gave me. At least, it gives us a place to start." Bill stretched out his big hand to Hooch and thanked him again as he went out the door, stumbling around a puppy or two.

"What are you going to do with all these little disposals?" Bill spreads one hand out towards the puppies ganged around him.

"Oh, I'll find a good home fer 'em, I 'spect."

Bill was finally able to get around the dogs and into his truck. He watched carefully as he started backing out of the driveway and drove away. He was thinking, *can't afford to run over one of Hooch's treasures. That old man would never forgive me!*

Bill liked dogs and had always had one or two when he was growing up on the reservation. Now that he was away from home a lot, he knew a ranger was not the best pet owner. His grandfather had taught him long ago that if you had a pet you had to take care of it. Someday he would have his own dog again.

His grandfather had been dead for many years now. Bill missed him. He had never known his grandmother. A few years after Bill's mother, Sunshine, had been born, her mother, Yellow Moon, died in childbirth. She and her baby boy died shortly after wards. Grandfather never took another squaw but raised his lovely little daughter alone, with the help of other women in the tribe and especially Buffalo Hunter's mother, Wild Flower.

Bill was glad to have had his grandfather for so long. He was saddened because he hadn't really gotten to know his parents.

The ranger was lost in thoughts when he suddenly realized he was back in town and needed to locate Harts Real Estate. He stopped at the Town and Country and looked through the phone book for an address.

Ah, here it is. Looks like just a couple of blocks from here. Good deal.

He drove the short distance to the Realtors and pulled into the parking space in front. The real estate office was located in a small building maintained by a receptionist and apparently had two realtors in house.

As he entered the office, he found a girl, in her late twenties or early thirties, sitting at the desk. She had curly brown hair and a big smile.

"Howdy, Ma'am." Bill greeted as he removed his Stetson. "I'm Texas Ranger Sullivan. I'm looking for Ms. Margaret Jeffers. Is there anyone around by that name?" Bill asked.

The girl eyed him suspiciously. "What do you want her for?"

"I'm doing some investigation work and need to speak to her about a case under investigation, if I may?" He smiled and seemed friendly enough.

"I'm Margaret. Everybody calls me Maggie though." She seemed to be relaxed now and actually gave him that charming smile again.

"May I call you Maggie, Ms. Jeffers?" he asked.

"Sure, all my friends do."

"I imagine you have heard about the Meyers' girl, down the road from you. She was murdered last night." Bill watched her expression change from disbelief to horror.

She didn't know!

"Oh, God! Not Suzanne? She baby-sits with my kids sometimes! What? How did it happen?" She questioned, her wide brown eyes tearing, as she tried to comprehend it all.

"Sorry, I thought you had probably already heard the news. Suzanne's throat was cut sometime last night in her own bed." Bill stated.

"How terrible! I saw several cars go by this morning but I'm always rushing around to get the kids ready for breakfast and school. I guess more traffic than usual never registered with me." She breathed a sigh and continued, "I live alone except for Mandy and Donny. It's so hard trying to get it all together every morning and get to work by 7:30. Mandy and Donny stay here with me at the office and walk to school around the corner about eight." She nervously chattered on in a attempt to explain.

"Ranger, are you married? Do have kids? If so, then you know what I am talking about." Maggie rattled on.

Bill didn't make any comments to her last question. He wasn't interested in anything at the moment except what was material to this investigation.

"Maggie, have you seen anything unusual in your neighborhood? Have you noticed a stranger cruising around?" Bill asked.

Maggie jumped to her feet as she exclaimed. "Oh, my God, are we in danger?"

"Not that I'm aware of. I would recommend that you keep your doors and windows locked at all times. Just be cautious until we catch this animal." Bill firmly stated.

"You can bet your life on that! You know, it's real hard for a woman alone to raise two kids. I just never really feel safe. Oh, I do the best I can for them. Never seems to be enough." Maggie shuffled a few papers around on her desk before she continued, "Texas Ranger, I'll do anything I can to help you."

"Maggie, your neighbor, Hooch, says he saw a stranger at your house a few days ago. Is that true?' Bill questioned.

"Oh . . . that must have been Bubba Green, an old boyfriend of mine. He needed a place to hang out for a few days. So, I let him stay with us. He was acting odd though and I finally asked him to leave."

"What do mean by the word 'odd', Maggie?"

"Well, he slept most of the day and was out prowling or drinking at night. I didn't want him around the kids. He said he was looking for work. I figured if he was, then he needed to be out and about in the daytime. Isn't that what you would think, Ranger?"

"Sure thing . . . Did he harm the children in any way or act inappropriately with you?" he asked.

"Well, no. He wasn't around the kids that much since he was sleeping most of the day. He came and went as he chose. My boy, Donny, said he smelled funny. I was afraid he might be on drugs, like he was when we were together before. Anyway, I just told him to get out."

"I assume Bubba is a nickname?" Can you give me his full name?" Bill asked.

"Yeah. His name is Bobby Fred Green. I don't know where he's staying but, since he left, I've seen him around town some."

"Can you give me a good description of Bobby Fred?"

"Good Lord! You don't think he murdered Suzanne, do you?" exclaimed Maggie, wringing her hand.

"Maggie, we have to check out everybody. We can't leave a stone unturned."

Maggie frowned. Bill could see she was worried. He needed to talk to this Bobby Fred. He was aware that his first job was to find him.

Maggie gave Bill a description of Bubba and his truck. She also told Bill that Bubba had told her he bought the vehicle from an individual . . . Somebody by the name of Brady something or other.

Preparing to leave, Bill said, "Thank you for your help. I may need to talk with you again later. I suppose the best time to catch you at home is in the evenings?"

"Oh, yeah, come on over anytime. I'll be there. With two kids, I am pretty much stuck at home at night. I'd be real glad to see you." Maggie said in a husky voice and handed him a piece of paper with her phone number on it.

Was that an invitation? Bill was thinking but he said, "See you later, then." Bill put on his hat and walked out of the office to his truck.

As he climbed into the vehicle, he glanced at his watch. *Oh my, I'm going to have to hurry to get to the junior high school by three o'clock.* He sped away. He was looking forward to seeing little Megan again.

Megan was standing on the sidewalk with a backpack full of books. He noted she wasn't so little anymore. She was talking to a petite blonde when Bill pulled up and stopped. Megan's companion whispered something in her ear and they both giggled. Megan waved and ran over to the truck and climbed in.

"My goodness, look at you!" exclaimed Bill. "You've grown up, young lady, and are pretty as a picture!"

Megan lowered her head. Although she was a little embarrassed by his compliment, she was pleased.

"Thanks." She said as she settled her backpack in the seat beside her.

She quickly changed the subject and said, "Susan thinks you're so cool!"

"What do you think, Meg?" he teasingly asked.

"Well-l-l, you aren't as cute as my daddy." she stated.

"Are you sure?" he questioned.

Megan grinned and got busy looking into her bag, moving books around.

Bill decided he was getting the foot and mouth disease again and he changed the subject.

"How is school? Are you learning a lot?" he asked.

"I guess it's okay. At least I'm staying on the honor roll. Mom says that's good."

"You bet your life that's good. Why, that's great! I'm real proud of you, Meg."

There I go again. Poor kid, her face is red as a turkey's waddle. Slow down, Bill.

By that time, Bill had pulled into the parking lot at the S.O. and Megan gathered her backpack and scrambled out. She said, "Thanks," and waved as she entered the building.

Dang, that little slip of a girl will have boys calling all the time. She's going to be a beauty; like her mother—a strawberry blond with the same green eyes as Max. If I were her daddy, I'd surely cull out her suitors. Why, no man will be good enough for that angel! I could protect her . . . if I was her daddy . . . Bill sighed. *If . . .*

Megan ran in and hugged Mary Bell and then hurried back to Maxie's office.

"Hey, Mom. That ranger is the coolest!" she said.

"Hi, Sweetheart! Got a hug for the sheriff?" Maxie asked.

"No, but I have a big one for you, Mom." Megan teased and walked over to give a bear hug to her mother.

Megan noticed the lovely bouquet of yellow roses, with tiny, white baby's breath blending in and around them.

"Mom, do you have a boyfriend?" Megan asked coyly.

"Not on your life! Oh, the flowers! That ranger got my dander up and this is his way of apologizing to me, I guess." Maxie replied. There was no guessing about it. The card said, "Forgive me for being an ass."

"Mom, that is so neat! I do think he really likes you. Susan thinks he's a stud!"

"Megan! You know I hate it when you use that word!" Maxie scolded.

"I know. I'm sorry, Mom." she said as she threw her bag full of books on a nearby table. She opened up a small change purse and dug out some coins before she looked up again.

"Mom, can I get you a coke?" she asked.

"Yes, thanks, Baby. I haven't taken a break all afternoon." Maxie said as she handed some coins to her daughter,

"I guess you heard the Meyers girl was murdered last night, didn't you?" Maxie asked.

"Uh huh . . . I didn't know her that well. It's really scary though . . . all these murders right here in our own hometown . . . You know I wish daddy was here. We felt safer, didn't we, Mom?" she said as she went into the hallway to find the drinks.

Maxie was thoughtful for a few minutes. *Yes baby, we do wish daddy was here . . .*

Megan brought back two cold cans of cola and handed one to her mother, plopped down into the nearby chair, opened it and took a sip. She sighed.

"Do you know who did it, Mom?" Megan asked.

"Not yet. We don't have the results of the lab tests. Bill is out questioning some of the neighbors, I think." Maxie unconsciously rubbed her head with the hand that had been holding the cold drink.

"Mom, do you have a headache?"

"I guess you could say that. I get so upset when anyone is murdered, but it sure does tear me up to see a young teen have her life snuffed out."

"That's sad," Megan replied.

"Mom, why don't we go grab a pizza, go home and watch a movie tonight? Just to relax and take your mind off this stuff for a while. Ok? You know you could use some down time." suggested Megan.

Sometimes, wisdom comes from the mouth of babes.

"Ok, kiddo, let's do that! What do you want to watch? I'll pick up a movie and the pizza on the way home." Her mother said and turned back to the file lying on her desk.

Megan was thirteen going on twenty. Perhaps due to the death of her father, she had just grown up before her time. She was a serious girl and she worried about her mother, who worked so hard and worried so much. *Maybe that's just what women do. Work and worry.* Megan thought.

She pulled out a book from her backpack and opened it and began to read. *History!* That was not one of her favorite subjects but she had to study for that test Mr. Ward was giving the class tomorrow. *Ugh! I hate history!* She sighed. *I may as well buckle down and do it.* As soon as she took another sip, she plunged into the history review to prepare for the test.

Sheriff Maxie O'Bryan was deep into the facts of the case when the phone rang, startling her back to reality. *Oh, dang it! It is probably that confounded ranger again, she said to herself. I'm not in the mood to talk to him! Not yet!* She picked up the receiver.

"Sheriff O'Bryan speaking." Maxie said in her most professional voice. "May I help you?"

"Max, it's me!" Bill Sullivan replied. He sounded peeved.

"Give me your name and phone number and I'll get back with you." Maxie ignored his sassy manner. She could almost hear the silent cursing on the other end and sighed.

"Oh, all right, I know it's you, Bill Sullivan! I knew that before I even answered the phone.

Bill chuckled softly and inquired, "And how did you know that?"

"Never mind." Maxie replied, ready to get down to business. She paused. *How did I know it was him?* She shook her head. *Is this man getting to me?*

"What did you learn from the neighbors? Anybody see anything to help us on this case?" asked Maxie.

"I have a bit of info that I need to run by you. Are you going to be in the office a few minutes?" Bill asked.

"I'm afraid so. Come on by and let's see what you have." she invited.

"Be right there." *Click.* He had already hung up the phone and was on his way.

About five minutes later, he walked into the office and sat down, waiting for Max to acknowledge his presence. He put his index finger across his pursed lips so Megan would be silent while he waited . . . waited and waited. *This woman is driving me crazy!*

"Damn it, Max, talk to me! Haven't I suffered enough of your silent treatment?" Bill complained rather sharply.

Megan pretended to read. She was enjoying this. *I think Mom really likes this guy!*

Maxie slowly looked up at Bill and forced a smiled. She was over her anger now. Almost.

"Bill, I'm sorry! I was just teasing you again. You big lug, you can sure dish it out. Can't take it though, can you?" she teased, her green eyes sparkling.

"Now then, tell me what you've learned today?" Maxie was all business now.

"I went by the home of Margaret Jeffers but she wasn't there. So I drove over and talked to Hooch. He really couldn't tell me much but did mention a guy that stayed at the Jeffers' place a while back. Hooch didn't like his looks at all. He gave me the name of Jeffers' work place, so I went there to talk to her. Got the name of an ex-boyfriend who stayed at her house recently and I'm checking him out." *At least she didn't toss them in the trash,* he thought as he glanced at the roses, then continued to fill Maxie in about what he had learned about Bubba Green.

"He is a no-good drug addict."

Bill had traced down the man who sold the old truck to Bubba. Rick Mathis and Bubba had gone to school together some years ago; but he couldn't tell Bill much about what Bubba had been doing the last few years. Bubba had just appeared one day at Rick's Wrecking Shop. Said he wanted to purchase an old vehicle. He had $400 cash that he dug out of his wallet and handed to Rick and left. Bubba hadn't said much. Bill told Max that Bubba did have a relative here in town. His grandmother was Maria French.

"That is about it, Max. Not much to go on, but a start. We have to start somewhere." He sighed.

"Have you gotten any information back from forensics?" Bill questioned.

"No, not yet. It'll probably be tomorrow before they get me any results of the tests," she stated, flipping though the file in front of her.

Maxie and Bill sat for an hour discussing the pros and cons of the case.

Finally Maxie turned to Megan and asked, "Honey, are you ready to go?"

"Sure Mom! Let's go pick up that pizza and a movie. Ranger Bill, you want to come over to our house for supper and a movie?" she asked innocently as she glanced at her mother who was frowning at her.

Bill sensed this wasn't the time to accept, smiled and said, "Thanks, Mugwump. I've taken at room at Aunt

Maude's Rooming House and I imagine she'll have supper ready for me when I get there. She treats me like I am one of her grandsons. I know she gets lonesome. I don't know if she has anyone else staying there right now, do you?" he asked as he turned toward Max. Maxie shrugged but didn't respond.

He swiveled around and said to Megan. "I'd love to have a rain check. How about if I bring supper over tomorrow night?" He avoided looking at Maxie.

Maxie was relieved for a second. She didn't feel like putting up with anybody tonight. About tomorrow night? Not if she could help it!

Before she could reply, Megan spoke up. "That would be great, wouldn't it, Mom?"

"Sure, that would be great." repeated Maxie flatly as she gathered up the files and notes on her desk to take home and look over later.

Megan glared at Bill and gathered up her books preparing to go home.

As they walked out of the office, Deputies Jack Rankin and Charlee Barnes were coming in. They looked subdued and tired.

"How are things at the Meyers' place?" Maxie asked.

"Well, I guess things are about the same." Jack replied. He talked briefly to Maxie about the tentative funeral arrangements and some statements the reporters had gotten which would be on television at ten. The Meyers' son, Brian, had come in from college so the family was all together sharing their grief.

Charlee asked, "Have you gotten any lab results or any other evidence to go on, Sheriff?"

"We don't have any forensic test results. I expect those in the morning." Maxie stated.

"You two go home and get some rest. Tomorrow will be another long day." Maxie added.

Bill gently patted Charlee on the shoulder, saying a few encouraging words. *Poor kid is still new enough on the force to get really involved with the crime victims. I can see she is taking this murder hard.*

"Meggie, let's go." Maxie turned to Megan and they walked out together.

"Good night, everybody." Bill yelled as he climbed into his vehicle, and headed down the street to the rooming house. He was looking forward to catching up on the gossip that he was certain he would hear from Aunt Maude while he enjoyed a delicious supper with her. *Still, I'd rather be with the girls.*

The headquarters for the Texas Rangers was in Waylon. Sullivan wasn't able to travel the distance back and forth everyday. He really had no reason to go back to his office until he had some tangible facts on this case. His expenses were paid by the state anyway. When he was working a case, he stayed in the vicinity of the crime to get acquainted with the locals and gain their trust. Everything worked satisfactory that way. Occasionally, Bill drove back to headquarters and checked in and by his lonely apartment to pick up the mail and pay a few bills. The place he lived in felt more like another motel than his home.

Chapter 4

Maxie was at the office by 5:00 a.m. The next morning. She hadn't gotten any rest. Before bedtime she had called Alma Cook, her elderly neighbor who was an early riser, to come and stay with Megan and take her to school the next morning.

She had a feeling then that this would be another one of those troubled days and sleepless nights. It proved to be just that.

Alma, a 68 year-old widow, was delighted. She spoiled both Megan and Maxie. She was always baking something and bringing it over. Actually, she kept their cookie jar full. Maxie smiled. She was sure that Megan would be off to school on time and with a solid breakfast to keep her going.

Twenty minutes after Maxie arrived Bill Sullivan came in and greeted her.

"I see you're here bright and early. Excuse me." He walked to the full coffeepot. "I've got to have a cup of that coffee before I get going. It's best if you don't talk to me till I do. Okay?" He looked at Maxie and grinned.

Maxie smiled, saluted and said in a sassy tone, "Yes, Sir! I'm guessing you are not a morning person. Am I right?"

Bill didn't answer her but continued to add sugar and stir the delicious smelling coffee. He plopped down in the chair by Maxie's desk and sipped the hot liquid for a few minutes as he picked up one of the unsolved case files and perused its contents.

They both sat silently as they drank their coffee and looked over the files in front of them. *I'm surprised. This is a comfortable silence.* Maxie thought, then dismissed such thoughts to concentrate on the case in front of her.

Finally, Bill spoke in a rather mild manner. "Well, Max, what are our plans for today?" he asked.

"Until I hear from forensics, I'm sitting tight right here," Maxie said as she poured them another cup of steaming black coffee.

"Well, I guess I need to locate our boy. The first thing I plan to do is see the grandmother. Bubba may still be staying with her." the ranger speculated.

"True. It would be nice if that were the case." Maxie continued, "But, that's not likely. Cases are never that simple, are they?" She turned as she heard someone coming in the front door.

She smiled as Jack who came in and pleasantly greeted them. "Well, did you two have a sleepless night? You're here mighty early."

Neither answered.

"Any developments in the case, Sheriff?" He directed his question to Maxie.

"Nothing yet, Jack. If the lab hasn't called me by 9 a.m., I'll call them." said Maxie.

"What about you, Bill, have you got anything?" Jack asked, turning his attention to the ranger.

"Well, I'm following up on a lead about a Bubba Green. You know him, Jack?" he asked.

"That name sound familiar. Hmmm . . . Is that old Bobby Fred? I haven't heard anything out of him for years. When he was a kid, he was always getting into trouble, juvenile stuff mostly. His parents divorced and his grandmother raised him, if I remember correctly. Let me think for a minute . . . I believe he got involved in drugs too, and was arrested a time or two. Never finished high school. Then when he was around seventeen or eighteen, he just disappeared. Haven't seen or heard anything about him since." Jack scratched his head as he was remembering Bubba.

"Maxie, can I borrow your deputy this morning?" When she nodded, Bill turned to the deputy. "Jack, do you want to come with me to talk to Bubba's grandmother?" Bill asked. "I'm going to start there."

Jack turned to Maxie and asked. "Sheriff, have you got anything else for me to do right now?"

"That's as good a plan as any right now. I can let you stay here by the phone and I'll go with the ranger. Which had you rather do?" Maxie teased, knowing Jack had rather be out in the field.

"What ever you say, boss." Jack replied.

Maxie glanced at Bill to see what his reaction was and then said, "You go ahead, Jack, and I'll see you two later." Maxie turned back to her desk just as the phone started ringing.

The two men stood silently waiting to hear if this might be the results from the lab they needed.

"Sheriff's office," Maxie answered. After a moment of silence, she added, "Hi, Sweetie! Are you doing all right this morning? Sorry, I had to leave early. Just couldn't sleep anyway." she added.

45

When they realized it was Megan calling her mother, the two men glanced at one another, grinned and walked out. Those two girls were very close and that pleased Bill and Jack

They walked silently to the parking lot. Jack climbed into the Bill's Silverado truck, pushed aside files, papers of all kinds and a black attache case. *This is the ranger's office—maybe even his home away from home. What kind of life is that?*

Since Jack knew Bubba's grandmother, he directed Bill to the little rundown house on Elm Street. It was early but there was a light on in what he thought was the kitchen.

As they walked to the door, Jack spoke softly out of the corner of his mouth, "We may catch her in her night gown, you know." They both laughed.

Sure enough, when Maria came to answer the door, she was clad in a faded, rose-print housedress, which buttoned down the front—where there were buttons left on it. She was a large woman with wrinkles on her face and graying hair. Her mouth was pursed with a cigarette hanging from her lips. She didn't look pleased to have company at this time of the morning.

"Ma'am, this is Texas Ranger Sullivan and you know me, Deputy Jack Rankin." Jack stated. "We need to talk to you for a few minutes, please. May we come in?" he asked.

"I don't know about that!" she replied in a gruff, unwelcome tone of voice.

Bill spoke softly, "Mrs. Franks, a young girl was murdered. You may be able to answer a few questions, if you will. I know you want to help us get this murderer, don't you?"

Maria's expression softened but she remained silent for a moment as she took a puff off the cigarette, blowing the smoke toward the ceiling. Then she said, "Well, I guess that can't hurt nothing." She unlatched the screen door and showed them the way into the kitchen.

They sat down around the scarred wooden dining table, taking in their surroundings. Both noticed a picture sitting on a shelf over the sink. It was a snapshot of a small boy and a young woman, both with sad eyes.

"What do you want to know?" she asked suspiciously.

Jack grinned and turned to her. "Is that a picture of your daughter and grandson up there on the shelf?" Jack questioned in a friendly manner. "Pretty little lady, she is." he added.

Maria glanced toward the photo briefly and then her face hardened and shut down. "That's not what you come to ask me is it, deputy?" She took a long draw on her cigarette watched the smoke curl overhead and venomously crushed the fire out in a nearby ashtray, which was already full of cigarette butts.

"No, Ma'am, it isn't what we came to ask about. Is Bobby Fred your grandson?" Bill asked.

"Yes, he is. What's he done now?" she frowned, leaning forward as though she was eager to know, yet afraid to hear. "That boy hasn't been nothin' but grief and heartache to me. What could I expect? His Maw left his Pa when Bobby was a young lad and I ain't seen him in some fifteen or twenty years. That no account daughter of mine only comes around when she needs money, which I have little to none. Never give me nothing when I was trying to do right by the kid and give him a home and food for his belly. I done my best. Never was good enough though. A boy needs his Pa. I reckon he is just pretty much rotten to the core." She bitterly added as took out another cigarette to light up, her hands shaking.

Bill watched her quietly, giving her time to settle down. She was upset. He just wasn't sure if it was anger or fear that prompted her trembling.

"Mrs. Franks, let me say that we aren't here to accuse Bubba of anything. I'm sure you did the best you could for the boy. You know about the murder of the Meyers' girl?" he asked. "Well, we have people who told us that Bubba stayed a couple of weeks with Maggie Jeffers after he hit town. He could be a witness to the murder. We have to cover all the bases. Maybe he remembers seeing someone or something that might help us in this case."

Maria thought about Bill's statement a moment, "Well, when he come back to me, wanting someplace to stay, he never mentioned anything, except that his old girlfriend had kicked him out. I suspect he's on drugs again. Can't stay away from them. He was driving an old beat up truck. Said he didn't have any money since he bought the truck and just needed a place to stay for a couple days." Maria ducked her head for a second and was silent.

Bill felt sympathy for the old lady. He was sure that she had done her best to raise her grandson right but knew she had failed in some way. It wasn't her responsibility but it was dumped in her lap.

That reminded Bill of his own circumstances, both his parents dying and leaving him to be raised by his old grandfather. Yet, he had turned out all right. *By the grace of God!*

Jack took up the slack in the conversation and asked, "Mrs. Franks, where was Bubba all those years he was gone?"

"A lot of those years was spent in the pen. He stole some things from a warehouse. He ain't really a thief. Just has to have them drugs. Not too smart, is he? As long as

Bubba was in prison, he stayed straight but he can't resist that heroin and crack . . . He'll never amount to a hill of beans!" she said with anger and disappointment, slamming a new pack of cigarettes on the table.

"Is Bubba staying here with you?" questioned Jack.

"Well, what few things he has is still here but I ain't seen him in about three days. He's always done me that way. Never tells me where he'll be. Never calls me to see if I need anything. He's rotten, I tell you . . . " Maria's eyes filled with tears.

Jack and Bill sat there to let her get control of her emotions. Finally, Bill spoke up, "Do you know where we can find him?"

"He has a couple of old friends around. But, like I said, I don't know where he stays or what he's doin'," Maria stated. "There was a couple of kids he ran around with in his youth . . . Hamilton and McGregor . . . best I remember. Though, I don't know nothin' about them boys now. May not even live around here anymore." She took a puff again, laid the cigarette butt in the ashtray and watched it burn while she prayerfully interlocked her hands.

Bill felt compassion for the old lady sitting across from him. She wasn't as hard as she let on. It was her difficult life, bitter outcome and present circumstances that had made her a crusty soul.

Jack asked, "Do you mind if we look though Bubba things? Maybe we can run across a clue as to his whereabouts. We really do need to talk to him, Ma'am."

She looked doubtfully at Jack and quickly at Bill then said, "He ain't got nothin' to speak of and he wouldn't like your prowling through his things, but I don't see no harm in letting you see." She pushed the chair back and braced herself on the table where she pushed herself up and led the officers to an adjoining bedroom. It was cluttered; the wallpaper was torn off in strips. There were two grimy windows with no curtains, partially covered by dingy torn shades. A few pieces of men's clothing were strewn around the room and an old beat up brown suitcase rested on a cane-bottomed chair with a hole in the middle.

Bill walked over and examined the suitcase and its contents. *Nothing there!* He continued walking around the room. On the chest of drawers he found some suspicious-looking powder. *Dope, I imagine.* He took a small sample to send to the lab for testing. A dirty hairbrush rested on the bedside table. Bill took a sample of hair from the brush. *Dirty blond, but is it the killers?* He speculated as he removed a sample for testing.

Jack was examining the clothing thrown around, hoping to find any evidence or body fluids. The things were dirty but he failed to find a spot that could be blood. He turned to Bill when he had finished checking everything.

"You about done here?" Jack asked him.

"Yeah, I think so," Bill replied as he bent over to examine a sock that was laying nearby.

"Let's go then," he said as they walked back into the kitchen and stood before Maria who was nervously wringing her hands.

"Ma'am, we really do appreciate your allowing us do this. You have been very helpful. Thank you for your cooperation. If you do hear from Bubba, will you give me a call?" Jack asked kindly as he handed her a business card, which she laid on the shelf beside the picture of her family.

Bill and Jack shook her hand and left the lady standing in the doorway as they drove away.

"Did you see any thing suspicious or unusual, Jack?" the ranger asked.

"Nah! Didn't see a thing. You got a few samples, didn't you? That might be a big help in tying this fellow to the murder or to exclude him all together." Jack was silent for a time. They had so little to go on.

Bill glanced at his watch. *It's 9:30 already! Max may have something for us by now,* "Let's go by the office to see if there are any new developments."

"Good idea! I could sure use another cup of coffee, too," Jack said and grinned at Bill.

Before long, Bill had pulled into the parking lot and the two officers went inside. Both stopped at Mary Bell's desk to inquire about her morning and her grandchildren. That always kept her happy.

"The sheriff is in her office and she may have some news from the lab," she stated.

The two men walked back to Maxie's office and Bill knocked on the facing of the door to make her aware of their presence. She turned and motioned them to come in.

They decided to pour a cup of coffee before they were seated.

"Max, do you need a refill?" Bill asked.

"No, thanks! I've had way too much caffeine this morning already," replied Maxie. Her faced changed as she picked up a couple of notes on her desk and addressed the officers with a very business-like demeanor. She was serious and not at all pleased.

"We don't have a lot to go on. But, here's what we do have," she said as she glanced down at the piece of paper in her hand and looked back up at the two, "The blond hair DNA brought results but no match has been found in the data base, so far. The knife was a Bowie hunting knife. The partial print outside on the ground was helpful but not enough to trace. They are still working on that. It appears to be from a very old athletic-type shoe. Apparently, the manufacturer doesn't make that kind any more. Forensics is not sure they have enough of the pattern to go back and track the make. They are trying, though. That's about it."

"No blood stains found?" questioned Bill.

"None!" Maxie looked at the two men and asked, "What did you two turn up?"

Jack spoke first. "Not much. Bill got a couple of samples, one of a white powder and the other a hair from a brush. It's blond. We can have it tested. However, we didn't find any bloodstains. Bubba's whereabouts is unknown. That's what his grandmother told us. Maria says he just comes and goes as he pleases. He stays there and is on dope."

Bill added, "His grandmother had no clue as to where we might find him but she was cooperative We have a couple of last names of friends. If we can locate them, Bubba could be staying there."

"Boss, what do you want me to do?" Jack asked, speaking directly at the sheriff.

Before Maxie could reply, Bill spoke up. "You know, I think I'll go to the local school and try to find a school annual that might have Bubba or his friends picture in it. Hamilton and McGregor are surely listed somewhere in them, too. Perhaps I will get some first names." Bill paused briefly and glanced at Maxie and Jack then added, "At least it's a place to start."

When the phone rang and Maxie quickly picked up the receiver and talked to the party on the line, she turned toward Jack and said, "There's been a little fender bender out on State Hwy 26 in front of old Jeb Wooley's place. They need an officer on board. Can you run out there and check it out for me? They haven't been able to get a trooper. Shouldn't take but a few minutes of your time."

"Sure thing!" Jack said as he got up and prepared to leave. He turned to Bill and said, "I'll catch up to you later, Bill." Jack turned and hurriedly walked out.

"So, do you think this Bubba may be the murderer?" she inquired looking directly into the depth of the piercing blue eyes. She sat silently for a few seconds. *It is almost like he can see into my soul!* She pushed aside her personal thoughts. *I don't have time for this!*

Bill's expression spoke volumes, showing compassion and concern for her. *She is taking this too personally. I see those dark circles under her eyes. She didn't get any rest last night . . . Hell, it just makes me want to wrap her in my arms and tell her everything will be all right,* he thought.

"Max, there's a chance that Bubba is the killer. Right now there isn't much to go on."

Bill changed the subject and asked. "What time do you want me to bring supper tonight?"

Maxie couldn't think of graceful way to get out of the invitation Megan had issued to Bill.

"Will seven be convenient for you?" she asked. She was wondering what they would do all evening. It would be a long one and she was exhausted, both physically and mentally.

"Seven it is!" he replied as he stood up, turned and asked, "You two Texas gals do like barbecue and the works, don't you?"

"Yeah, that's fine. I'll furnish the dessert. Okay?" She supplied in a subdued tone of voice.

"Sounds good, I may not see you again until tonight but I'll be there at seven with my spurs jingling." Bill gave her a smile that made her heart do a little flip-flop. He grabbed his file and left the office, heading to the school with a happy heart.

Bill decided he would go to the high school first. *Although Bubba didn't finish school, he probably made it into high school, unless he failed a few grades. That was possible,* he thought. He turned on Commerce Street that led him to the school a few blocks away. In a few minutes, the ranger pulled into a parking space and sat there for a few minutes just observing.

The redbrick school building was old but it looked well kept. The grounds were vacant and decorated with paper and various other trash. There was a large billboard on the left that stated the bulldogs had been state champs in football two years earlier.

During the football season, the small town totally supported the team. The bleachers were filled with parents and grandparents who came to watch their sons and grandsons play. There were many fans that simply went to see the bulldogs play, just for the pure enjoyment of it. Someday Bill hoped to have a son whose games he could attend and feel the pride that these folks felt.

Bill climbed out of the truck and entered the rustic building. The smell of sweaty bodies mixed with light colognes touched his nose. "Kids have their own particular odors," he said to himself as he continued down the hall to an overhead sign that read Library.

As he entered the door of the library, he was instantly greeted with a cheerful, "Hello there. Can I be of any assistance?" the woman inquired. Savannah Brown was a shapely blond with glasses that rested near the tip of her nose. Bill guessed she was probably in her late fifties, although she tried, with make up and her clothing, to appear younger. She had a pretty smile. That counted the most with him.

He cordially greeted her and stated, "I'm Texas Ranger Bill Sullivan. I'm assisting the sheriff's department in investigating the murder of the Meyers' girl. I'd like to see some school yearbooks that date back several years ago. Just point the way." He suggested as he turned toward the many shelves of books.

"What year are you wanting to see?" she asked as she walked over to a shelf at the back of the room where stacks of yearbooks were stored.

Bill gave her the information. She pointed to a section and hurried away speaking over her shoulder, "If I can be of any assistance, holler."

Bill took out a handful of books, marked the spot so he could put them back in the their proper places, and walked to a nearby table. He placed them in the middle of the table, sat down and began to thumb though each annual, each grade, searching for the names he sought-Hamilton, McGregor and Green. As he completed looking through a book, he placed it to one side and began another.

Thank goodness the classes were small. At least it won't take me as long to search as I thought it would, he thought to himself. Several minutes later, he came up with a name, James Hamilton. He took out his book of notes and made a notation of the name and year. As he turned another page, he saw the Hamilton name again just a grade below the first. *They could be brothers.* He was pretty sure they weren't twins because they didn't resemble. *They could be from totally different families,* he thought as he jotted down the name in his book. Bill continued through several books, writing names down as he found them. After he located the Hamiltons, he ran across Bobby Fred Green's round face looking straight ahead. His expression was sullen but revealed little. Willie McGregor's picture was found two pages over from Bubba's. He was a hefty boy, *probably a football jock,* Bill thought.

Bill glanced toward an available copy machine and ask whether he was permitted to make copies. She assured, "That's fine. Do you need assistance?"

He walked to the copier and turned to tell her that he could figure it out. Copy machines were a necessary part of his job.

After making copies of the pictures he had located, Bill put the annuals on the shelf and walked up to the librarian's desk and asked, "Is there a charge for copies? I made four." Bill reached back to his hip pocket and pulled out a brown wallet with an eagle embossed on the front.

"We do have a small fee for copies, but don't charge if they are for an investigation. I hope it will help get the killer. Do you think it is one of our ex-students?" Savannah was curious. She looked at the handsome man standing before her. *I'm not so old that I don't appreciate a tall, good looking guy, like you, Ranger Bill Sullivan,* she thought to herself and blushed slightly.

"Thanks Ms.Brown . . . These may help us on our case." Bill noticed her pink cheeks, wondering just what this little lady was thinking. "Your cooperation and these pictures will be very helpful," he added.

The librarian tried and failed to get a look at the pictures Bill had made before he stuck them inside a folder.

She asked, "Do you have a suspect? That was a terrible thing that happened. Right here in our own county, too."

"Yes, it was," he replied. He proceeded to change the subject.

"Ma'am, did you know the girl, Suzanne Meyers? I was hoping to talk to some of her friends while I am here. Do you know if she had a boyfriend?" he questioned her politely.

"No, I'm sorry. I really don't get closely acquainted with the students. Don't know a lot about their personal life. I guess you can find out some of that from her parents," she added. "I know she was an 'A' student. Sorry, Ranger Sullivan, I can't help you with more than that."

Bill told Savannah again how much he appreciated her help and left the old school. He went over what he had learned and made the decision to drop by the SO for a few minutes before lunch. As he pulled into the parking space, Max hurried out the front door. She looked troubled.

"Hey, where are you off to in such a hurry?" he called across the tops of a couple of rows of parked cars. She knew it was Bill but continued to fish out her car keys and then turned just as he walked up beside her.

"I thought I would run by the Meyers' house again," she stated.

"Mind if I come along?" he asked and then without waiting for an answer he added, "I have some questions of my own to ask."

"Sure. Get in." Maxie climbed into the driver's side of the vehicle, unlocked the passenger door, and waited for the long-legged ranger to get in and fasten his seat belt before she inserted the keys and started the engine.

Glancing at his atomic watch, he asked, "Would you like to stop for a little lunch? I'll bet you didn't eat a bite of breakfast. I know I didn't." He rubbed his two large hands together like a little boy outside the candy store. "I sure could go for a burger and some fries; how about it?" he cheerfully inquired.

"Oh, I haven't even thought about food. Now that you mention it, I am hungry." Maxie pulled into the Drive In and waited for Bill to give her his order. She pressed the button for service and listened for a response, then quickly gave the order to the employee. Then she scooted down into the red-leather seat and tried to relax while they waited.

Bill glanced at her, waited a few minutes before he spoke. When he did it was a subject he just picked out of the blue. "Have you ever wondered how many miles these gals walk everyday, waiting on customers? Must be a lot. There aren't very many business places today that have curb service, are there?"

Maxie, with her head resting on the seat and her eyes closed, laughed softly. "I've thought about that same thing." She continued to relax until the burgers arrived. Maxie was about to doze off. The tiring day and sleepless night had taken its toll.

"Are you ready to share this cholesterol junk food together?" he softly asked. Slowly, Maxie pulled herself back to the surface of consciousness and opened those beautiful green eyes. She had a relaxed expression and a drowsy look in her eyes.

"I must be boring as hell or you are one tired lady," chuckled the ranger, as she handed the hot burger and fries to him.

The food smelled delicious and her appetite surged. *I'm famished,* she realized. Bill opened the drink holder and set in her drink, handing her a red straw. She carefully took the paper off her hamburger and took a big bite. "Umm, this is delicious! I didn't realize it but I am starving. Can't remember when I last ate. Last night I think I had a small piece of pepperoni pizza. Right now I am not even sure of that." She turned and gave him a drowsy smile, her eyes half closed.

Bill stared at Maxie with blue eyes, filled with concern for her. Then he gave his attention to the meal at hand, trying not to think about how sexy Maxie looked. He could visualize her just waking up to a sunny morning after a long night of steamy romance. He body grew tight just thinking about it. "Don't think about it!" he commanded his body. Until Maxie glanced over at him, he didn't realize he had spoken out loud. His face took on a sun-kissed glow. *Damn!*

"Don't think about what?" she asked innocently. Judging by the color of his face, she couldn't imagine what he was thinking. She was silent for a moment waiting for his reply.

Bill paused to try to think of an explaination. Then he said something that made no sense, "Well, ah, I, ah was thinking about that poor kid that was murdered," he stammered. He realized that this was not good dinner conversation. He quickly tried to recover and get in control of his thoughts and his body. "Hey, let's don't talk business right now. I'm sorry, my mind just keeps going over and over the events of the past few days," he apologized and tried to change the subject.

"Is Megan looking forward to my visit tonight?" he inquired, hoping to get Max's mind away from her duties.

"Well, I suppose she is; she made a remark at breakfast that she couldn't wait to tell her friends that you were coming over. In her words, 'I can hardly wait. All my girlfriends think he is a hottie.' At times, Maxie was absolutely shocked at some of the words that came from her innocent little teenage girl's mouth.

It suddenly occurred to her that Megan would soon be fourteen. *Oh, my gosh! Fourteen!* She would like to go out on dates, as many of her friends. However, years ago she and Matt had discussed and made the decision that Megan would be fifteen before she car-dated and that would be to school-sponsored events only. They knew in this generation there were so few rules for teenagers. Maxie was of the opinion early car dating resulted in more kids hooked on drugs and many pregnant, unwed mothers, who were yet children. Maxie knew she could not give in to Megan's pleas. She was so tempted to at times when Megan turned on the charm, of which she possessed an over-abundance. She sighed.

Bill and Maxie continued to consume their unhealthy lunch in a comfortable silence. Both lost in their own thoughts and desires.

Bill is a really nice guy. We're friends as well as co-workers. I like that! Oh, he pisses me off at times when he thinks he knows what's best for me. The flowers were a nice touch, Mr. Bill Sullivan.

Finally, she spoke. "Bill, I really loved the yellow roses and your card was sweet. Thank you for the apology. Since when am I the yellow rose of Texas?" she chuckled and tossed the wrapper into the brown paper bag and wiped her hands again on the thin white paper napkin.

Bill sat looking down and said something corny. "Yellow roses are beautiful but thorny. Do you find any connection there?" He teased to keep the moment from becoming too serious. *Beware! Proceed with caution! This little lady is too scared to even think about a relationship right now,* he was thinking. *That's fine with me . . . hell no!, it isn't fine with me, but do I have any choice?*

Maxie giggled, like a young girl, but then frowned and she warned, "You better be very careful, too, with all those thorns you could get hurt. You know, Bill, I really wouldn't want that to happen."

Bill sat back and listened to her words. *She's issuing me a warning! My chances with her aren't really strong right now, but I intend to work on that one. I've never been a quitter.*

Don't intend to start now. He turned his head towards her, smiled that sexy smile and didn't say a word.

For awhile Maxie sat quietly, staring straight ahead. As she ran her words through her mind, she was afraid her heart was already in jeopardy.

When she married Matt, it was for good or bad and forever. The couple had made plans to buy a little summerhouse or a condo on the Gulf, near the spot where she had been born and grew up. Early on they had put aside money for that. When little Megan was born, they set up a saving account to be used for her education. She was still contributing to that fund. However, she sold the summer house as it only reminded her the dream was dead and gone. One thing she had told herself after Matt was killed was that she would never marry again and certainly not to another law enforcement officer. *Do I still feel that way?* A small voice repeated the words Bill had spoken earlier, '*You deserve to be happy. You know Matt would want you to,*' he had said. *Did she deserve happiness?* She asked herself . . .

Her thoughts were still tormented with the visions of Matt's death. That horrible feeling returned to haunt her. When she had heard the gun explode, dread washed over her again and again, flooding her soul with fear. At that moment, she knew that Matt was gone, before she even knelt at his side. She would never forget how white his face was as he lay there in a pool of crimson. She trembled and then screamed for someone to call 911 . . . and waited for the EMT's to tell her what she already knew. Matt was dead! *It was my fault! It should have been me, not Matt. How can I go on with my life after that? Am I sentenced to a lifetime of loneliness and guilt?*

Time goes on but that moment was with her everyday. She was advised to go to counseling over those issues. She did. She was even assured that God had forgiven her of any wrongdoing if she was to blame. Maxie just couldn't forgive herself.

Chapter 5

After Jack had handled the fender-bender, he went back to the office or SO as officers generally referred to the sheriff's office with initials only. He asked Charlee if there was anything new in the murder case. She told him the lab had finally gotten a make on the old shoe print. However, the company had gone out of business some years ago.

"I do have some good news," she added. "Mary Bell and I found some old records and got an ID on Bubba Green. I don't suppose he got a license until he was grown but I can see that not having one didn't keep him off the streets. He was arrested several times for misdemeanors: theft, driving without a license, criminal mischief and such. He made a few trips to jail for possession. The kid never had much supervision and his poor granny couldn't keep up with him. He just wouldn't mind her, was never home on time, took her car without permission. Finally, she just quit trying and turned him completely loose on society."

"We have a social security number," she said as she handed Jack a slip of paper with a pencil scrawl on it.

"Well, I guess that is better than nothing. See if you can get the skinny on him. Maybe you can come up with a DL number. You never know," he said. After jotting the social security number on the manila folder he held in his hand, he handed Charlee the slip of paper, "I'm going to that used clothing shop. You know, they could have an old sneaker with that tread design and they might have sold a pair to the killer. Who knows."

Jack slipped out the side door to his Expedition parked on the west side of the building. He cruised downtown and parked near the used-clothing store. As he entered, several volunteers cheerfully greeted him, asking about his wife, Marge, and their son, Jason. He, in turn, asked about their grandchildren, as most of the working ladies were of the older generation and many were widows.

After ten or fifteen minutes of PR work, Jack got down to the business at hand and asked the ladies, "You do have a box of old shoes available, don't you?" They nodded and led the way to a large box of assorted shoes.

Pricilla teased, "Jack, are you needing shoes so bad, you have to come to us? What's the matter? Doesn't that lady sheriff pay you enough to buy new ones?" Everybody in the shop laughed and Jack chuckled right along with them. They all knew why Jack was here—to search for evidence of some kind. This wasn't his first time in the store to do that.

"Dig!" Pricilla demanded, as she pointed to the full box of assorted types of shoes.

"Yes, Ma'am! If I don't come up for air by one o'clock, better call 911," he teased.

The ladies all smiled and went back to their jobs of sorting and folding the donated clothing from a nearby box that had recently been brought into the store. Some items that were torn and soiled got tossed as trash. Clothes in decent condition were sorted by sizes, folded in neat stacks and placed on shelves to be sold from $.10 to $1.00. For the desperate party, such as victims of fires, there was no charge. The ladies worked companionably, side by side, talking softly to one another.

Jack began the task of pulling out every pair of old athletic shoes. As he checked the bottoms, he placed them on the floor beside him. There were at least a hundred of them. Just as he was about to hit bottom, he located a pair that looked very much like the half-print sent to forensics. He laid this pair aside and continue to check those remaining. Finally, he gathered the shoes on the floor and haphazardly tossed them back into the box. He picked up the worn pair, walked up to the front and placed them on the counter. "I'll take these. How much do I owe you lovely ladies?" As he asked, Jack took out a black-leather wallet from his jacket pocket.

Avis, looking pleased, said, "We aren't charging you for these, Jack. They are on the house. This is your lucky day!" The other volunteers agreed and smiled at Jack.

"Any of you girls remember Bobby Fred Green or Bubba, as he was called?" questioned Jack. One or two said they remembered him. "Has he been in the store buying anything, that you remember, in particular, shoes?"

Avis said, "We don't work everyday. There are different volunteers designated and scheduled for the whole week. But, I remember him though. I haven't seen him in years." The other ladies said about the same thing. Some didn't know that he was back in town. Most hadn't seen Bubba since he was a kid. Those who remembered him, did so because he was always in a lot of trouble. Jack got the name and number of the person he needed to call for a list of all the volunteers. One of them might have seen Bubba come into the store over the past two weeks.

Jack thanked the women and left the shop with a pleasant smile on his face. After stopping for a snack at the drive-in grocery, he drove back to the sheriff's office. He devoured the chicken salad sandwich before he arrived at the S.O. He grabbed his drink, shoes and went inside. Mary Bell was still out for lunch, he supposed, since her desk was unoccupied.

Jack went into his office near the back and placed the old shoes on the floor, upside down. He took out the picture of the shoe print located at the murder scene. He speculated. *I do believe the tread is a match.*

Once Jack got the other names of the volunteers of the used clothing shop, he spent the greater part of the afternoon making calls to them. However, he struck out when none remembered seeing Bubba come into the shop.

Chapter 6

The sheriff was at her desk, with Jack standing next to her, when Charlee came in and sat down in a chair nearby. Maxie was tired. Actually, at this moment she felt like she could sleep lying on a taunt barbed-wire fence. They were discussing the murder, all the evidence and speculating about the killer.

"Speculations don't count!" Maxie said as she slapped her hand on her desk. "You know we have to have the facts." She had no reason to jump Jack. She added politely, "I'm so sorry, Jack. Right now, I'm very frustrated about the whole thing. We're getting nowhere! In the meantime, this pervert may be out there stalking his next victim!"

"Sheriff, can we bring in Bubba Green? I think Bill has him located at the Hamilton place on First Street. At least, his old truck in the driveway. We don't need to arrest him, just bring him in and talk to him. Can't we do that?" he pleaded.

"Well, we can't arrest him! We have no evidence that he is involved in this case. If you can find him, talk to him. He may refuse to come into the office. I'm sure, with his history, he is nervous of jails. He may have an alibi. Ask him for a DNA sample. Swab his mouth or get a hair sample. The sample found at the scene turned out to be one of Jennifer's blond hairs. Ask to see his sneakers and check the bottoms. See if he owns a hunting knife. Get whatever you can from him. If he has any idea that he may be a suspect, he will take off for parts unknown. You know he will. So be nice, Jack." the lady sheriff cautioned.

Jack grinned and said, "I'll take Charlee along. She can charm the feathers off a rooster, and will have him eating out of her hand in no time," he turned towards the deputy as he made the last statement. He watched her face turn red and turned his attention back at Maxie.

"Sheriff, you need to go home and rest. You're barely able to stay upright in that chair. I can't leave you sitting here; you might fall out and hurt yourself," Jack teased.

"Jack, for once you may be right. I think I'll call it a day. See you two in the morning."

Maxie started closing files and straightened her desk as the deputies glanced at each other and walked out. Both of them were surprised. Maxie didn't take advice readily, but, left shortly afterwards to go home and rest. At least she wanted to rest. Could she? That was the question.

About 4:00 p.m., Charlee came into Jack's office, carrying a slip of paper. She sounded cheerful when she stated, "Hey, I got results on the social security number. NCIC ran it through the computer and came up with this driver's license number and identification. Guess what? I ran the criminal history on this guy and found out he just got out of prison at Huestonville. Served about five years on a felony possession charge. His MO is a mile long," she said as she handed him the printouts.

Jack quickly scanned the offenses on the criminal history and turned to the deputy and complimented her, "Good job! This will help us track old Bubba down, for sure. At least this," pointing to the list in hand, "sure tells us what kind of guy we are up against, doesn't it? He has quite a track record, doesn't he? No violent offenses apparently. That's unusual." Jack added, as he continued to look over the list of offenses.

To receive a full compliment from Deputy Jack Rankin made Charlee's face turn slightly pink. Jack was crass at times and blunt at others but seldom complimentary. That was not a part of his matter-of-fact demeanor. Working with him had certainly been a learning experience for Charlee. The twenty-five-year veteran peace officer had knowledge that was invaluable to her. She had a lot of respect for Jack and they worked well together. *Perhaps, he likes me because I take orders well,* she mused.

Jack was thoughtful and finally added, "I am going to find the ranger." He picked up the rap sheet and started out the door but Charlee called out to him.

"Hey, Jack, I'm going out and grab a bite of lunch. I'll be back in about an hour?" she said.

Jack peered around the doorframe and said. "Sure thing, Cha Cha." Being called by her nickname, Cha Cha, didn't surprise Charlee anymore. He was well known for nicknaming his friends. Jack grinned and left the building. It just meant he liked her. *Imagine that!*

Charlee Barnes was of German descent, which showed in her fair-skin and blond good looks.She stood a good five-feet, ten inches in height and was solidly built. At twenty-five years of age, she was an attractive, single girl, without an inch of fat. True, most guys were shorter than she, but that didn't bother her at all; however, it was a factor that seems to disturb most men. As a result, she just chose not to date anyone right now and concentrated on her career. Occasionally, she dined out in the evening with one or two of her friends from the church. Charlee was a good cook and at times she prepared dinner and invited a few friends to her tiny apartment for companionship.

Deputy Barnes lived about eight blocks from work, with her calico cat, Patches. She loved her job and the folks she worked with. She liked trying to make a difference in people's lives. Charlee Barnes was a true public servant. She is dependable, a little naive and very ambitious. She knew everybody. Charlee made a point of getting acquainted with folks and when she did she gained their trust immediately. *That can't hurt, can it?* That is what she told herself anyway.

Her favorite color was bright orange, a decor that was very evident throughout the combination living room and kitchen. Down a short hall on the left was the tiny bedroom and bath. The rooms were small but big enough for her and Patches. It was convenient to work, the post office, café and a family-owned laundry and dry cleaning business. She was happy there. Her neighbors were middle-aged but they were friendly. Charlee could call them all by name.

Granny Sue, a sweet elderly lady, lived across the hall. Although she was not really Charlee's relative, she kept Patches for her when Charlee had to be out of town a few days at a law enforcement seminar in Austin. Granny affectionately told her friends she was taking care of her grand kitty.

When Charlee had finished her lunch and visitation hour, as Jack sometimes called it, she was back at the S.O. bright eyed and raring to go. As she came down the hall to

Jack's office, she could hear two men's voices talking in low tones. Bill and Jack were in a serious conversation.

"What's up?" she questioned, looking at first one and then the other.

"I called Bubba and scheduled him to come in tomorrow morning. He promised he would. Swears he knows nothing about the murder. Blah, blah, blah. Sure wanted to arrest him right there on the spot. He has a smart mouth and that just makes me want to smack him all the more!" Jack stated

"You know there is a chance he will run, don't you?" Charlee asked.

"Sure! I tried to be nice, Cha Cha. It is just not part of my nature." Jack said.

"Jack, why don't you and I run over to the Hamilton house and see if we can just catch him there. We can fire a few quick questions his way and feel him out." Bill suggested.

"All right with me! Do we need to take Charlee with us?" Jack asked, speaking to Bill.

Bill was weighing the pros and cons and finally said, "Why not!"

The three of them told Mary Bell they wouldn't be back to the office before she left to go home and then they left.

It was a fifteen-minute drive to the little blue house with white shutters on the corner of Main and First Streets. Sure enough, as the officers approached they could see the old truck that was now registered to Bubba. They got out and walked to the front of the house. Jack knocked on the door that at one time had been a bright red, but was now a faded pinkish orange color. After the second attempt at getting someone to answer the door, Jack called, "Bubba, I know you are in there, come and open this door. We need to talk. This is the sheriff's department."

The door slowly opened a crack, and a tiny little girl with the blackest eyes Jack ever saw looked up at him. "Mister, what do you want?" a small voice asked.

Jack knelt down to the child's level and spoke more softly, "Honey, we just want to talk to Bubba. Please, tell him to come to the door, will you?" The little face disappeared and in a few minutes, the door swung open wide and there stood the one and only Bobby Fred Green in the flesh, which he had in abundance.

Bobby Fred wore a grungy white tee shirt that failed to cover his rotund belly and a dirty pair of jeans with a hole in both knees. He was barefooted. His brown hair was oily and dirty and he looked as if he hadn't shaved since his release from the pen. A cigarette hung out of one side of his mouth as he asked, "Well, Jack, what can I do for you?" His brown eyes rested on Bill as he spoke even though his question was directed at Jack. Then, they slowly slid over Charlee in a lusty way.

Jack introduced his companions, telling himself to keep his cool, "This is Texas Ranger Bill Sullivan and Deputy Barnes."

A moment of fear or hatred was registered in Bubba's eyes, which he quickly covered up.

"What can I do for you, Ranger?" he removed his cigarette and ran his tongue nervously across his lips.

"We want to ask you a couple of questions, Bubba." Bill said in a pleasant manner. "We are investigating the murder of the Meyers' girl. You were staying at the Jeffers' place, next door to the Meyers, for a while and were wondering if you saw anyone messing around the their house See anything going on that just didn't seem right?"

"Nah. I was sleeping most of the day, working some at night. Nah, I didn't see nothin'," Bubba stated, looking down at his feet. He started closing the door when he added, "I don't know nothin' about no murder. I told you, Jack, I'll be in tomorrow. I got work to do." The door slammed.

Jack and Bill looked at one another and then at Charlee. With eyebrows raised Bill asked, "What was that all about?"

"Don't look at me!" Charlee exclaimed. "He is hiding something but I got the impression it's drugs and not a murder. How about you two, did you get any vibes?"

"About the same as you. He is probably flying high. I got of drift of the smell of marijuana same as you." Jack said.

"Yeah, I'd say he is trying to hide something but I don't think he knows anything about the murder," Bill remarked as they walked back to the their vehicle. They discussed the aspects of the case as they drove back to the office.

"Where do we go from here? He was our only suspect!" Charlee exclaimed loudly.

"If we have to, we start over. Bubba isn't off the hook yet. We will see what he has to say in the morning." Bill said wearily. "Let's all go home and get some rest. We can start fresh in the morning." He climbed into his truck and drove away deep in his own thoughts.

The Texas Ranger drove to the boarding house, showered and changed clothes. He was really undecided whether he should take supper to Maxie and Megan or take a rain check. He sat around in his room, reading and relaxing, for an hour or so. Then he called their residence on his cell phone. Megan picked the receiver and answered, "Hello."

"Hey there, Kitten," he greeted. "Is your mother still sleeping? I was sitting here wondering if I should take a rain check on supper tonight."

"Mom is taking a shower. I don't think she slept much but she rested a little." Megan sounded concerned. "Ranger, we're ready to eat when you get here. I'm going to make the tea. We'll be waiting for the food; so hurry up." Megan said.

"Do you want to go ask your Mom about that?" Bill was hesitant to just come in unannounced.

Megan knew what her parent would say if she did ask, *Punkin', I'm just not up to company tonight. Tell him some other time.* Megan wasn't about to give Maxie the chance to say no. She said softly, "It'll be fine. Please don't discuss business though. Mom needs to get her mind off that stuff. She's really been upset over this case, you know?"

"I know," agreed the ranger. "Listen, I will be there in about thirty minutes. OK?" Megan agreed and hung up the receiver. Maxie came into the living room looking more rested.

"Honey, who was on the phone?" she asked her daughter.

"Bill. He'll be here in half and hour with the barbecue," Megan replied.

Darn! I had forgotten all about that, Maxie thought, *I don't feel like entertaining tonight!*

Maxie asked, "Megan, why didn't you come and ask me about that?" sounding a little cross.

"Mom, if I had, what would you have said? No, that's what! You need to think of something besides the murder case." Megan pleaded.

"You're right. I do need to think of something else. I don't know why I can't get any sleep. I close my eyes and

I see poor Suzanne. Maybe that picture will fade away in a day or so." Maxie said wishfully.

"I hope so, Mom," Megan hugged her mother and went into the kitchen to brew the tea for supper.

Maxie sat on the sofa and picked up a Good Housekeeping magazine and thumbed through it, not really aware of what she saw and unable to concentrate on the words before her. *I've got to get a grip on myself. There is no way I can do my job if I can't be objective about this case. Dear God, help me,* she prayed.

After her shampoo and shower, Maxie put on gold sweat shirt and a worn pair of Levi jeans. She was barefoot and comfortable. She certainly wasn't going to dress up for the ranger. Her face was free of makeup, although, she had dotted on a little peach—colored lipstick. She was blessed, so her grandmother said, with a few freckles scattered across her nose and cheeks that made her appear a picture of an innocent young girl. *I'm far from innocent, much less a young girl,* she mused

When the knock came, Maxie got up and opened the door to greet the big hunk, Ranger Bill Sullivan. He had both hands full and she held the door open as he brushed passed her and headed towards the kitchen. There he greeted Megan cheerfully and started setting out the things he had purchased to put together a meal for the three of them. He even thought of paper plates and cups.

Guess he doesn't like washing dishes, Maxie thought. *Well, neither do I!*

The two of them, Megan and Bill, shooed her out of the kitchen and suggested she just sit and rest while they finished up. Maxie went back and plopped down on the sofa. She could hear the hum of their voices making light conversation and Megan adding a giggle once in a while.

Maxie leaned back into the soft cushion and closed her eyes and listened. *They are good together. Not many men have a rapport with teenagers. Most don't speak their language. Bill seems to know all the things to say and just what to ask about to draw Megan out of her quiet shell. He'll make a good father someday,* she sighed. *Megan needs a dad. Wait a minute, self, that's not a good reason to get involved with anyone-just to get Megan a dad. She has one already.* Maxie was angry with herself for even having such a thought about Bill. *What would he think if he knew I was having these thoughts?* That idea amused her.

The small kitchen table was laid out with some succulent babyback ribs, pinto beans and German potato salad. Megan had sliced French bread and made the tea. The table was set with the red-plaid paper plates and red cups and napkins to match. It was all very cheerful and appealing.

"Thank you, guys," Maxie smiled when she entered after being summoned by Megan. The three of them sat down. Megan said a short blessing over the food and they began their supper together. Bill kept the conversation going and steered away from anything that might be construed as business. He teased Megan and glanced at Max every now and then, who had little to say. However, she did eat her share of the food. It was a delicious and comfortable mealtime.

Bill didn't stay long after he "washed the dishes" as he called it when they were tossed into the garbage. Megan put away the leftovers, which were slim pickings. The two girls went into the living room and sat down.

"Do you have homework, Meg?" asked her mother.

"I did that while you were resting, Mom. Want to watch television?" Megan inquired.

"That's fine, Sugar. Just pick something not so serious; a comedy maybe." Maxie suggested.

"Here's an 'I Love Lucy' rerun. That alright with you?" Megan asked, turning to her mom.

"Fine," Maxie replied. The two of them sat on the sofa, cuddled up together, and watched Lucy and her antics. Once in a while they made comments to one another. Megan giggled a lot. Maxie just savored the moment of companionship between them. She knew it probably was asking too much for it to remain that way. After all, Megan was a teenager. This was a stage when teens got so smart that they thought they knew more than the parent did. This companionable moment meant the world to Maxie. She simply sat and enjoyed it, knowing they would always be close even when they were miles apart.

Chapter 7

The killer was scanning through the newspaper. He chuckled. *It looks like I've gotten away with this murder, too!* Other than the obituary, there was no mention of the police having a suspect or any leads in the case. *That was just too easy*, the skinny guy was thinking. *I reckon I'm too smart for the dummies around here! Half of them don't know their ass from a hole in the ground.* He gloated at the thought of his clever moves at the scene. *The secret is not to leave any evidence-just quick and clean-that is the secret!*

The assailant was feeling very good about the whole thing. He held in his hand a ladies diamond wrist watch. Looking at the face and at the back he was speculating what it might be worth at the pawnshop. When he needed cash, he would take it in and see. It looked expensive but you never knew this day and age, even nice looking watches could be purchased at a supercenter for under $20. He would check it out. Right now, he had a lawn to mow. Since his release from prison, that is what he did for a living because he claims he was unable to find a real job. This one put groceries on the table and let him get a look at what might be his next victim. He smiled as he rubbed his hand across a jagged scar on his cheek.

Chapter 8

The next day everybody was back to work in full force at the sheriff's department. Bubba was true to his word but came in about an hour late. He had cleaned up some. At least his hair was recently shampooed and beard was trimmed. He wore clean jeans and another tee shirt, that didn't quite cover his large stomach, and a dirty pair of sneakers. He was nervous. Bill imagined he was in need of his morning fix. That was enough to make his hands shake. The ranger smiled thinking about it. *Too bad, Bubba!*

After a grueling question and answer session, which gave them few results in the murder case, Jack requested Bubba to remove his sneakers. Bubba did as he was asked, glancing at Charlee whom he notice looked good this morning. Jack pulled out the photo of the partial print at the murder scene to compare with the tread on Bubba's shoe. They didn't match the footprints. *So much for that clue,* Jack thought to himself.

Bill bent over face-level with Bubba, glaring him right in the eye and asked, "Do you own a hunting knife of any kind?"

Bubba twisted his hands together and answered, "Yeah." *I don't like the way this ranger looks at me; he has the coldest, icy stare that I have ever seen. He gives me the willies. I haven't done anything wrong!*

"Where is the knife now, Bubba?" asked Bill, never taking his eyes from the man.

"It's in my truck, I guess. Want me to run out and look for it?" he was hoping to get away for a few minutes so he could smoke a cigarette or something.

Quickly, Jack got a permission slip signed to search Bubba's truck. He got up and said to the man, "If your truck isn't locked, I'll go out and see if I can locate your knife."

What could Bubba say except, "Go ahead. It may be under the front seat on the driver's side. I didn't lock my truck. Should be safe parked right here at the sheriff's office, shouldn't it?" he said, sarcastically as Jack left the room.

Maxie, who had been silent, spoke up, "Bobby, do you have any information concerning this murder? I get the feeling you aren't telling the whole truth. I don't believe you committed the crime but there is something else, isn't there?"

"No," he said as he ducked his head and squirmed around in his seat.

Jack came back into the room, carrying a large hunting knife in a brown leather holster. "Forensics will want to see this," he said to Bill and Maxie, since there appears to be a blood stain near the handle."

Defensively Bubba replied, "Well, it's a huntin' knife after all. I went coon huntin' and skinned that sucker out. Guess I didn't clean it up very good. No law saying that I have to, is there?"

The lady sheriff, deputies and ranger were silent for a minute. *Let Bubba squirm a while,* thought Maxie.

The Texas Ranger asked Bubba for a swab for DNA so he could be struck from the list as a suspect, if indeed he was innocent. Bubba opened his mouth for Charlee to swab. She swabbed the inside of his foul-smelling mouth, put the swab into an evidence bag, sealed and marked it for evidence. She glared at him in disgust. He grinned wickedly at her. Bubba licked his lips as he was thinking. *What a juicy broad! I'd like to get a piece of you! I could show you what a real man is like, girlie,* and he pondered on the things he could do to the deputy given the opportunity.

The sheriff asked, "Are we through with him?" They all agreed that they had about exhausted the efforts to find any clues that he was connected with the murder. The next step was to check his DNA and the evidence on the knife. Bubba was dismissed and allowed to leave the office.

"Bill, what is your opinion? Do you think this scum had anything to do with the murder?" asked Maxie as she looked directly at him. She was thinking, *he looks rested and refreshed this morning.* His coal black hair was neatly combed and he wore a light, manly cologne. *I guess I have never noticed just how good looking he is. He was so sweet last night. Brought in all the food for supper and helped clean up. I appreciated that he didn't hang around after supper or talk business. I was really tired and not good company. However, his visit gave me a chance to really see him as just a good man. Megan likes him. That is important, too. Ummm . . .*

Bill sat quietly, staring into space. "Max, I doubt the DNA will turn up anything. I don't figure Bubba knows a thing about the murder, but he may have some information we could use." Bill added, "I get the feeling he is hiding something. It may be the drugs. If he is out on parole and using he could go back to jail for violation of his parole. I'm sure he knows that. Enough to make him nervous, don't you suppose?"

"Well," Jack injected, "I didn't say anything but I confiscated a bag of crack when I searched the truck for his hunting knife. I thought we might could use this as a bargaining tool later," Jack said nonchalantly as he placed the baggie on the sheriff's desk.

"Good idea, Jack," Maxie commented.

Jack looked from Bill to Maxie and asked, "What did you learn yesterday at the Meyers' home? Any new developments?"

Maxie stated that they had very little additional information. The key thing that had come up was that the family had not been able to locate an expensive watch that was given to Suzanne for her coming graduation from high school. It was possible that the killer had grabbed it. The girl evidently wore the jewelry all the time to school, although her parents had cautioned her that it was too valuable for everyday wear. The family was still searching the house to be sure it was missing. They gave me a name of the boy Suzanne had dated a few times. He was from a nice home and a good family that the Meyers had known for years.

"We don't really think that will lead anywhere but we want to check him out." Maxie sighed.

"Ranger, what is our next move?" Jack questioned. "Got any suggestions about where to go from here?" He glanced at Maxie and back to the ranger. Charlee stood quietly nearby.

Bill answered thoughtfully. "I think we should check the pawnshop to see if the watch is there. It may be a little early to pawn the watch though. We can check locally first and then call the shops in the surrounding towns. He would be a fool to pawn it here. Like we said, at this point, we aren't even sure it's gone. Sure won't hurt to alert the pawn brokers about the watch and give them a description of it."

Bill turned towards Maxie and asked, "Max, do you have something for Charlee to do?" Maxie shook her head in reply.

He then addressed the deputy, "You want to check all the pawn shops, Charlee?"

Bill could see that she was eager to be of service when she replied excitedly, "Sure thing!" and immediately left the office. Bill smiled, *Aww, the eagerness of youth!*

Jack gave his full attention to the sheriff and asked with concern, "Boss, did you get any sleep last night. Looks like you bumped into two doorknobs with those circles under your eyes," he said teasingly.

"Jack, I did get some sleep. I rested a little yesterday afternoon, too. Thanks for your concern. Really, I'm all right. Don't worry about me." Maxie smiled affectionately at her number one deputy. She asked Jack, "What are your plans today?"

"Well, first I'm going to Waco to the forensic lab with these things," Jack said, as he held up the DNA samples and knife.

"Jack, why don't you let me do that. I should go anyway and check in at the office and see what is going on." Bill stated.

"Okay with me." Jack shrugged. "Let's go ahead and take the bagged evidence to have it tested while we are at it."

"Good idea." Bill said turning to Maxie, "Sheriff, I will probably be gone for a day or two. If anything comes up and you need me, call my cell phone number, will you?"

Looking directly at her he softly added, "You will call if you need me, won't you?"

He truly cares about that gal! Jack was thinking and he turned and stepped into the hall to give them a moment of privacy. A huge smile crossed his face. *About time!*

Before she thought, Maxie said, "I'll miss you." She realized how suggestive that sounded and added in a more business-life manner, "I mean, you've been a lifesaver on this murder investigation. You know, I think I must be getting too old to work these murders anymore. They drain the very life out of me." She looked up into those bright blue eyes and saw worry. Before she knew what was happening, Bill leaned over and planted a sweet kiss on her forehead and grinned as he left the office.

Maxie could hear him whistling as he walked down the hall. She smiled. *My daddy used to whistle. Suddenly, I really miss him. He would say that if we forget to whistle, maybe life was getting too serious.* She sat quietly, deep in thought, for a few minutes. She was remembering the days of her youth and the good times with her family. *Family meant everything to Pop. He was so proud of his sons because they followed him into law enforcement. You died, Daddy, without knowing that I wanted to be just like you, too. I hope you know that now, but Daddy, it is so hard at times. How did you do your job all those years and keep your life pulled together? Where did you get the courage and strength?* The answer came to her suddenly, *from God.* She sighed and said a silent prayer for God to give her strength to get through this and help her find the killer before he murdered someone else.

Another thought popped into her head, *Bill, I miss you already. You are steadfast and dependable. Someone a girl can lean on. I could get use to that.*

Maxie had other duties to attend to and quickly read over the few notes that Mary Bell had handed her when she came in earlier. One was about a stray dog chasing a sheep out on County Road 306. She made a quick call to the animal control officer. She gave him the necessary information about the dog. He told Maxie he would drive out and pick up the animal.

Then the sheriff had a call that there was a family disturbance at the Fuller's place again. After Maxie looked over the other notes she got up from her cluttered desk, emptied and washed her coffee cup and told Mary Bell she would be out at the Fuller's place for a little while. *Jake Fuller is probably drunk again,* she speculated as she drove out to try to make peace between the man and his wife of twenty-five years. This wouldn't be the first call she had made to that residence.

When she approached the old farmhouse, all appeared to be peaceful around the place. There was a crowing rooster sitting on the fence post, telling the world he was boss. A black and white collie dog lay in the sun on the front porch. She could hear the buzz of a lawn mower at the back of the house. She was certain that it wasn't Mr. Fuller mowing, because he was probably nursing a hangover. Maxie knocked loudly on the front door that could use some paint, like the rest of the house. After the second knock, the front door opened, and Mrs. Fuller stood there, her hair in curlers, wearing a faded, print house dress and sporting a beautiful black eye.

She whispered to Maxie, "Shhh, Jake's sleeping it off. We don't want to wake him up. He would really be mad at me!" She put her hand up to her swollen eye, ducked her head in shame and added, "You know, Sheriff, he's a good man. It's the liquor that makes him crazy."

"You want to file assault charges, Mrs. Fuller? Maxie asked. "That may be the only way to straighten him out, you know."

"Oh, no! I'm scared he'll kill me!" she said a little louder than she meant to. She quickly glanced toward the hallway. "You knew he fought in the Vietnam war? Well, he's never been the same since. I don't know what but it did something to him. Well, you may be too young to remember, but the soldiers were treated awful when they came home. All that made Jake ashamed, I guess. He started drinking heavily then and has never quit." Sadness enveloped Lola Fuller's face.

"I thought he got some counseling or attended AA for a while. Is he still going?" the sheriff asked Mrs. Fuller.

"Yeah, he did go for a while. Jake said nobody understood what he had been through, so Jake just quit going."

"Do you want to leave him? I can help you get a restraining order or find you a safe house, if you like." Maxie sounded concerned.

"Goodness no! I'm all he's got. If I were to leave, that would just about kill him. I could never do that. In spite of all this," she said pointing to her black eye, "I still love the man," she firmly added.

"Why did you call dispatch? Look at yourself. You know he could kill you, Mrs. Fuller."

"The reason I called is because it's the only way to get him to stop beating me. I call to get him to stop," she said flatly.

Maxie didn't think she would ever get Mrs. Fuller to file assault charges on her husband. Perhaps she could find a support group for war veterans. That might be the answer.

Maxie took information for a report and left the house, glancing at the man mowing the yard. She drove away wondering how in the world anyone could sleep with that noise under the bedroom window. They would have to be in a drunken stupor.

Chapter

When the Texas Ranger arrived at Waco, there wasn't a lot going on. He did follow up on an old case he was working on, answer a few phone messages. He was anxious to get back to his investigation and to Max.

His thoughts kept drifting back to her. *You've got it bad, Ranger,* he told himself. *That little yellow rose of Texas has me thinking about rocking cradles and mowing lawns. Darn that petite, flaming redhead, she has really gotten under my skin. Be careful, heart,* he cautioned himself, for all the good it did.

Bill visited the medical examiner's office to determine whether there was any new developments in the murder case. Also, he delivered the evidence Maxie sent for testing, including the baggie containing the unknown substance.

"Morning, Brad. Did the autopsy show any kind of drugs or anything unusual on the Meyers' kid?" he asked the ME.

"No drugs. Death due to the knife wound. Apparently, she bled out quickly."

"Any signs of rape?"

"No signs of rape or sexual intercourse. In fact, she was still a virgin," he stated.

"So, the killer is just that, a brutal killer?" This was more of a statement than a question.

"Looks like it. I'm sorry, Bill. We need more evidence than this. We got the shoe print but I imagine that came to a dead end . . . old and worn, company out of business."

"Yeah, it is pretty much impossible to track anything that old. In fact, we have such a small amount of evidence to go on in this case. It really bothers me."

"The stuff you brought in for testing today, is it from a good suspect?" the medical examiner questioned.

"Not really. So far, the guy is our only suspect . . . my gut feeling is that he is guilty all right; guilty of doing some hard stuff. Damn!" Bill was discouraged. He glanced at the body lying on the cold slab. *She is so young. I'm determined to get that murderer! Such a senseless killing!*

He turned to leave the room and headed toward the lab. The tech was running a drug test and looked up as Bill entered.

"Bill, I'll get to your tests later this afternoon, hopefully," she said a little doubtfully.

"Just when you get to it, Babe." This was not a term of endearment but a nickname.

Bill was disappointed and thought, *I'll not be able to get back today. Sorry, Max.*

He went back to his office and automatically picked up the phone to call Maxie, changed his mind, and started through the notes he had pending. He couldn't stop thinking about her but he decided he wouldn't call her. Not yet anyway. She could call him, if he was needed. *Don't rush things,* he cautioned himself.

Bill was busy most of the afternoon. After four o'clock, he went back to the lab. As he walked past the window glass surrounding the lab, Babe looked up and saw him. She looked weary and not very happy to see him. He mouthed, "Got mine ready?"

She shook her head, "No."

He waved and turned to leave the building. He would pick up a bite to eat on his way to the apartment, do some laundry and check any phone messages he might have received. He needed to stay busy and would make use of the extra time with which he found himself confronted.

When he entered his apartment, somehow it didn't feel like home. It never had. The place lacked character, looking so much like a thousand motels that he'd stayed in on his travels. The furnishings were sparse. A brown leather sofa and recliner sat on one side of the paneled room, with walnut side and coffee tables. Across the room stood a new 36" Sony television, which was seldom turned on. The kitchen area was compact and served the purpose. Bill did very little cooking. He was gone too much. That's what he told himself anyway. He went to the answering machine and punched "play" and listened to four or five messages. One call was from a buddy with whom he played golf. He sat down and dialed his number, but before the phone rang, he disconnected the line. He wasn't in any mood to make light, general conversation.

There was a call from Brittany, a female companion. He listened to the message while he was relaxing as he was reading the sports page of the newspaper. The phone rang and he hoped it was Max so he quickly answered. It was

Brittany. She wanted to see a movie and ask if he would be free to go with her. He explained that he was in town just briefly and was working on a murder case that was likely to tie him up and would probably be out of town for several weeks. He apologized and hung up.

Brittany was a nice enough girl and good company. She was a tall, slim blonde of the country club variety. Her father had money. Her mother was well known and was involved in one charity or another. Brittany had reluctantly joined her dad's law firm after law school. She seemed to have settled in, taking cases that none of the other partners of the business were interested in handling. She got most of the castoffs. She never complained. Bill imagined that, because Britt was ambitious, she would one day be running the office. Right now she was biding her time, getting the experience necessary to prepare her for that day. She was very smart. Since she was easily impressed with money, power and prestige, Bill couldn't figure why she occasionally chose him for a date or partner to attend a function at the country club or a political fundraiser of some kind. Brittany seemed to be content with a casual relationship. At times, he was not available to her and Brittany never complained when he refused. It was almost as though she preferred things to remain platonic between them. That suited Bill as well.

Bill had kicked back and was snoozing in his big leather chair when the cell phone rang in his jacket, startling him. He fumbled in the pocket of his jacket he had tossed on the arm of the sofa and said, "Hello," trying to get his thoughts together.

"Bill, this is Maxie," a soft voice said. She waited for a reply.

"Hey, Max, what's up?" He brighten up at the sound of her voice.

"Nothing new. I was curious as to whether you have any results on the samples taken in my case," she asked.

"Lab tech was busy today and had some ahead of me but Babe will have results in the morning, I imagine. Nothing much going on around here. I'm at my apartment trying to get some laundry done, you know, checking mail and paying bills; the usual everyday stuff." Bill was silent for a few moments, waiting for her reply. Her tone was very professional.

"I'm sorry to have bothered you . . . I . . . Megan was missing you tonight. She couldn't stop talking about you. Mister, you have charmed that little girl of mine." Bill could hear the smile in her voice, finally.

"I had fun last night with both of my girls. Makes a man feel special to be surrounded with all that beauty," he said in a husky voice.

"I'm the one to feel special. Hey, you sent me beautiful flowers, brought in supper, and cleaned up afterwards! I have to tell you that those things are about the most romantic thing a man can do for a working woman. A girl would be a fool to let you get away, Bill . . . Will you marry me?" she teasingly asked. No sooner had the words left her mouth did Maxie wish she could just suck them back in and unsay them. She quickly added, "I'm teasing you, Bill. But, you know you were a knight in shining armor and came to this damsel's rescue in my time of need. I truly appreciate it, Bill."

"Yes!" Bill was shocked because he would marry her in a minute but he laughed and repeated, "Yes, I guess I was the knight that saved you yesterday. You were one tired, worn out, sleepy damsel. Megan is a sweetheart. I would love to spend more time getting to know her. She is a lot like you, Max, very special."

"Well, I don't know about that but she is like me in some ways. She has her mother's temper! Sometimes I think she got a double dose of my bad points. I can see a lot of her dad's personality, though, as she gets older. However, I can't deny she belongs to me. Look at that red hair! That in itself, is a dead giveaway, isn't it?" She laughed softly and then added. "I need to get some sleep . . . Will you be home tomorrow?" *Now why did I say 'home'?* She scolded herself.

Bill was very much aware of the word 'home' himself. He smiled to himself and decided not to make an issue of it. "I should be back by nightfall, if something doesn't come up in the meantime. It'll be Friday. Would you two girls like a date with this Texas Ranger? I thought we might take in a movie. What about it? You need a life. Hell, you deserve one!" he said with the excitement of seeing the girls sounding in his voice. Then he pleaded, "Please, don't refuse."

Maxie was a sucker for his charm and little boy antics and she quickly agreed to a movie. He told her he would call or look her up when he got back to town.

She said goodbye. He said, "I miss you," and hung up the phone. She sat for several minutes thinking about the last statement. *I miss you, also, you big handsome galoot!* Somehow, he was weaving her into his blanket of life. She wasn't sure she was ready for that. *I'll take this relationship slow. When we finish working on this case together, he will leave and go back to his own life and I will resume mine. In the meantime, why shouldn't I just let myself enjoy his company? I don't believe that he is looking for a commitment anymore than I am. Perhaps he was sincere.* She pondered the possibility of that thought. *Take the ball and run with it, Max,* she challenged.

Bill sat for some time thinking about Max and their conversation. *I think my old southern charm is finally getting to her. I have to be careful and not scare her off. We can develop a deeper friendship and go from there. I can't wait to get 'home'.* He smiled, folded his paper and rose to take a cold shower.

Afterwards, he lay in bed thinking. *Tomorrow is a new beginning and the first day of the rest of our lives, Ms O'Bryan.* He drifted off to sleep with a smile on his face, dreaming about his thorny, yellow rose of Texas.

Chapter 10

Bill awoke bright and early and was at the lab before the door was unlocked. He walked down the hall to grab a cup of coffee and sat down in the lounge. While he waited, he read the newspaper. He was anxious to get the test results and finish up his business here so he could get back on the murder case and Max. Actually, it was more 'get back to Max' than anything else, he admitted.

By noon, he had the test results in hand and walked out ready to leave when his Captain dashed out and stopped him as he was climbing in his vehicle.

"Bill, we have an emergency! I've just been called about a kid holed up in an old farmhouse outside of Kingsburg. Apparently, he is high on drugs or something. He has a weapon and is threatening to kill his parents, himself or anyone who comes to the house. He's fired a couple of warning shots. The sheriff's deputy and a trooper went out to assist. They have requested a ranger to talk him out. You've been elected to do that," his superior firmly said. It may have sounded like a request but Bill, from experience, had learned it was issued as an order, which he couldn't refuse. Not that he would have. He served where he was needed.

"Sure, tell me what you know about the kid. Where are his parents? I'd like to talk to them at the scene in case the boy is willing to negotiate. Of course, they would have to remain at a safe and secure location."

He told Bill that the parents were at the scene or nearby at a neighbor's home. "I don't have any additional information right now, Bill. You need to get on the road since it is forty-five minutes drive."

In thirty minutes Bill was driving down the county road a mile out of Kingsburg. Ahead he observed a local law enforcement county vehicle and a State trooper's car. He pulled up and parked his truck. Standing behind them were two uniformed officers, all with weapons ready and sighted on the farmhouse. Bill detected a shadow as the party inside the house paced the floor. He could make out what appeared to be a pistol in one hand and a cell phone in the other. Bill spoke to the officers, identifying himself. They stepped back, putting Bill in charge.

Bill got the boy's name, all the particulars and took the megaphone and yelled. "Chris, this is Bill Sullivan. I'm a Texas Ranger. I've come to help you, son." Bill spoke with authority in his voice and yet it was laced with concern.

From inside came a booming voice screaming, "You can't help me! Nobody can. If you try to come in here, I swear, I'll shoot myself." The shadow inside the house threw the phone down and raised the weapon to the side of his head. "Just leave! I mean it, I'll kill you and myself, if you try to come in!" Chris threatened.

Bill began by telling the boy that his parents loved him and wanted to help him work out his problems. Killing himself would not solve anything. After about twenty minutes of talking back and forth, the kid agreed to talk to his father on the phone. Bill walked over to the trailer house standing several hundred yards away and tried to reassure the kid's parents. They were distraught and anxious. The step-father dialed his son's cell number and began pleading with him to surrender.

Chris was saying very little. Suddenly he yelled, "No! No! You don't understand. You have never understood me! I'm never coming out!" and disconnected.

Bill comforted the parents as much, as he was able to under the stressful circumstances, and returned to the site. He got on the megaphone again and began trying to convince Chris to let him come in and talk to him. He told Chris he would put down his weapon and enter the house unarmed.

Finally, about ten minutes later, the boy consented. Bill laid his pistol on the hood of his truck and started up the walk. He knew that he was in danger. The boy could fire off a shot and he could instantly die. At this point in a stand off the perp seldom had rational thoughts. Bill said a little prayer as sauntered up to the door. He spoke to Chris in a polite tone, "Chris, I'm unarmed. Let me in, son." In a couple of seconds the door swung wide, a scared teenage boy stood behind it. When Bill entered, Chris quickly slammed the door and pointed the gun at Bill.

"Sit over there," Chris motioned to a chair next to the front wall and one that left Chris in a position to see out the window, in case this was just a trick. His hand was shaking slightly, his eyes were pink and puffy and his nose was red. He was a basket case at this point and had a hair-trigger finger. Bill knew he was in a tight situation and this kid was wired just like a time bomb, ticking off the minutes, ready to explode. 'Handle with Care' was written all over this scene.

"Chris, you look like an intelligent young man. Why are you doing this? What's troubling you, son?" Bill sounded sympathetic enough but Chris wasn't ready to back down and he certainly wasn't in the mood to be talked down to by an officer of the law. Bill noted the anger that flared up in his bloodshot eyes. Chris kept his gun pointed directly at Bill although his eyes shifted to the view outside every few minutes.

Finally he said, "Life sucks, you know. I don't have anything to live for. My step dad hates me, my girlfriend broke up with me and my grades are failing so I've been kicked off the football team. I don't want to live anymore. It is too damn much trouble!" Chris said, with anger rippling through his young body.

"Now Chris," Bill replied calmly, "Life is worth living but you have to be willing to put some effort into it. What makes you think your father hates you?"

"He's not my father!" Chris said adamantly. "Most of the time he pretends I don't exist," he added bitterly. "That's a pretty good clue, don't you think? All we had going for us and our relationship was football, now that has been taken away from me. So, tell me, Mr. Smart Ranger, what's your opinion?"

"Listen, Chris, let's get one thing straight," Bill said firmly, "Your stepfather isn't to blame for your flunking and getting kicked off the team. You are! You have to own up to that. That doesn't have to be the end of your football career. It just means you've got to get down and dirty to study hard to get those grades up to passing the next six weeks. You, and you alone, are responsible for the situations you are in, not your mother, not your father and not your coach or your girlfriend. Admit it!"

Chris ducked his head for a brief moment and looked up and swallowed, his Adam's apple gliding up and down his skinny neck. He shook his head, negatively, cut his brown eyes in Bill's direction; but he remained silent, thinking about the things that Bill had just said.

After a few minutes pause, Bill continued, "Chris, I have to ask you this, are you on any kind of drugs? Drugs do things to your thinking process, but, you can get help for that."

"Naw! About a year ago, I did smoke a marijuana joint but decided that wasn't the route I wanted to take in my life. You know if you're in sports, you should take care of your body. I've tried to do that." Chris stated. The gun was wavering as his arm was beginning to tire.

"Why don't you put the gun down, Chris."

Chris readjusted the weapon and shook his head to indicate he wasn't complying.

Bill continued, "Okay!" and raised his hand to indicate to Chris to disregard that statement, for now.

"Chris, what about your mom? How do you think she's feeling right now? I can imagine her heart is breaking. She's wondering how she has failed you. Son, trust me, you don't want to do this. Your mother has stood by you, encouraged you and cared for you for seventeen years. Hell, you can bet she's willing to take the bullet for you to save you from making the biggest mistake of your whole life." Bill was hoping this was getting through to the boy. All he knew for certain was Chris was listening.

"You are one lucky cuss, you know that? You have a mother who is here for you. I wasn't as lucky. My mother and father burned up in a fire when I was six years old. A good man raised me. My grandfather was an interesting character. He loved me. He took care of me. He saw that I got an education. He was also a full-blood Indian. We lived on a reservation in Oklahoma. Big Hunter taught me to be self sufficient, to hunt for food, to study nature and to always be true to myself."

Finally, Chris was listening and had his mind on someone other than himself. "One of the lessons I learned was that I was responsible for my actions, good or bad. I was taught respect for others and myself. That's not a bad thing, Chris."

"Are you telling me the truth? Were you really raised as an Indian?" Chris asked, showing a small amount of interest, as he was looked at the physical features of the ranger. *He has dark hair and skin. But he has blue eyes, and that certainly wasn't common for a full blood Indian*, Chris was skeptical about Bill's story.

"You're lying!" Chris yelled, "Indians don't have blue eyes. Good story, Ranger, but I don't buy it." Chris rubbed his arm and then switched the gun to the other hand.

"I'm not lying to you. The truth is my dad was an Irishman with blond hair and blue eyes. He was riding around Oklahoma when his horse threw him and that busted his leg. One of the braves from grandfather's reservation found him and brought him into their camp. The medicine man splinted his leg but Dad couldn't travel for a couple of months. My mother was the one chosen to take care of him. They fell in love, married and moved to Texas. That's a true story." Bill waited patiently for Chris' response.

"How come you didn't die in the fire with your parents?" Chris still doubted the story.

"Well, I was visiting with Grandfather at the time . . . which they often let me do so that I could learn the heritage of my Indian ancestors. I wasn't there with them at the time of the fire . . . " Bill paused as memories came tumbling back and the same pain and guilt flooded him again. Guilt, because he had felt he might have been able to alert his family had he been there. Of course, commonsense said Bill could have died with his mother and father.

Chris stood watching Bill closely. He noted the brightness of his blue eyes. *Why, the Ranger blames himself for his parents' death! What a thing to live with.* Chris was thinking. Suddenly, his own situation came to mind and he began to think about his mom. *Will Mom blame herself if I kill myself? Would she live with that the rest of her life—feeling guilty—just like this officer. In fact, the whole thing might kill her. Can I gamble with her life that way? Mine isn't worth much, but Mom is important to the world. She's a doctor!* He began to have doubts about his plans.

"Chris, let me help you. Your Mom and step-dad are waiting for you to come out. There isn't anything here that can't be fixed. They want to support you and help you deal with your problems, son. There are solutions." he pleaded. "Please, hand me the gun." The mere fact that Chris had called 911 to tell them he was killing himself was a call for help. "Help is available, Chris, reach out for it now."

Chris was letting all the past day run through his mind and wondering how he had let himself get in this situation. He had to take responsibility for his grades and get them up. He had to work on his relationship with his dad. *My dad? This is the first time I have ever thought of him as such. But, he is my dad. He is the only one I have and I'm going to make the most of that and, with his help and Mom's, I can do it!*

Chris lowered the weapon, carefully released the shooting mechanism and handed the revolver to Bill. He was ready to surrender and he supposed he would be going to jail. He heard the words repeated in his mind, *take responsibility for your actions. Yes, I can do that.*

Bill opened the front door and heard the click of guns cocking and saw them trained directly on himself and Chris. He waved his hand and shouted, "He is unarmed and coming out. Stand down." He turned to Chris placed a large hand on his shoulder and said to him, "Chris, this is a new beginning. Don't let the past drag you down. You're a good kid. You sorta lost your way for a while. Now you hold up that head and know that I am proud of you. It takes guts to do what you are about to do. Surrender. This tells me that you have an inner strength that will carry you through life. Fall back on that strength when you need help. Be proud of who you are, son. You are important to others and you should feel important to yourself. Set high standards . . . but give your parents a chance to get closer to you. Communication is important in any relationship. Talk to your folks. Don't feel ashamed to ask for help. Be happy and know that if you need to talk to someone, I'm here, Chris."

"Thanks, Ranger, I have every intention of doing just that." Chris reached out and gave the tall ranger a quick hug and walked out with his head held high.

Bill took a deep breath and felt relief. *He is going to be all right, with a little luck and God's helping hand.*

It was getting late by the time Bill completed his report of the incident. He had an appointment to talk to Chris' parents on Sunday afternoon. He knew he wouldn't get back to Maxie today. He made a quick call and left a message on her voice mail at home to that effect. Like it or not, he was spending another night in Waco. He looked forward to seeing her Monday. Suddenly, the weekend stretched out and would be a long one for him.

Chapter 11

Maxie had arrived home later that she had expected and found the phone message box lighted. One short call was from her mother, which she was sure could wait a while. The second message was from Bill. Basically, he said simply that something had come up and to please forgive him for he wouldn't be able to get back and take his two favorite girls to the movies as planned. He asked for a 'rain check' and told her that he would see her soon.

Megan came into the room and heard the message play out. She was disappointed. *Darn it! I'm disappointed as well!* Maxie thought.

"Sorry, Baby," she said as she hugged her daughter.

"Do you want to go ahead and go to the movie or wait?" Maxie questioned.

"No, not really. Let's wait until Bill gets back. Okay? I really like him, Mom, and if you would give him half a chance, you would also. He's so nice to both of us."

Maxie stood looking at her daughter as though she were a stranger and so grown up. "Come on let's get something to eat . . . what sounds good to you? Pizza? I think I have a pepperoni in the freezer."

"Yum, pizza sounds great! Want me to make us a salad to go with it, Mom?" she asked cheerfully. Maxie pulled out the frozen pizza and was tearing away the wrapper when she turned and looked thoughtfully at her daughter.

"A salad would be nice . . . "she paused and then continued, "Is something bothering you, Meggie?"

Megan busied herself with salad makings, chopping the green pepper, tomatoe, and celery on a small chopping board to add to the pre-packaged iceberg lettuce salad mix. When she finished putting that in the bowls, she sat down on the nearby oak barstool.

She wore a serious expression when she asked her mother, "Mom, do you ever get lonesome? You know, do you want a man in your life? It has been over two years since Daddy left us. Don't misunderstand me, I still love him and I miss him like crazy. But, you know, he's not coming back. Frankly, I don't think he'd be very happy to see us right now. We're sad sacks most all the time."

Her mother felt grief and loneliness bubbling to the surface, which she had thus far manage to push back and not really deal with it. Megan put up her hand, to stop her mother from interrupting and continued. "Don't get mad at me, Mom, but I think it is time for the two of us to move on and maybe let some nice man into our lives."

A shadow of anger, intermingled with the other feelings, drifted over Maxie at these words. *How could you suggest such a thing! . . . All right, Maxie, just calm down and think about what she just said,* she scolded herself. It wasn't often that the two of them sat down and actually talked about their fears. They hadn't in a long time. Maybe it was time to lay it all out on the table. It hurt to think about it and it was easier to ignore the tragedy and pretend it didn't happen. *But, it did happen!*

Maxie took a deep breath and said calmly, "You do, huh? Got anybody in mind? It's not like I have men knocking down my door, you know."

"Mom, you hardly have anybody knocking, man or woman . . . Your job! That's what you have and that is what you live for. I know it and you know it. I think you deserve to be happy again."

Maxie remembered the words that Bill had spoken, *'You are a beautiful young woman and you deserve to find happiness again.' That confounded Texas Ranger is worming his way into my thoughts and feelings at every turn . . . Of course, he could be right, couldn't he?*

After Matt had died, Maxie decided she would dedicate her life to getting the bad guys. Within the past year, she had gone out with a friend or two, but avoided any relationship that might bring her closer to the opposite sex. She realized it would hurt too much to let her heart get all tangled up with emotions and commitment again. *When that happens, they up and leave. Like Matt did!* Exactly like her husband had done. *I can't believe it but I'm still angry at Matt for leaving me! My gosh!*

Megan broke into her thoughts with, "Besides, I need a daddy. I need a man in my life to teach me about things . . . especially boys. I'm a teenager, for gosh sakes! I know that you and Daddy decided I would have to be fifteen to date. I respect that. I just think if you married again, I could lean on my new daddy for that male companionship I'm looking for." She paused and drew a troubled breath. "I don't want you to even think about me though. I want you to find a good man, date, and let yourself fall in love and . . . " Megan smiled, "the daddy part would just come later." She smiled at her troubled mother.

Maxie walked over to the barstool and pulled Megan into her embrace. "Meg, are you playing cupid? I tell you what, I'll work on it, I promise. You're right, Megan, it's time we got on with our lives." *Where was I while she was growing into a sensible young lady?* Maxie asked herself.

Megan looked up into her mother's pretty face and smiled that impish smile of hers. *I'm going to work on that too, Mom, starting with that ranger.*

The timer sounded. The pizza was ready and the two girls sat down the bar, eating while they continued to exchange thoughts, more like sisters, than mother and daughter.

Megan got to bed about 9:30 and Maxie continued to sit and stare at the television. She felt more relaxed than interested. After the ten o'clock news, she plodded down the hall in her fuzzy house slippers and crawled into bed. She lay there wide—awake for a while, thinking about the things they had discussed. It made sense. While lying in the dark, she whispered to Matt for a few minutes, then smiled sadly and slipped off her wedding band, laying it on the bedside table. *Yes, Meggie, I promise that I will work at being happy. Matt says I should go for it!* She turned to her side and quietly sobbed into her pillow until she was spent and then drifted asleep.

A little after midnight, a shrill ringing woke her. She sat straight up in the bed, threw the covers back and grabbed the phone. *Who would be calling this time of night?* She wondered. Maxie picked up the receiver and said, "Yes?" Any calls coming in this time of the night usually meant problems. She was silent for a couple of minutes as she listened . . . "Calm down, Mrs. Fuller. I can hardly understand you.!"

Mrs. Fuller told her that she thought somebody was in her house. Mr. Fuller was out, as usual, and she was frightened. At first she thought he had come home, but she had tiptoed down the hall to her husband's bedroom and saw a male figure in black, rummaging around the room, looking for something.

Maxie quickly reassured Lola that she should hide and wait for Maxie who would be right out. She threw on some clothes, told Megan she had to make a run and would be back shortly. If she didn't, Megan was to call the neighbor next door.

Maxie jumped into the truck and took off at a high rate of speed, reaching for her radio to call for a backup unit. The city policeman on duty responded.

Please, dear God, don't let there be another murder, she prayed.

It took ten minutes to reach the Fuller's residence. The lights were all on and there was a truck parked in the driveway. Maxie didn't see any other vehicle. She jumped out of her truck and dashed to the front door, heart racing. She didn't knock but drew her weapon as she opened the door and ordered, "Sheriff here, put down your weapons." She was preparing for any situation that might confront her. She was relieved to see Jake sitting on the sofa, holding his wife and comforting her. Mrs. Fuller's eyes showed the fear she was feeling.

"Is he gone?" asked Maxie. The couple nodded and said, "We think he is." Maxie had to be sure so she would check the house herself. The perpetrator could easily hide in a closet. She carefully went down the hall, checking the baths and the bedrooms, with her gun cocked, pointed and ready. If necessary, she would use it. When she didn't find anything except a foul body odor in Jake's bedroom, she holstered her weapon and went back to the couple seated on the sofa. Lola was still shaking, but the fear had all but disappeared from her face, although she looked troubled.

"Tell me what happened." Maxie asked just as the city unit drove up and a young, black-haired cop walked in with his hand on his holstered weapon. He relaxed when he saw the sheriff had the situation under control. She told him how much she appreciated his response and the circumstances as they appeared to her thus far. "Looks like a break-in. I'll be checking everything out in a little bit. We don't know if anything was taken at this point. Would you look around outside the house?"

At that moment, the officer received a call on his radio, attached to the shoulder of his blue uniform. When he responded, dispatch asked him to check out a disturbance on March Avenue. He answered, "10-4, be right there." He hurried out and with his flashlight looked around the house and yard finding nothing. Then he made his apologies to the sheriff and left the residence.

Maxie observed that the intrusion into his home had sobered Jake and he seemed to be totally aware of their present circumstances. She asked, "Mr. Fuller, was the intruder still in the house when you got here?"

"Yes, he was. The house was dark and quiet when I entered the kitchen door. I heard a noise down the hall and just figured it was Lola, but decided to check. I saw this black shrouded figure running to my bedroom. When he saw me, he made a mad dash across the room and jumped out the window. I went in search of my AK47. I was ready to kill the bastard!" he exclaimed.

"Where were you, Lola?" she asked.

"I was hiding in the closet in my bedroom. I had a lock put on my door a while back." She looked up at Jake, a little nervous at that admission.

"Sheriff, I get drunk and then I get mean. Lola does it to protect herself from me, I'm ashamed to say." He was matter-of-fact about the admission, but bowed his head in shame.

Maxie had to stick with the facts of the incident and she continued her questioning, "Lola, what happened after you called me?"

"Well, I tried to be as quiet as I could but I was shaking so hard. Sheriff, I was so scared! Anyway, the man banged around a little in the other room and I heard him coming down the hall, he grabbed the doorknob and tried to get in where I was. I was crying but buried my face in my jacket hanging in the closet to muffle the sound. I think he heard me. It sounded like he shoved his body against the door, you know, like he was trying to break it down. Then, I guess he heard Jake's truck pull into the driveway. He waited to see if somebody was coming into the house, I think, because everything was quiet for a couple of minutes. I was worried. Jake doesn't usually get home very early after he has been out on a binge, so I wasn't sure it was him. Anyway, I waited and listened. In a few minutes, I heard the kitchen door open and someone come in the house. I could hear footsteps and scrambling noises. I was afraid he was hurting Jake but I was more afraid to come out and see what was going on so I stayed put and prayed. After a few minutes, Jake came to the bedroom door and called to ask me if I was all right." She gazed lovingly at her husband.

It dawned on Maxie, *My gosh, she really loves the drunk!*

"I want the two of you to sit tight while I look around for any evidence. Then, I want you both to search to see if anything is missing."

She spoke softly to Lola and suggested she make some coffee. Lola went to the kitchen.

Maxie went to her truck, picked up her supply case, went down the hallway to check for prints or any other evidence. Other than a grass clipping or two, she found nothing. She dusted the bedroom doorknob for fingerprints and found two or three, which she speculated belonged to the residents. She was thinking, *could this have been the murderer?*

In her thoughts she reviewed what she believed happened. *The intruder climbed into the window. Lola just happened to be in another room at the time. She was lucky that she slept somewhere else . . . What was he looking for?* She went to the window where the entry took place and carefully searched the sill. She was always surprised that most folks didn't lock their windows. Around here, they left keys in their cars, doors and windows unlocked. *People are too trusting! Crimes don't just happen in the big cities anymore.* She knew that for a fact, *but how do you get people to break their long-practiced habits that are instilled in them over years?* She found no answer to the question she asked herself.

Later, after the Fullers looked around, they found a few small items missing. However, they were of little value. A 22 caliber rifle was standing beside the window where the man had entered. He probably intended to take it when he left. It was unloaded. Jake stored it in his closet.

As far as they could determine, there was nothing of value missing. The chest of drawers was half open and clothes strewn around the room. Maxie looked for footprints outside the window but found nothing usable. The lawn clippings were thrown up against the house and some grass was found on the windowsill. *I'm finished here.*

As Maxie prepared to leave, she picked up her case and went out the front door. When she started down the steps, Jake followed her outside. She stopped and turned back towards him. She looked concerned. He looked troubled.

"Sheriff, I need to ask you a favor . . . Lola said that you told her you could find me a support group for Vietnam vets. It's time for me to get some help. This thing tonight scared the hell out of me! My wife means the world to me. Today made me realized she could be taken from me. I couldn't bear that! If you can find a vet group, please call me?" he pleaded.

Looking a little surprise, Maxie assured Jake she would find him some help and soon. She smiled to herself as she turned and continued down the steps to her vehicle. *I'll be a son-of-a-gun! That man has some good in him after all. He loves his wife!* The world was full of surprises, some of them nice ones.

The lady sheriff arrived at the SO promptly at 2:20 a.m. She needed her sleep but was wired after all the excitement. She wrote up her report and readied the bag with the fingerprints for mailing to the lab. As she tidied her desk, she was thinking about the party who had caused all the excitement tonight. Suddenly, she had a fierce longing to go home and see Megan. She shivered, got up and left the office as she drove quickly to her home. The house was dark and still. She breathed a sigh of relief. *I'm paranoid, I guess. I'm going in and check all the locks on my windows and doors!*

Sometimes, I would like to take little Meggie and just go away somewhere safe, just the two of us. A voice of commonsense came to her, *You can't put her in a box. That would smother her. She has a right to grow and live a normal life. Teach her to protect herself.* Max sighed.

Once she'd peeked in and saw Megan sleeping soundly, Maxie double checked all the doors and windows before she collapsed in bed and drifted into an exhausted sleep, shutting out all the cares of the world.

The next thing Maxie heard was a shrill ringing. She lifted her head to determine if the ring was the phone or doorbell. Sleep vanished. She groaned when she realized it was neither. It was the alarm clock. Reluctantly, she crawled from the warm covers and staggered to the bathroom. Maxie shivered as she stood under the slightly warm shower spray, to get awake. She was remembering all that had transpired last night . . . *well, actually about five hours ago*, she thought as she glanced at the wall clock while she dried off with a white fluffy towel. She was naked as she entered her bedroom and searched out clean panties and bra. She didn't wear a uniform to work, as such, but today she pulled on brown slacks with a tan shirt. After dressing she strapped on her gun and holster and pinned on the badge.

She walked to Megan's bedroom and called, "Meggie, time to rise and shine." She ambled on to the kitchen to prepare a piece of toast and coffee.

Do I ever need that cup of coffee this morning!

She had been surprised to find the newspaper on the front porch for a change. *Must be my lucky day . . . yeah, right.* She flipped through the morning paper while she waited for Megan.

Megan skipped down the hall and into the bright, butter yellow kitchen with a big smile on her face. She appeared to be happy. *Is that the results of our little talk?* Her mother wondered.

"My, don't you look pretty today, Meg. Is something special going on? You never want to wear a skirt. Must be a young man you are trying to impress, huh?" Maxie spoke to her daughter in the teasing manner she often used. However, she was surprised when Meg's face turned crimson. *Oh my! My little girl has a boyfriend! I'm not ready for this!* Maxie felt a moment of panic. She told herself, *calm down, it isn't the end of the world and you knew it was coming sooner or later.* She took a couple of deep breaths.

"Well, Mom, there is this one boy. He's so cute, but, we are just friends. Sometimes he walks me home from the library, that's all," Megan said casually, not looking at her mother. She was wondering how her mother was taking this news. After all, she had tried to tell her last night when they had their 'mother/daughter' talk. *Get use to it, Mom! I'm thirteen!*

Maxie hoped she sounded better than she felt when she asked, "Who is he? Do I know him or his parents? Is he nice?"

"Mom . . . for goodness sake . . . just ask one question at a time! We're only friends! Not a crime, is it?" Megan appeared to be agitated.

"I'm sorry, Meg, I guess I wasn't expecting this. Tell me about him while you eat breakfast," she requested as she poured her second cup of coffee. *I can see it's going to take of lot of coffee to get me through this day.*

"His name is Jimmy Jackson. Most everybody calls him J.J. His mother works part time at the library. You know them, I bet, because they go to our church." Megan stopped to smear the strawberry jam across her toast and then continued, "Cyndi is her name. That's short for Cynthia, I think. She has dark brown hair and eyes and sings in the choir. Remember?"

"Oh, yes, I do remember her. We served on the food committee together once. Cyndi is a very nice person. If I remember right, her husband, Bob, travels all over the world and is gone a lot. I think he is an engineer or something." Maxie pondered as she recalled the things she had learned in her association with Cyndi.

"Well, I don't know about that but you are correct, J.J.'s dad is gone a bunch. Sometimes, I have to go to the library to do some research. J.J. is usually there, waiting for his Mom to get off work. At times, he leaves early and walks home with me when she has to work late. They live a few blocks over from us so we walk along together and talk."

"He sounds nice. When do I meet him?" Maxie said. She was curious about this boy.

"Oh, Mom! We are just friends!" she firmly stated. "Don't make a big deal out of it, please."

"You don't want me to scare him off, huh?" Her mother teased. Megan smiled shyly.

Maxie looked at the time. Grab your books, we have to get moving," she stated. *It is going to be a long day! I have a gob of things to think about,* Max was going over a long list of things she should attend to and mentally added, *"Megan has a boyfriend,"* as they went out the door and sped away.

Chapter 12

Jack had interviewed Suzanne Meyers' boyfriend, but, failed to learn anything new that would be of value in the case. Josh Whitman seemed to be a really good kid and was upset about the murder. He told Jack that, since Suzanne had a test to study for, she and gone straight home the day she was killed. He knew because he had dropped her off at the house. He hadn't seen any strangers around the school or hanging out at the pizza parlor or malt shop where many teens met after school. Suzanne's folks weren't at home at the time he dropped Suzanne off. He mentioned some guy was mowing the backyard, which could prove to be significant. The deputy made of quick note of that information and dismissed it. He returned, empty handed, to the Sheriff's office.

On Monday, Maxie was later than usual getting to the office. Coffee and a little time would get her back in shape for the day. She made a call to the local Veteran's Service Officer and got a name of a possible contact to get Jake set up for some group therapy. She dared not put this off.

He was ready to commit to counseling and AA meetings. Now was the time. After a short discussion, she was given a phone number of a therapist who held meetings in the basement of one of the local churches. She called and after some discussion she gave him Jake's number to contact. Jake would have questions about the meetings and attendees that she couldn't answer. She said a silent prayer, *I hope Jake is ready for this.*

About the middle of the morning, Bill walked in with his Stetson sitting on the back of his head. He came in grinning. *Lordy! You're looking mighty good, ranger. That smile could charm the fleas off a hound dog,* Maxie thought. She watched him glide in and sit in the chair next to her desk. Suddenly, it dawned on Maxie that for such a big, tall man Bill moved smoothly and with grace. He was comfortable with himself. That was not a bad thing either. In fact, she thought it made him more appealing.

"Did you miss me?" he teased. *Damn, she looks tired! I wonder what has been taking place around here while I've been away.*

"I missed you like I would miss a wart on the end of my nose," she jokingly answered.

He grinned at her as he poured his coffee and seriously asked, "Seriously, what has happened around this place while I was gone? Max, you look like you haven't gotten any sleep the past twenty-four hours." His tone of voice showed concern for her.

She briefed him about her night and told him about the intruder in the Fuller's house. "He could be the murderer."

"His MO was similar in that he evidently came in the window and was looking for something of value, I expect. He scattered some things around, found a 22 rifle in the closet, which he placed near the window. Probably, his

117

plans were to grab it as he left. Jake and Lola haven't slept in the same room together in a while. Jake, as usual, had gone out drinking when she retired for the night. Lola was in the south bedroom asleep when she heard a noise that woke her.

At first she thought it was Jake and got up and checked the bedroom door to be sure it was locked. Lola said she glanced at the clock and noted it was just after midnight, much earlier than her husband usually came home after a drinking binge. She got back in the bed, pulled up the covers and prayed that Jake would just quietly go to bed. There was something different about all the sounds coming from the other room. She got up and tiptoed to the door, put her ear against it and listened. Then she quietly walked down the hallway to the door of Jake's room. That's when she saw a man wearing black clothing and a black ski mask. He carried a small penlight and was rummaging in drawers. She almost yelled out but quickly covered her mouth with her hand and hurried back to her room and quietly locked the door. She was scared. Grabbing the phone she crouched in the closet and called me. The perpetrator either heard her or was expanding his search as he came down the hall to the closed door. He rattled the doorknob, found it locked and he tried to break it in by ramming the door with his shoulder. Apparently, that was the moment Jake returned home. Thank God! Jake came in the kitchen door and stumbled around for a few minutes. He said he thought he heard Lola, still up, and so he started down the hall to check. When he got to the doorway of his room, he witnessed a man crawling out of the window. He quickly went in search of his AK47 with every intention, he said, "of killing the bastard." Since Jake was drunk, he couldn't put his hands on the weapon or his

22 caliber rifle. Later we found the rifle standing by the window. Jake ran to see about his wife at that point. After pounding on the door and calling her name several times, Lola got the courage to come out. By this time, old Jake was as sober as a judge. When I arrived they were wrapped up in one another's arms, cuddling on the sofa. Lola had been crying and was still shaken and scared. Jake was doing his best to comfort her."

"That's about it, Bill. Just another day in the life of Sheriff Maxie O'Bryan." She reached over to fill her coffee cup again.

"Wow! That was some night you had, Max. Is the moon full?" he chuckled; he had learned from experience that it wasn't uncommon for strange events to occur during the full moon period.

"Could be," she replied. She sipped the hot liquid and asked, "How was your trip?"

He took a few minutes to fill her in on his exciting afternoon while she listened with interest. She really loved looking at him. *He's a prime specimen of a man.* She scolded herself for the distraction and drew her full attention to his story about the young boy and his standoff.

As the two of them were discussing the possibility of the intruder, at the Fullers, perhaps being one and the same as the murderer at the Meyers' place, Jack and Charlee came in chattering to one another.

Jack eyes got big when he saw Bill, "Well, look what the dog dragged in!" He turned and addressed Charlee. "Who unlocked the kitchen door to let in this stray?" She shrugged her wide shoulders and smiled at Bill.

"Isn't it a little late to be getting to work, Jack?" Bill said returning the friendly banter as he glanced down and pointed to his watch.

"Damn it, I've already put in my day! Hell, I should go on home and spend the day playing with my little woman," he said suggestively and grinned wickedly.

Turning back to his boss, he remarked, "I hear you had quite a night. Maxie, why didn't you call me?" he demanded and sounded more than a little teed off.

"Jack, I couldn't see any reason for both of us to lose sleep. Besides, one of the city boys responded to my back-up call. Anyway, by the time I arrived, the intruder was long gone."

Maxie filled the deputy in with details of her busy morning.

Jack reported the results of the interview with the boyfriend of the murder victim. "I didn't get anything there. The kid wasn't aware if Suzanne had any enemies. She was quiet, polite and an A student."

The officer's exchanged a few ideas about where to go from here and the sheriff said to Charlee, "I want you to check back with all the pawn shops here and branch out to the surrounding towns. See if that watch has shown up anywhere."

Charlee said she would take care of it and immediately left the room to do the job she was hired to do.

Bill handed Maxie the lab reports that he had brought back from Waco. She read over them. "Except for the bag of cocaine, it looks like a dead end, Bill. I guess you can pick up Bubba. The drugs are certainly a violation of his parole."

"Well, I contacted his parole officer and gave him the information. Bubba may be long gone by now, especially if he has missed his drugs. He is smart enough to figure out that Jack found his dope the day we searched the old vehicle."

Jack rose from his chair and spoke seriously to the others, "You two realize that if the intruder at the Fuller's home was the killer, he didn't get any satisfaction from that illegal entry. I'd say he is primed to kill. I expect we may see something again real soon. This is my gut feeling, people . . . thought I'd better warn you." With a scowl on his face and worry in his eyes, he turned and left the office saying, "I have things I need to take care of before noon."

Max and Bill glanced at one another and shrugged. They could see that Jack was upset. Maxie shoulders drooped as she turned to concentrate on the report in front of her. They sat silently for a time, deep in their own thoughts about the murderer. The ranger sipped his coffee and took note of the worry on Maxie face.

About fifteen minutes later, Charlee came rushing back into the room and exclaimed, "One of the pawnshops has taken in a ladies watch. Do we have a good description of the one stolen?"

Maxie looked through the file and found a slip of paper with make and type of watch that belonged to Suzanne. She handed this to Charlee, who hurried out of the office.

"Keep your finger crossed. This may be the watch we are looking for," she said.

"We could use some good luck for a change." Bill said.

"What if the killer is out there right now plotting his next murder? Do you think he is a serial killer, Bill?" Maxie asked, with concern and her worry apparent.

"Well, there is always that chance. I'm more inclined to think Suzanne was just a victim of circumstances; she woke up and he couldn't afford to leave a witness of any kind, so he killed her . . . Who knows what a killer thinks?" Bill knew Maxie was not reassured.

"What do you say, shall we drive back out to the scene of the murder and look around again. Maybe we missed something." Bill said sounding more optimistic.

Anything was better than sitting around here, doing nothing, Maxie thought. She agreed by rising from her desk, grabbed up the case file and motioned Bill to follow. He grinned and did.

The house was empty, except for Suzanne's mother, who opened the door. When she peered out, there was a sadness around her eyes that touched Maxie's heart. "Come in," she said and stood back to let the two officers enter her home.

"Have you got any good news about the case?" Betty anxiously inquired.

Maxie took Betty's hands in her own and squeezed them affectionately. "No, I'm sorry, Betty. Charlee is tracking down a lead on a watch that might lead to something. Bill and I want to look around again, if we may. Perhaps there is something that we missed the first time. Do you mind?"

"Of course not. We left the room just as it was. I can't bear to go in there so I just close the door. Will it ever get any easier, Sheriff? Please tell me that it will!" pleaded Betty, her eyes welling up with tears.

Maxie put a comforting arm around the mother and hugged her. Bill was standing behind them and Maxie saw compassion in his eyes. *He really cares about people! I like that about this man.*

Bill went to the scene of the crime. There was a terrible darkness that enveloped him when he walked into the room. It was as if Suzanne's spirit still lingered there. He spoke softly, "We are going to get this guy, Suzie, I promise. Then, your spirit can rest in peace." He renewed his pledge to do that.

"Who are you talking to, Bill, yourself?" She came into the room, looking about with interest.

"Yep," was his only response and he continued wandering about examining an article here and there on the white chest of drawers and bedside table. He went to the window and got down on his knees, looking at the wooden sill and the rose-colored carpet under it, examining every fiber. Maxie walked to the closet to browse around for a few minutes, finding nothing.

"Bingo!" Bill exclaimed, holding up a dark hair that he had pulled from the crack between the carpet and baseboard. "This might be it, Max!" he exclaimed sounding hopeful.

"That would be wonderful! Here, I have an evidence bag for it," she said, handing him a small plastic bag.

Bill put the hair in the baggie and sealed it. He rose to his feet with a smile on his face. *All we have to do now is find the guy that matches this. In a world full of men, how easy will that be? At least it's a new starting place. When I get my hands on that pervert, he will be in for a world full of hurt, Suzanne.* His thoughts directed to the presence he felt in the murder room.

Since Bill was part Indian, he was raised to believe in the spirit world. In his adult years, he had concluded that the spirit world of the Indian and the God of the white man were one in the same. He seemed to have a special connection to the spirit world during a crime, whether it was a spirit of the white man or Indian was of little concern to Bill. His aim was to get the perpetrator as quickly as possible.

Maxie and Bill talked to Betty for a time. They told her not to get her hopes up but that the new evidence could help them solve the case. Betty looked expectantly at both of the peace officers.

Mrs. Meyers told them about the funeral arrangements for her daughter. "I got a call from the funeral home. Suzanne's body is back. The funeral will be in the Chapel tomorrow at 3:00 p.m." Betty sighed; her bottom lip quivered. She downed her head for a moment, without speaking.

"Mrs. Meyers, we want to look around in the yard, too."

"You do what you need to do," she replied and turned away, dismissing them as she struggled to get her emotions under control.

They walked outside and Bill suggested that they separate. Maxie was to take the eastside and he would go to the west of the house, looking for any evidence. This process took them a good thirty minutes of scanning and walking the yard. When the two of them came together at the back of the house, they looked at one another expectantly.

"Did you find anything?" Maxie asked.

"I found another one of those footprints here at the back of the house. Doesn't make good sense that he would walk all around the house. Maybe he was looking for a window or door that wasn't locked."

"That sounds reasonable, doesn't it?"

He walked over and placed an arm around Maxie's shoulder and said, "Let's go where we cuss and discuss the facts." He led her back to the front of the house, not removing his arm. She enjoyed the closeness for a moment and then shrugged his arm off, went to her patrol unit and got in, slamming the door. Bill grinned.

When they arrived at the cafe, there were only a few other patrons. A majority of the coffee drinkers had come and gone. They scooted into a booth, ordered and sat in a comfortable silence for a few minutes, hardly aware of the cool beverages they sipped. Both were thinking about the case.

"You know, Max, even with the evidence gathered this morning, we have to have a suspect to match. Have you got any suggestions? Where do we go from here?"

"Bill, I don't. What really bothers me is what Jack said this morning. More than likely, the killer is out there stalking his next victim. Jack has good instincts for these things and many times his hunches have proved right on the mark. It is discouraging not to be able to put our hands on a suspect. What can we do? Where do we go from here?" Maxie asked Bill, looking directly into the depths of those caring eyes, searching for answers that neither of them had.

In an hour, the two were back at the SO. Maxie looked over her messages and picked up the phone to do some callbacks while Bill went in search of Charlee. The deputy's office was at the end of a long hall. He knocked softly and entered. She was on the phone. He propped himself up against the stark-white door jam and waited for her to complete the call.

After she hung the phone up, she turned to Bill and said, "Sorry, I've got cows out on the highway east of town." She hurried out and down the hall to take care of it before some innocent traveler crashed into an animal, causing serious damage to him and the cow in question.

Bill smiled. He remembered when he had first entered law enforcement. His enthusiasm was every bit as great as Charlee's, even if it was just a bovine out on the highway. That was a good thing about a young, inexperienced officer. They loved all of it. Most were not hardened and cynical like the veteran officers, who sometimes got that way after years on the force. The innocents believed that most people were good and behaved like they should. Often, it took years for it all to soak in . . . a law enforcement officer's work is never done. You put away one criminal and at that moment another one is born. Your pay is small and your risks are great. Things never seem to balance out. After years of this, some officers experienced burnout. They aren't much help to the department, or the public, when that happens. Some supplement their income with payoffs. Were they any better than the criminal on the streets? To his way of thinking, they weren't. It troubled Bill.

Bill had decided years ago that all work and no play wasn't healthy. He spent some of his off time with boy scouts, involved in church affairs, teaching children the right way of life and that any policeman was a friend. He believed that all the officers needed to be exposed to good people, because what they saw daily was the bad ones. If a man was married, the wife was usually the aspect that kept the law enforcement officer sane and on track. A good spouse was certainly an asset. The police officer comes home and when he gets through the front door, if he's lucky, he leaves all the bad stuff in his life outside.

Home. I want one; I need one, were his longing thoughts.

As Bill came back by Maxie's office, she turned toward the doorway and asked, "Did Charlee get anything?" She noticed that Bill looked spent, just as she felt.

"I don't know. She rushed out saying she had cattle on the highway. Most folks think their situations are more important than the other fellows, you know. However, livestock running loose can be a real hazzard to the public. I've seen serious accidents happen with cows, horses, and deer dashing across a road. It isn't a pretty sight as you know."

"Yep, know what you mean." Maxie acknowledged.

"Are you going out for lunch?" Maxie asked.

"Why do you ask, you want an invitation?" he teased. "The answer is, yes, I'm going to grab a bite."

"I have a few paper trails I need to follow up on so I'm ordering in today." Maxie stated.

"Max, you look tired. Maybe you should go home get some rest." Bill suggested.

"Can't. I guarantee I will hit the hay early tonight." She reassured him when she noticed the concern written on his handsome face.

"What are your plans after lunch?" She politely inquired.

"I have a lead I want to check out." He rose from the chair and put on his hat and added, "I'll see you later, Max." She nodded, he turned and was gone.

She called the nearby Subway for a delivery of a turkey salad sandwich and a cola. Maxie turned back to scan through the written messages that lay before her and began working through them, one by one. It was hard to keep her mind on the business at hand. Her thoughts were consumed with the murder. She wore a worried frown as she was thinking, *We've got to get this man before he kills again. Jack is right. I can feel it in my bones, too. The perp is ready to commit another murder. We can't let him! We must stop him now!*

Chapter 13

The killer car was parked across the street from a group of red brick houses, which all basically looked the same. Butch had been staying outside of the city limits to commit his crimes. That was safer. *That drunk, Fuller, spoiled my last attempt.* He'd left that house empty handed and that teed him off big time.

Today he was staking out his next victim. He had watched the young girl walk home alone from school several times. There were no cars in the driveway. He assumed the family worked outside the home and were gone. He needed to get their schedules down so he would know when it was safe to come back and do his best work, kill. He reached into a paper bag for a candy bar to munch on as he passed the time in comfort and sipped his warm beer.

Those dumb cops don't have a clue. He chuckled softly. *Hell, I'm too smart to leave any evidence behind. I've done murdered twice. Every time it gets easier and more thrilling!* Thinking about it got him sexually aroused and he touch his private parts longingly. *The high I get watching my victims die is better than a drug high. Cheaper too! Although, there's nothing wrong with crack now and then.* Butch longed for a fix. He opened the glove box and pulled out a dainty ladies watch, encrusted with what appeared to be diamonds. The man fingered the jewelry and had vivid visions of his victim. *Wonder if they are real diamonds? Maybe, it's time to sell this baby. I could use a little cash in hand.* With that decision, he slid the watch into his shirt pocket. He finished the candy, tossed the wrapper in the floorboard, took a big swig from the can of lukewarm beer and scooted down into his seat, his dark, greasy hair fanning out across the headrest. Butch figured he had time to catch a few winks while he waited. He wasn't in any hurry; he had plenty of time.

The driver of the Buick was drifting in and out of sleep as he was remembering his time in prison. It was hell on earth there. He had one buddy, Al, who taught him the tricks of the trade. When it came to murder and burglary, Al was a pro. His description of his murder victims was vivid and it excited his listener as he talked about those he had committed. He described every bloody, gory detail. *Al was smart and he taught me everything I know. He hated women. Said his maw was nothing but a whore, about like my old lady. Al would be proud that I learned so well under his instruction,* he mused. As he fell into a deeper sleep, his head lolled to one side with his mouth open, saliva oozed from the corner of his lips and ran down his whiskered chin.

Bill returned to the Sheriff's office and sat down in his office. He was thinking about the murder, searching the crime scene in his mind for something that he might have missed. *The blond hair belonged to the girl. Footprints turned up nothing. No weapon left at the scene. One item may have been stolen—the watch. No leads on that either. The perpetrator used rubber gloves. At this point, our only hope lies with the dark brown hair that we recently found and sent to the lab for testing. Dang! I feel like there is something I have overlooked . . . I'm going back to the house and double check one more time.*

He got up, left the office, telling Mary Bell where he was headed so she could reach him.

She watched him closely as he left. *Something is bothering him. I guess he's just worrying about this case. He is a good officer and always gets results from his investigation.* As he drove away, she turned to see Maxie come into the office.

"I thought I heard someone come in." Glancing out the window, she added, "Oh, I see it was Bill. Something is bugging him, Mary Bell," she said in a troubled voice.

"I could tell. He didn't say much but I feel like he's worrying about this murder, don't you?" Mary Bell asked.

"We all are! Even Jack said that it was time for another killing. You know how his gut feelings usually pan out. Truthfully, I feel the same. It's frustrating to say the least." Maxie replied. She looked concerned as she returned to her office.

As Bill cruised down the street, preoccupied with his thoughts, he passed a beat-up green Buick parked on the wrong side of the street. There was someone inside the car asleep, sick or dead. The man's head was bent at an unnatural angle. Deciding he needed to check it out, Bill turned his truck around and came back, parking in the front of the vehicle. He made note of the license plate and jotted the number down on his notepad. Bill got out of his truck and stepped to the driver's side, away from the street traffic. He noticed the open can of beer in the cup holder. *He's probably drunk and is sleeping it off.* He rapped his knuckles on the partially raised window glass. The man jumped, shook his head and looked around. He lowered the window and stared blankly at Bill.

"Yeah, what do you want?" He wasn't happy about being disturbed.

Bill told the man that he was a Texas Ranger, had driven passed, saw him in the car and stopped to see if he was alright or needed help.

The man acted a little nervous, his hands shaking as he lit a cigarette and took a puff and exhaled, blowing smoke out the window and into the ranger's face.

"I'm fine. My buddy lives here," he pointed to the house he was parked in front of and continued, "He gets off work in a little while. I'm waiting for him to come home. I had a little time on my hands and fell asleep. That's it, Ranger."

"You been drinking?" Bill inquired. He didn't look drunk and Bill saw only one beer can. "You know it's against the law to drink and drive, buddy. You can hand me the beer can."

The grungy looking man handed him the half-empty can and said, "Sure thing. A buddy of mine left that in my car this morning," he lied.

Bill poured out the remainder of the beer, said a few words of caution and left. It wasn't his job to work traffic or drunks. He felt he had more important things to handle right now. He left the driver, walked back to his own vehicle and tossed the empty can in the back as he slide into the seat of his truck.

The man drew a deep breath and thought, *I gotta to be more careful. I don't want no suspicion thrown in my direction. I need to lie low for a little while.* He turned, looked across the street at the house of his next victim and smiled.

You won't have to wait very long, babe, he promised as he drove away.

Bill pulled into the driveway of the Meyers' home. He sat silently, hoping to see something that might give him a clue. Slowly, he got out of the truck and walked up the drive.

Mrs. Meyers heard him drive in and met him at the door. She wore an anxious look on her pale face.

"Ranger, have you found him?" she inquired.

"No Ma'am, I hate to say that we don't have anything concrete. I would like to look around again, if I may?" Bill asked politely. "Would you unlock Suzanne's bedroom window for me, please?" He saw her expression and quickly said, "Never mind, I'll do it, Ma'am." He walked passed her and into Suzanne's room to unlock the window.

Bill went around the house and looked into the window, trying to put himself in the killer's shoes. Bill was tall and would have trouble climbing into the small space but he saw that a skinny guy would have no problem. When he pushed the window up, he saw something he had overlooked. There appeared to be a speck of blood on the bottom side of the window frame, which would not be visible to anyone from inside the room. He took his gloves out and put them on, scraped off some particles of the discolored spot and stored it in a baggy. He hoped it was enough for the tests. *Maybe this was it, the necessary evidence that could identify the murderer, and not lead to a dead end like all the others.*

Bill closed the window and returned to the front of the house. "Mrs. Meyers," he called.

She hurried to the door and invited Bill to come inside. He sat down with her on the sofa and reported what he had found. "Don't get your hopes up . . . we'll have to test it at the forensic lab and that takes time. Also, I wanted to ask you if you found the watch?"

"Thank God for the evidence!" she sighed and placed her hand over her heart wearily. "We haven't found the watch. I'm positive Suzanne had it on that day. At night, she laid it on the nightstand next to her bed. First thing every morning, she would put it back on before she went off to school. She was so proud of it!"

"Bill patted Mrs. Meyers on the hand. He rose and went back to the bedroom to lock the window, then he said his farewell and departed. He was excited to have the new evidence. He looked at the tiny bag and hoped it contained the answer. *There is only one other thing I'd like to put my hands on right now, the killer!*

Chapter 14

Jack was working on a report while Charlee was sitting by his side chatting excitedly, when Bill came in Jack's office. Both deputies turned to greet him and Bill asked, "What's up?"

"The bad news is Charlee and I went to a pawn shop and checked out this ladies watch they had. Well, it isn't the right one. The good news is that another ladies watch has cropped up in Kearns County at a broker's business, which might be the right one. Let's hope."

"It's about time for their shop to close for the day so we are driving over bright and early in the morning to have a look at it." Charlee added.

Jack and Charlee exchanged a few ideas with Bill, then Jack asked, "You got anything, Tex?"

"Matter of fact, I do. I went back to the scene and standing outside the raised window, I discovered what appears to be a drop of blood on the underside of the window frame. Hopefully, it'll be the killer's blood. Of course, we won't know for a little while." He took out the baggie and handed it to Jack.

"Hot dang!" Jack responded. "That's great, Ranger! I'll see this gets to the lab in Waco pronto." Turning to Charlee, he asked, "We haven't sent the black hair from yesterday, have we?"

"No, Chad, who works the night shift, is going tomorrow. It's his day off but he says he doesn't mind. It seems there is a certain young lady who works there in the lab that he has taken a shine to." Charlee smiled as she told them about the crush Chad had on Babe.

Bill smiled, *Babe's a cute kid, freckles and all.*

Maxie rushed in the office inquiring about the status of the case. She said she was on her way to the school to get Megan. Bill told her he would ride along with her as he had a few things to discuss. They hurried out.

Megan was surprised to see the two of them pull up at the curb. She grinned and turned and said something to her girlfriend. They both laughed as Megan ran to the vehicle and climbed in the back seat.

"Hey, Mugwump, how was your day?" Bill asked pleasantly.

"Great! I made a ninety-six on that old history test; second highest grade in the class, Mom."

"Wow, look at you!" Maxie said as she turned to the back with a big smile. "I am so proud of you. Didn't I tell you that you could do it? Study time pays off, huh?"

"Yeah, I guess it does." Megan replied.

"I think we need to celebrate." Bill suggested. "How about a chocolate milkshake, girls? I'm buying."

"In that case, how can we refuse." Maxie teased. "Megan, is that all right with you?"

"Yep! Super!"

Maxie drove into the nearest drive-in. All three of them ordered a small chocolate milkshake and chatted as they waited for the order to arrive. She realized just how comfortable they were together. That was good.

"Mom, do you know what? J.J. asked me to go to the movies. I think he likes me." Megan was hoping that having the ranger present might soften the blow.

"Oh, he did, huh." Her mother didn't sound pleased. "What did you tell him?"

"I told him I would have to check with you but that the rule is that I can't car date until I am fifteen. That sounds so old, Mom!"

Bill was listening to Megan's pleading voice. *She's naive but this little girl has a lot of common sense and maturity—more so than most thirteen-year-old kids that I know. Maybe I can get by with making a suggestion.*

Bill interrupted the mother and daughter as they affectionately argued the point by saying, "Why don't we compromise? I suggest that we all go to the movie together—the four of us. How does that sound?"

Max gave him one of those, 'This-is-none-of-your-business' looks. She waited a few seconds as she considered his suggestion.

Megan, feeling she had someone on her side, begged, "Please, Mom. It would be like double dating, but not exactly. Remember our talk the other night?"

Feeling put out over this man sticking his nose in her private life, Megan calmly replied. "Yes, Meggie, I remember our talk very well . . . " She paused thoughtfully and continued, "I'll think about it."

Meg smiled. *That's good enough for now. I think the ranger really likes us. That makes me happy. If Mom will give him a chance . . . if . . .*

Bill changed the subject and they talked about school, teachers and activities. He was cautious when he brought up J.J. and asked questions about him, and his mother and father. He would check them out before a firm decision was made. Bill wasn't taking any changes with this little gal. J.J. would have to come out looking like a knight in shinning armor before Meg could go anywhere, anytime with that boy. He would make darn sure of that.

Maxie listened to the banter between the two of them. Bill was funny. Megan laughed and enjoyed his company. Maxie had to admit that she also was comfortable being with Bill. That was a plus. At least, it couldn't hurt the situation anyway.

Chapter 15

Deputy Barnes and Betty Meyers drove to the little town about thirty miles away to check with the pawn broker who had called the SO about a ladies watch that came through their shop. Charlee identified herself and asked to see the watch. The owner came from the rear of the building and held in his hand a dainty wrist watch. Charlee examined it and felt sure it was the watch taken at the murder scene. She handed it to Betty, who lovingly fingered the face of the watch. The young deputy saw the grief flood her face. Betty turned the watch over in her hand to check the back. She burst into tears seeing the initials, S. M., engraved there. Charlee led her to a stool and seated her while she asked the owner a few questions about the person who brought the watch in and got a name and address. There wasn't a lot of information. The clerk couldn't give a description, except he was hispanic.

Charlee handed the watch back to the clerk, asking them to release it to the Sheriff's Office for evidence in the case. She signed the necessary release forms, bagged the watch and gently took Betty by the arm and led her to the car.

Charlee felt sad for the grieving mother; but it was hard to contain the excitement at finding the watch. She drove back to the Meyers' home. *Finally, we have a name of a suspect.*

Mr. Meyers opened the front door to let them inside. He was anxious; hoping something had turned up when he asked, "What did you find?" He glanced from Charlee to his wife, recognizing the grief there. Then he pulled Betty into his arms trying to console her.

Charlee could see he was bitter and angry. *Why shouldn't he be? They lost a daughter to a no account killer.*

Charlee understood his anger. It made her mad when she thought about the way the poor girl had died. "Mr. Meyers, your wife identified the watch but I have to keep it for evidence in the case."

"Can I see it?" he asked.

"Sure, I'll get it." Charlee ran to her vehicle and pulled out the evidence bag and came back to the house. "I'm sorry, but you can't take it out of the bag."

Mr. Meyer's and his wife stood huddled together examining their daughter's most prized possession. Emotions spilled out as tears, filling the room with sadness. Charlee couldn't say anything for a few minutes. She struggled to get control of her own feelings of the heart. Finally, she told the family that she had to go. The couple reluctantly handed the bagged watch to Charlee. They joined hands as they walked her to the door, sadness evident in every step.

Now, what the deputy had to do was find this Joe Rodriguez, the name written on the pawn receipt she had gotten. The worst part was he had listed his address as General Delivery, which would be no help at all in locating him quickly. *That's what I get paid for!* Charlee thought as she pulled out and drove down the dusty road.

The weather the next day turned wet and gloomy. The winds were blowing hard, funneling the rain into areas it wouldn't ordinarily have traveled. The men who wore western hats, had to hold them tightly to their heads or jam them down to the tops of their ears. They certainly didn't want to take any chances of losing them. Cowboy hats were an investment and without his hat he felt like a city slicker without a suit, underdressed. Most housewives stayed in on days like this. Those who had jobs to go to were dressed in rain gear and carried colorful umbrellas, which provided very little protection from the wind and hard rains that traveled sideways. Most ended up with wet feet and legs if they were out for very long.

Jack fairly blew in the back door of the law enforcement building, along with the wind and water. "Whewww! This is typical Texas weather, fierce and uncomfortable, Charlee."

"Yeah, this is one of those days I would prefer to have remained in bed," she sounded wistful. "Just, wait around and it will change. Texas likes variety."

"Well, Cha Cha, what are you working on so earnestly?" Jack questioned.

"Jack, I went to the pawn shop with Betty Meyers. She identified the watch as Suzanne's. I have a Joe Rodriguez's name on the receipt. That's the good news. The bad news is that the address says, General Delivery."

"Damn!" Jack stated as he pulled his chair up to his own desk.

"Are you checking files or records, Charlee?"

"I am. I gave the info to Dispatch about ten minutes ago. Without an I.D. it could take a while or we may come up empty handed. We just have to wait and see."

"What have you got on tap today?" Charlee inquired.

"Same old same old. Well, I won't take up your time. I'm supposed to see Rob Graham this morning. While you are waiting for results of the state records, I'll go take care of that." He picked up his hat and left the office.

Charlee called after him, "See you later." She was searching through some of the SO files to see if Joe Rodriguez had a criminal history case. Rodriguez was a common Hispanic name in Texas. She speculated that there could be hundreds of them. She noted several "Rodriguez" files as she filtered through the drawer. Before she finished searching, she did locate four possible suspects with the name Rodriguez. She pulled those files and placed them in a stack on her desk to look over later.

Her mind kept drifting back to yesterday at the pawnshop. Mr. And Mrs. Meyers were glad to see that the watch was actually the one that belonged to their murdered daughter, Suzanne. However, just looking at it made the grief and suffering re-surface. She remembered the sadness that spread across their faces as each caressed the precious object belonging to their child.

We have got to get this creep behind bars and soon! She felt a renewed determination to do just that.

When the phone rang, she grabbed the receiver and greeted the caller, "Sheriff's Office, this is Deputy Barnes. May I be of service to you?" It was Maxie. She said she wouldn't be coming into the office because Megan was sick with the stomach flu or something. Maxie didn't want her out in this weather. She asked Charlee to call if she needed her.

"If it is absolutely necessary, I'll have the neighbor come and sit with Megan, but, only if the SO has an emergency." Maxie sounded tired.

Charlee told her not to worry and that she would call if necessary.

The telephone rang just as Charlee hung up, startling her. *I guess the Sheriff forgot to tell me something,* she was thinking as she greeted the caller.

This call was from the lab. They had results on the dark hair sample that was submitted. DNA was not the same as the family DNA. That could mean it actually was a hair belonging to the killer. This was progress, but the problem now was finding the person to match that evidence. *Like looking for a needle in a haystack,* Charlee sighed. She jerked up a file lying in front of her and began checking out the Rodriguez cases. All had Joe or Jose as a given name. The pawnbroker said the man was probably in his mid-thirties and on the heavy side. That certainly didn't match the MO they had on the killer. A large person wouldn't be able to climb through the windows at the Meyers' or the Fuller's homes. The officers had speculated that entry was by the same person. That meant the killer let someone else pawn the jewelry. It was essential to the case that the man be found and questioned. *Sooner the better.*

Charlee was looking at dates of births and other physical attributes when she finally found an incident that caught her eye. This file was Criminal Docket No. 1107 in District Court, about a year ago. The defendant was Jose Rodriguez. His address was listed. That certainly didn't mean that he was still living at that residence. The charge was Theft of Merchandise valued above $2,500. *He is on probation for ten years, to pay a fine of $1,000, restitution and court cost.* Charlee decided she would check this fellow out.

She grabbed the file, her umbrella and headed for the back door, radioing Jack on her way.

The Texas Ranger had checked a few leads that resulted in dead ends. He hadn't heard Maxie on the radio this morning and that concerned him. As he was passing near her home, he drove down her street and saw that her work truck was still parked in her driveway. His heart did a flip-flop thinking something might be wrong. He swung into her drive and parked behind her truck. The rain pouring down upon him was of no concern, as he walked calmly up the sidewalk to the front door. He rang the doorbell, praying all was well.

After two rings, the front door slowly squeaked open and Maxie stuck her nose out, not wanting the wind and rain to be ushered into her house. There stood that Texas Ranger looking much like a drowned rat, rain pouring off that Stetson like a small waterfall. *Darn him! He looks so good anytime, even drenched,* Maxie thought as she opened the door and invited him inside, quickly closing the door behind him.

As water trickled off his hat and shoulders, Bill had a worried expression on his rugged face. He realized Max looked exhausted but was all right. He had jumped to conclusions. Glancing down at her floor where puddles were forming, he figeted. *Dang it! Look what a mess I've made!*

He said, "Max, I'm so sorry. I've made a mess, but, I promise I'll clean it up. Will you bring me a mop and a towel, please?"

Maxie was thinking how much he looked like a little boy caught with his hand in the cookie jar. She nodded and returned shortly with a huge white bath towel and a sponge mop. "Here you go, Bill." She handed the dry towel to him and started mopping the water that had pooled around his expensive-looking cowboy boots. He slipped them off and stepped aside before he did anymore damage.

"What are you doing here, Bill, beside making a terrible mess?" Maxie teased.

"Max, I'm sorry about that. Really, I am. I just didn't think. I didn't hear from you today and I just happened to be driving by your house and noticed that your truck was still parked out front. My first thought was that something was wrong. Maybe, the killer had found out where you live or maybe you were dead. I panicked." She was standing close, too close. He caught the faint scent of shampoo and noticed her hair was damp. Suddenly, he pulled her into his arms and held her, wet clothes and all. He was so relieved that she was all right. As he held her close, he was struggling with emotions he didn't understand. It seemed right when Maxie put her arms around him and returned the hug.

She looked up into those serious blue eyes that had tears shimmering there. *He really cares about me!* The thought hit her like a ton of bricks. She pushed herself from his embrace and smiled up at him. "Thank you for caring, Bill. That means a lot . . . and you weren't just passing by, were you?"

"Hell no, I had to see about you," he admitted, still gripping her arms, not wanting her to move away just yet. She stood there for a few minutes, thinking about his admission. Then she put her hand in his and pulled him toward the living room. There he saw his other little lady, Megan, lying on the sofa, a quilt up to her ears, looking pale and listless.

He rushed over to Megan and grabbed her tiny hand, squeezing affectionately. "Mugwump, you're not looking too frisky today, what's the matter, hon?" He carefully placed a hand on her forehead and turned to her mother, "Max, this kid is burning up with fever! We need to get her to the doctor." He was worried, no doubt about it.

Maxie held up both hands, "Whoa! I have called her doctor. He says she probably has the flu that is going around. Dr. Bruce said to give her lots of fluids and something to bring the fever down. I did that a few minutes before you came bursting through the door."

Bill sat on the edge of the coffee table, talking softly to Megan. She smiled weakly. There was a wet cloth above her head and he took it and gently bathed her face. In a few minutes, Megan had drifted off to sleep. He stood up and Maxie motioned him to the kitchen. He followed her and sat down wearily in an oak, ladder back chair, sticking his sock feet out in front of him. Maxie placed a steaming cup of black coffee in front of him and the sugar bowl. Then she sat down opposite him, not saying a word.

After dumping in four spoons of sugar, he stirred vigorously. As he lifted his mug, Bill grinned at the Daffy Duck character on the side, smelled the aroma and took a swig, burning his tongue in the process. He swore silently but continued taking sips until he began to feel human again. He smiled at Maxie and said softly, "Thanks, you saved my life, my friend." When she grinned and took a sip of her own coffee, he said, "Sorry. I worry about you two gals so much. Maybe it isn't my place to do it, but, by George, somebody needs to!"

"So, you've appointed yourself to do the job, eh, Ranger?" She said teasing him. "I'm big enough to take care of myself and I have been taking care of my child for nearly fourteen years." She sounded like the strong, independent lady that Bill knew best.

"Max, open up and let me into your life, will you? I want to take care of you and Megan. Honey, you are a desirable woman-a little sharp-edged at times," he grinned and continued, "I don't mind that. Megan likes my company, even if you don't." He sounded a bit hurt.

"Bill, I don't dislike you! You're so good to Megan . . . and to me. I appreciate it." She stared at her hands wrapped around the warm cup. "I'm not ready to let go of the past. But, I promise you and Megan that I am working on it."

Bill noticed then that Max had taken off the wedding band that she had worn for years. *Maybe, just maybe, I am finally getting through to this beautiful little lady seated across from me.* He silently hoped for patience. *Hell, I don't even know if I'm ready for a commitment myself!*

Maxie was watching the man across from her. Only a few weeks before, he was practically a stranger to her. *This is what it would be like if we were married. I do feel relaxed and comfortable around him. He is kind and affectionate to Megan. He cares about me. Is it possible to fall in love with this man?* She asked herself. *I have to admit there is some strong chemistry between us. Neither of us can deny that.* She knew they needed to take only a step at a time in this relationship.

Bill was sitting across from a thirty-eight-year-old red head that wore the expression of a twelve-year old that had just gotten the birthday present of her dreams. *Be careful,* he warned himself, *that you don't come out of this with a broken heart. This old ticker couldn't survive another breaker,* he cautioned, remembering his first love and all the pain involved which left him scarred.

"Max, let's take this slow and easy. Our relationship is growing but we don't know where it leads. Will you nurture it just a little? Please, give me a chance." he pleaded, reaching across the table and taking both her tiny hands in his. He squeezed them affectionately and released them.

Maxie nodded her head in agreement.

She figured it was time to change the subject so she asked, "What have you been doing this morning? The weather is crappy out there, isn't it? Megan woke me in the night, gagging over the commode." She was speaking rapidly. "Then her fever starting coming up. You've exposed yourself in coming here."

"Don't worry, I'm never sick. Too mean, I suspect." He grinned shyly.

"I had some people to see. First, I stopped at the PD, checked MOs that match our killer, drove to the prison, thinking I could find an inmate-someone released the past two years—and so far, came back empty handed. Bill looked at Maxie and questioned, "When did you say these other murders began?"

"About three years ago, I think. We aren't certain the same person committed all of those unsolved murder cases. So, what did you find, anything worth while?"

Bill smoothed his hand across his pant's legs to check for dampness then he looked up at Maxie and wearily said, "Well, I looked at the files of several inmates. I found one or two that were suspicious, though not anything concrete. I asked the warden about murderers of women. Well, there are literally hundreds of those so that dog won't hunt. It would take months to check out all of them. We don't have months, Max!"

"I know . . . we've got to have more evidence to go on. If the watch deal doesn't pan out, where do we go from here; just sit on our behinds and wait for the killer to strike again? I don't buy that!" Maxie said adamantly. She got up, walked over to the small kitchen window surrounded by white curtains. As she stared out she was thoughtful, *I feel so helpless . . . I'm the sheriff of this county and I'm the one who needs to do something.* She turned while leaning on the counter, with a doubtful expression on her face.

"Max, we can't give up! We have to go over everything again and again if necessary. No crime is perfect and we've overlooked something. We have to find it; the one thing that will make the difference in this case." He rose from the chair and walked over to take her in his arms. He looked down into the sad green eyes of the woman he loved.

Damn, I do love her! When did that happen? I've built a wall around my heart for these many years! Could she have gotten through it? He was taken back at the very thought of it.

As he lowered his head slowly, she felt his heart beating strongly beneath her hands. Max was surprised to see a look of total devotion in those gorgeous blue eyes, but, she was puzzled by it. Just as quickly as it appeared on his handsome face, the wanting look vanished. However, his concern was still apparent.

When their lips met, things began to heat up quickly. Maxie was taken in completely by it. The kiss was hot, wet and sweet. Bill raised his head as if to ask her consent. He read desire in her face, pulled her closer and gave her the kiss every woman dreams of full of love and devotion. This one was the real thing. They were breathing hard and the two hearts were beating at a fast clip. Max knew Bill was aroused as his hardness rubbed against her, melting their bodies together.

We can't do this, she silently protested as she shoved Bill away. Turning her back to him while tears trickled down her cheeks she sobbed, her shoulders quivering from desire or the pain of not completing the thing they both craved. It had been a long time for her. *Too long.*

After getting his emotions, as well as other parts of his body, under control Bill walked over to Max and put his strong, muscular arms around her and held her, not saying anything. *I understand, Max, we both feel like we are being unfaithful to our former loves. I do understand.* His thoughts raced back to his youth when he was so easily aroused. He smiled to himself. *I'm an adult now, so act like one,* he scolded his body parts that didn't want to listen.

The phone rang twice before Maxie could get to it to answer. It was Charlee. She sounded far away. "Charlee, what's the matter?" Maxie asked with concern in her voice. She could tell that Charlee was upset about something.

"I'm sorry to bother you, Max. I've had a little accident. Messed up my Expedition pretty bad." Charlee said.

"Are you all right?"

"Yes, just a little banged up. I was tailing a vehicle that I believe may belong to a Jose Rodriguez. He could be the suspect involved with the pawning of the watch."

"Oh, by the way, the watch at the pawnshop was Suzanne Meyers. Her mother and father positively identified it."

"Anyway, the streets are wet and slick today. When I made a corner a little fast, I skidded into an electric pole. Needless to say, the guy got away from me. I'm sorry, Sheriff." Charlee was apologizing but she was mostly angry with herself. *Stupid stunt, for someone who knows better!* She scolded.

"At least you're not hurt. That's the important thing, Charlee. The vehicle can be fixed or replaced. You can't be . . . Do you need a tow truck?" Maxie asked.

"I've already called them. They should be here in five or ten minutes. I just wanted you to know what is going on . . . By the way, how is our girl, is she feeling better?"

"Meg had a pretty high fever when she got up in the night sick but I've talked with her doctor and he thinks she has a stomach flu that is raging. It may last for two or three days. Poor little thing, she is out of it right now, sleeping on the sofa in the living room. So, we'll consuming liquids and a fever reducer for a time, I imagine. When Meg feels better, I will call in our neighbor to sit with her until she feels like going back to school. Until then, I'll be right here, Charlee, if anything comes up, call me. You hear?"

"Yes, Ma'am." Charlee answered briskly and in a professional manner.

"Charlee, shouldn't you go to the ER, to be sure there are no injuries?" Maxie inquired.

"That isn't necessary. I'm fine. I've asked Jack to come by to pick me up. I'll probably be at the office the rest of the day. I expect I'll have a few bruises and be sore tomorrow though." Charlee said sadly.

"I'll talk to you later then . . . and Charlee, please, be careful." Maxie slowly hung up the receiver.

Bill showed concern when he asked, "What happened, did Charlee have an accident?" Max nodded and he continued, "I gathered that much. Do I need to go see about her?"

"She just skidded off the slick, wet road. Unfortunately, a pole was there to greet her. She said she was following someone she thought was Jose Rodriguez, a suspect in the pawning of the victim's diamond watch. Could he be the killer?" Maxie thought about the case.

"Listen, since I can't do anything here, I'll run by the office and see what Charlee was working on. Maybe I can help her. I'm not any help here. If there is a chance this character might be the one, we have to follow up." He leaned down and kissed Max on the lips. It was a quick, friendly kiss, but Maxie could feel the heat rising in her cheeks. "I'll be back to check on Meg later, if that is all right with you, Max?"

"Sure, Bill. She'll feel better this evening. Why don't you come by after supper? I would ask you to eat with us, however our meal will consist of chicken broth and gelatin, I'm afraid," she laughed.

"I'll pass on that and grab something before I come. Are you sure I can't pick up something for you-some solid food?"

"Oh, no, I figure my best bet is the soup thing. If I have to hang my head over the pot, I don't think I want to have to watch a parade of solid foods pass before my eyes the second time." Maxie smiled up at Bill as she spoke softly to him.

"You take care of yourself, Max. I don't want you to get sick . . . We need to talk, you know." Without another word, he walked out to the foyer, pulled on his boots, and slipped quietly out the door.

His mood brightened. *Ah, good, the sun is going to shine! We sure could use a little sunshine in our lives about now.*

Jack and Charlee were in a serious discussion when Bill came to the office unannounced.

Charlee had a pretty bodacious black eye that would be a real beauty tomorrow.

"Cha Cha, I heard about your little bump-in. What happened? Did that mean old electric pole jump out in front of you?" Bill teased, a broad smile spreading across his rugged face.

"That is one way of putting it, I guess." Charlee reached up to her swollen eye. "I came out of this with some beauty mark, didn't I?"

"Now, you did! Are you sure you're not hurt anywhere? You know people have walked away from accidents only to discover later that their leg or arm was broken."

"Actually, I was making a turn, not driving very fast. The weather was just right for the slime on the pavement to create a treacherous situation for driving."

"I guess it was just one of those things . . . That sounds like a song title, doesn't?" She smiled at the two guys before her.

"Except for the black eye, you look great!" Jack added, "She was just telling me that the watch was pawned by a Jose Rodriguez, which is a rather common name in our part of the country. She checked defendants of some of our old cases and found a few files. She was in the process of locating one of those to talk to him about the watch."

Charlee told them, "I'm pretty sure he isn't the killer. I'm told this feller is a big man. He couldn't get through a window without having some trouble getting his gut through. However, he could be involved. I wanted to talk to him, you know, ask a few questions. The address in the case was for a Pedro Hernandez, a cousin of Jose's. Evidently, Jose has been in prison once and stayed with them a little while after he got out. Pete said his cousin was living with a lady friend on Hopkins Street. He described the vehicle as best he could. He couldn't give me the name of the female, except he thought it was Rita something."

She continued. "Anyway, I was driving up and down the street searching for a red, four-door mini van, when he backed out into the street. He took off like a bat out of hell. My feeling is that Pete called him and warned him that the sheriff was after him. The Hispanics are pretty protective of family . . . That is about all I have for now." Charlee glanced at both the officers who showed interest in this incident.

"Why would he run? What does he have to hide if he is innocent?" Jack asked.

"Well, if he is involved, and that is possible, he could be on parole. We know he was in prison and we know where.

Sounds like he has something to hide. Is that your opinion, Jack?" asked Bill.

Jack agreed. "Sure 'nuff. What about you, Charlee? What is your gut feeling about this guy?" Jack looked her straight in the eye.

"I'm thinking he knows something he doesn't want us to find out."

"I say we concentrate on finding this man so we can get him in for questioning." Bill supplied.

Bill turned to Charlee, "Did you get a LP number?"

"Because of dried mud or dirt a part of the plate was covered, but I did get a partial number. Here it is." She handed the scrap of paper to Jack. "I've reported that but I didn't put out an APB on the guy. Heck, I don't even know if the driver was Jose. I'm not even sure he knew I was following him. One thing I do know is he was in a big rush when he drove away. We don't have enough evidence for a warrant though."

"Let's wait and see what comes back up on the partial, shall we?" Bill suggested.

"Have you gotten results of the hair and blood samples we sent for DNA testing?"

"Yes, we have the results of the hair sample. Of course, we need someone to match up with.

That may be the hard part. The lab is working on the blood sample. Maybe we will have that back tomorrow. Anyway, the hair isn't from a family member." Charlee added.

Chapter 16

The scrawny man with dark hair and eyes was seated in an old green Buick not far from the spot where the Texas Ranger had seen him. He fingered a long jagged scar across his left cheek that was red and ugly. Because of it he seldom looked into a mirror. As a result his hair was dirty and uncombed, spikes sticking up here and there. He wore jeans and a blue tee shirt, which had not seen soap and water for a while. Body odor was strong. He was used to it. Prison had been a place filled with many bad odors: body and breath, secretions from male sex organs, feces, and puke. Not a pretty picture, but it was real life in a place like that. This man was remembering that he was Al's bitch while he was in there. They got their sexual release from the fumbling encounters in their cells at night. *Sometimes, Al was brutal and when his big organ stuck in me, it hurt like hell.* Just thinking about it excited him, though, and caused the him to become aroused. *It was almost like the more pain Al inflicted, the better the sex was. The orals were the best, at least for me.* He reached down and rubbed his rock-hard sex organ. He was ready. He was primed for his next victim. Always after a bloody kill, he was hyped up and would achieve a good release as a result. *I need it! You know I really miss you, Big Al.* The unkept ex-con was remembering the reason Albert was called Big Al—the name described his male member perfectly. *I should know!*

It was late now and the neighborhood was quiet. Very few lights were burning in the homes and traffic had all but ceased. Except for the streetlight down a block away, it was a dark night. It seemed nobody was stirring. The red brick house was black now. The killer carefully got out of the Buick, he was dressed in black clothing and barely visible. He crept down the sidewalk toward the home of his next victim, a black ski mask tucked in his back pocket. He felt for the hunting knife in its leather holster. The rubber gloves were poked into his shirt pocket. *I've thought of everything, little gal. Get ready. Here I come!*

Bill had gone by later that afternoon to see how Megan was only to discover Maxie was pretty sure she was coming down with the flu, too. As she opened up the door, an odor of sickness was evident. Maxie looked weak and ill. Her eyes had little expression and her cheeks were rosy.

"Go home, Bill, I think I've got the bug now."

"Please, let me come in and take care of you and Meggie. It appears that you two ladies need someone to see to your needs, don't you think? By the way, how is our little girl?" He was feeling awkward standing outside on the front step.

"I could use your help but I don't want you to get sick with the rest of us. Somebody has to work!"

She sounded cross but Bill realized she was feeling that the whole world was falling in on her. He merely took hold of the door, pushed Max aside and entered the foyer.

Maxie sighed, turned and trudged back to her bedroom, dragging her fuzzy slippers across the carpet. She was wearing a green tee shirt with a kitten on the front. It struck her right below her cute rear. *Man, you're sick. You've got the hots for an ill woman.*

He followed Max into the room and tucked the covers up around her. Her skin was hot and feverish. Bill stepped into the bathroom to wet a cloth. He folded it and laid gently on her fever-ridden forehead.

"Umm, that feels good. Thanks," she said weakly.

"Have you taken something for the fever?"

"I've tried but everything comes back up as soon as it hits my stomach."

He didn't like that picture. "Your skin is really hot, Max. Have you checked your temperature?"

"Yes, doctor. It's 101 degrees."

"Try to rest. Be sure you are getting enough liquids, Hon."

"I will . . . not that it will stay put . . . " her voice trailed off before her sentence was finished.

Bill decided he needed to check on his other patient, just to be sure she was all right.

He tiptoed to Megan's bedside. She seemed to be resting, breathing evenly. Carefully, he touched her head and decided her fever had gone down. *Thank goodness for that! She looks like an innocent, little angel lying there; and, why not? She is. I intend to keep her that way!* He touched her gently, tucking the covers around her, she moved slightly but didn't open her eyes. He said a silent prayer, *God, protect her and help her get well soon.*

He left the room and trudged wearily into the living room. He removed his boots and gun then lay, fully dressed, on the sofa. The lights were out except for the kitchen light over the sink, which was enough light for him to see how to get around, just in case one of his girls needed him. He was tired. *I better get a little shut-eye while I can.*

The man who drove the green Buick had gone to the back of his next victim's house. He was checking the windows for entry. He wore old sneakers for comfort and for the silence that he needed as he moved about. Finally, he found a window slightly raised. Bringing a lawn chair over to climb up on, he carefully put on his rubber gloves and ski mask *Now, I'm ready for action. Are you ready for me? I've spent hours watching you going and coming from school, on the school grounds, at the malt shop, and staking out this place where you live. It has been worth all my time, little darling, but I need you to pay now. I saw you flirting with that football jock. He brushed against your perky breast. I thought you were a good girl, an angel! Yeah, now you gotta pay for being bad.*

He jumped from the chair to the window ledge and crawled through the window. It was dark in the room. He stood still for a minute to let his night vision kick in and to get his bearings.

There the girl lies over on the other side of the room. His breathing was rapid by then. He was hungry for the sight of blood. He drew his weapon of death and crept over to the side of her bed. His eyes had adjusted enough that he could see the still form and hear the soft breathing.

Suddenly, the form took on life and sat up on the side of the bed, taking him by surprise. *Damn! That's not the girl. It's her mother! This bitch is a big ole gal.* That was all he had time to think before the figure plunged at his legs and took him down. They wrestled on the floor, as she yelled for somebody to call 911. *This bitch is stronger than she looks,* he thought as he struggled to maintain control.

She held his knife arm away from her muscular body. One thing registered with him and that was he had to get out of there, NOW! He scrambled away from her, swung his knife hand and felt the blade gouge into her right shoulder. She writhed in pain, which gave him enough time to scurry out the window and leave the premises.

Not a second too soon either. He saw the flashing lights and heard the siren wail, about a block and a half away, as he hurriedly jumped into the Buick and sped down the street.

Only his taillights were visible in the distance, as the police unit pulled up, followed by another vehicle. The police officer picked up his radio to tell the unit in the rear to follow the taillights. They needed to talk to this party. The Buick lights suddenly disappeared.

Officer Black jumped out of the patrol car and dashed up the front walk to the door, knocked and yelled, "Police! Open the door!" All the lights, inside and out came on; the door opened a crack and a young, frightened teenage girl stood before him in a blue nightshirt. She was shaking from head to toe.

"My Mom, please help my Mom. She's been hurt and is bleeding!" She pointed toward the hall. The officer ran down the hall to the first bedroom and found the victim lying on the floor. There was a lot of blood. The policeman knelt down beside her, "Ma'am" and touched her gently. She opened her brown eyes and he saw fear in them. "I'm a police officer, Ma'am, don't be afraid. I hear the ambulance coming now to take you to the hospital. I need to know if you saw the perp who did this to you?"

"No, he wore a ski mask," she replied weakly. "I woke up and turned over toward the window and he was just standing there looking at me. You know how you sometimes get a gut feeling that somebody is looking at you? That's what happened I had just gotten to sleep when that awful wave of fear washed over me. Maybe he made a noise or something. I couldn't believe somebody had come into my room so quietly. I have had some defense classes so, when I saw the knife in his hand I didn't think, I just dove at his legs and he fell back. We wrestled on the floor. He was trying to kill me! I was yelling for Brittany to call 911. I tried to pull off the mask, but, he stabbed me in the shoulder, jumped up and practically fell out the window. That is about it, Officer."

The EMTs came into the bedroom carrying a stretcher and quickly examined her for transport. When they saw how much blood she had lost, they hooked up an IV and used a large gauze square to compress the wound. Officer Black got what information he needed as they stabilized the victim. When she was ready to transport, they picked up the patient and loaded her in the ambulance. She weakly called to her daughter, "Brittany, go stay with Grandmother."

The officer in charge told her that he would see her at the hospital later. Also, he reasured the worried mother that he would be sure her daughter got safely to her grandmother.

Brittany was still sobbing. Officer Black knew that she was scared and worried about her mother. He suggested she call her grandmother to come pick her up. She did, although her hands were shaking so much she had difficulty punching in the numbers on the receiver.

"Brittany, go get dressed and pack a few things to stay at your grandmother's a few days." Officer Black suggested. "Your Mom is going to be fine, Brittany. I promise. She's a fighter. However, she may have to be in the hospital a few days."

Officer Black secured the scene after the girl left and checked for evidence. He wondered whether the intruder was a burglar or a killer. *Did he pull his knife when the victim woke up or was he there to kill her?*

He was amused when he pictured the surprise on the face of the man when he learned his victim was a fighter. *She could have been killed though. She is one lucky lady - a fighter and a woman after his own heart!*

The officer found the turned over lawn chair under the window. He discovered a single cotton thread. When he continued to search the room for other evidence, nothing was found. He took samples of the blood, which could belong to the victim or the intruder.

Chapter 17

Bill woke to the soft voice of Dispatch on his radio he had placed beside his weapon. It was after midnight. He arose slowly, listening for any sounds from the girls. He had slept a few hours anyway. Raking his fingers through his thick black hair, he walked down the hall to check on them. Megan was still resting. Max was awakened by the radio, although Bill had turned the volume down to almost a whisper.

He wet a wash cloth and washed her face gently as he sat down beside her. She was pale and listless. From experience, he knew that fever would do that to a body.

"Hey, there, Sleepy Head, how are you feeling?" Bill asked Max.

"Rotten to the core," she replied. "It was so quiet in the house, I thought maybe you had gone home. I got up twice to up-chuck, but it has been a couple of hours since the last time. I think I may be passed that point. Now, I can hardly wait for the diarrhea to make its presence known."

"Sorry, Sweetheart . . . " he said gently as he held her hand, massaging it lovingly.

"I just checked on Megan. She doesn't seem to have any fever and is resting quietly. Don't worry about her. Anyway, I grabbed a little shuteye on the sofa. My radio woke me and probably you, too. Sorry."

"I thought I heard voices . . . Oops! I've got to run." Max quickly got up and ran to the master bath that connected to her bedroom and slammed the door.

"Hello, diarrhea!" *Time to make my exit for a while. Sickness, I can deal with. Diarrhea is something else entirely. I don't even like my own.* He shivered in disgust at the mere thought of it and quietly left Max's bedroom, saying to the closed door, "I'll see you later." *Some nurse you are,* he scolded.

He went back to the kitchen and grabbed a coke from the fridge, returned to the sofa where he gulped it down. He listened to discussion between Dispatch and the police. *Sounds like they are having some excitement tonight. Someone broke into a house on Adams Street.* He gave his full attention when he heard there was a stabbing. *What if this was the same man who murdered Stephanie?* He knew that a police radio gave out very little information. No names mentioned to protect the innocent parties. This was the case in this incident as well. He would have to go to police headquarters to check this out. In the meantime, he would sit tight with the girls. *No reason I can't make a phone call though.* He picked up the cell phone that lay next to his other paraphernalia, punched in the police department number and waited for an answer.

"This is Texas Ranger Bill Sullivan. I heard a report on the radio about an Adam Street break-in. We have been working on a murder case at the SO. I want to know who the victim is and whether this is another murder? Dispatch mentioned a stabbing?"

The police department personnel told him what she knew. "A man climbed in the window, stabbed a lady with a knife. She is in the hospital at Duncan Regional." She added, "I don't think she is seriously hurt but she lost a lot of blood." Reluctantly, she gave Bill the name of the victim.

Bill thanked the girl for the information. He lay back on the sofa, with his hands behind his head, mulling over the few facts in the case he and Maxie were working on. *This sounds like more than a coincidence. I think the killer is still an amateur. In this incident, he couldn't figure out how to handle the situation. When things didn't go his way, that threw the perp off. He panicked, slashed at the victim and got out of there in a hurry. I'll have to get more details about this case. Maybe, we can tie them together. This MO is too close to the murderer's to ignore.* He drifted into a light sleep with his mind dwelling on the killer.

Bright and early the next morning, Bill arose and took a quick shower. He carried a fresh clean shirt in his truck for times like these. He looked in on Max. She said she was better. "You go to work. I feel so much better this morning, Really, I'm capable of taking care of Megan and myself. I've checked on her. She said she wanted to go back to school. I told her that she needed to stay home today and rest. Meggie has a little stomach upset. You know, the rolling and growling that follows, but she says she is hungry. I'm going to the kitchen to heat some broth and hot tea for her. We've got to keep liquids going in so I may try a few sips while I'm at it."

She smiled and said, "Thanks, Bill, for your help last night. I don't know what I would have done without you." She took his strong hand in her own and patted it. He leaned over her, placed a light kiss on her forehead and told her he would see her later.

He put on his belt, gun and other paraphernalia from the coffee table and left. First, he drove to the café to get that much needed coffee and a breakfast burrito. Afterwards, he drove to the Police Department, and entered with a purposeful stride to the desk of the officer in charge.

"Good morning," he sounded more cheerfully than he felt. "How are things going this fine day?"

A sleepy-eyed officer looked up at the handsome ranger and replied, "It has been a busy night." She noticed his badge pinned to his white shirt. "Are you the Texas Ranger that called me earlier?"

He stretched out his hand, "Yes, I have to confess, that was me. I'm Texas Ranger Bill Sullivan." He shook her hand and continued, "I really appreciate your information last night. I'm sure you know the SO is working on a murder case and, from what you said, this guy sounds like the same one we're after. We've been feeling that it is time for another murder. The victim was lucky if she escaped serious injury, I can tell you that. I believe this guy gets his kicks when he kills."

"That's sick! I do know that there are a lot of crazies out there . . . What can I help you with this morning?" She pointed to a full pot of coffee, "Help yourself to coffee. It's fresh. Made it for the day shift who comes on at seven o'clock"

"Ranger, I was ready to conk out, so sleepy headed. I'm glad you arrived. Talk to me. Keep me going for another thirty minutes. A soft bed sounds wonderful right now. Most nights I have to drink a gallon of coffee to keep going all night. However, there was enough excitement last night that I didn't have a problem staying awake, until now."

Bill realized the young lady was beat. He sat down beside Janice Johnson's desk and sipped the strong black coffee. Understanding the night hour syndrome that can attack, they chatted. He kept her occupied until her shift had ended.

Officer Johnson was in her early thirties. She told the ranger she had three kids. She talked about them. Bill sensed she was very protective of her children and admired her for that.

"Do you have information about the case that you would share with me, Janice?"

Dang! He is cute . . . but a little old for me, I guess. Like many of the other office girls, she appreciated a goodlooking man—no matter what age or walk of life.

"Ranger, the investigating officer is Willie Black. You need to talk to him, I imagine. He came in during the night and wrote up a report. I don't feel right about letting you see it without his permission. He told me when he left that he was going home to get some rest. He left about thirty minutes before you came in." Janice replied sleepily.

"Will he come on tonight?" Bill asked the girl.

"Oh, yeah, he'll be back at seven. I believe that's right," she said reaching for a sheet with all the designated shifts of each officer. "That right, Black will be on again at seven."

At that moment a fresh, bushy haired black woman rushed and to Janice's desk. "Sorry, Jan, I know I'm a few minutes late. Couldn't get the kids to cooperate this morning."

Bill made note that she was probably in her mid to late twenties, a little on the stout side, but she had a smile that would break the bank.

"Oh, hello! Who are you?" the officer asked, appraising Bill. Her black eyes locked on to the badge he wore and she put on her professional manner. As they talked, Janice was gathering up her belongings. She left the room, yelling that she would see them later.

After explaining all that had transpired in the early morning hours, Bill excused himself. He would catch Officer Black later.

About mid morning, Maxie came dragging in the office. Bill was sitting there, drinking another cup of strong black coffee, and reading the morning paper. Today, he found it was hard to stay awake.

"What in the world are you doing out of bed?" Bill asked Max, folding the paper and laying it aside.

"I feel better today, but, I am weaker than I thought I would be. I've been up an hour but decided I should come and check up on everyone." She grinned as she collapsed into a nearby chair.

"Bill, you don't look too perky this morning either . . . I'm sorry. You didn't get any sleep last night, I'll bet," noticing the dark circles under his eyes.

She continued chatting. "Megan is feeling much better and I suppose I'll let her go back to school in the morning. However, I know how this stuff works. After the fever passes, you feel almost normal. Ain't so! I found that out this morning."

"Who is with her today? I can go stay the rest of the morning, if you want me to,"

Bill suggested.

"No, she isn't your responsibility, Bill," she replied wearily. *Oops, me and my big mouth! I believe I hurt the ranger's feelings. After all he has done for Meggie and me, I need to be more considerate.*

Bill rose, stood beside her desk and said, "I'll see you later . . . You probably don't know that somebody broke in through a window after midnight of the residence on Adams Street. I've got a feeling this is our man. He had a knife and wore a ski mask."

Bill was amused when thinking about the attack that the man had gotten and added, "He had a surprise when his victim jumped him. She tackled and wrestled him down trying to get the knife away from him. He managed to roll away but knifed her in the shoulder before he left. City PD is working the case. Officer Black doesn't come back on duty until evening. Meanwhile, I want some information and I'm going to the hospital to question the victim."

Maxie's color was ghostly by the time Bill had finished his story. *Oh, my gosh! Jack and my gut feeling were right. The killer tried to strike again!*

"Bill, I'm sorry but I'm not in condition to help you right now. For just a second, I thought I would pass out just listening to details of the incident. I need my strength back so I can do my job!" She ducked her head for a moment, trying to maintain control over her surface emotions.

Bill put his arm around her shoulders and said softly, "Go home, Sweetheart. I understand how you feel. Rest today, will you? I'll come by later. I promise." Before she could protest, he was gone.

She felt sick. *Common sense tells me you are right, Bill.* She thumbed through messages and made two short calls. She stopped at Mary Bell's desk and left a note telling her she had to go home. She felt rotten.

Bill drove quietly to the local hospital where the nurse at the desk unwillingly told him the room number of last night's victim. There was a guard posted at the door. Bill identified himself to the policeman, then he entered the room. As he entered he saw a muscular woman thoughtfully staring at the ceiling. When the door opened and a tall man entered, fear flooded her mind.

Bill spoke a few words to reassure her that he was an officer of the law. Handing her a card to identify himself, he said he was there to ask her a few questions about last night's incident, She immediately began to relax. He noted her dark brown, tousled hair and expressive sad eyes. *This lady has had a lot of hardships in her life.* He observed the firm set of her mouth and the few shallow creases that decorated her forehead.

As Bill talked, he was sure that the victim was beginning to relax when he asked, "How do you feel this morning?"

Before she could answer, he added, "You are a very brave lady, you know, although perhaps a foolish one." The ranger smiled and said, "He could have killed you."

"He was there to carve me up! I was fighting for my life, Ranger Sullivan. I have no doubt about that. If I had been asleep, I'd never seen the light of day. I swear!" She was agitated and nervous just thinking about the intruder in her house. She felt he had desired to do bad things to her or her daughter.

"I'm a widow just trying to get by, raising a teenage daughter the best I can. It is tough enough without this incident. Brittany and I have always felt safe in our home. Not anymore!" She was thoughtful for a moment. "It was foolish of me to open the window for a little breeze, wasn't it? I guess it was even more foolish to attack that guy. I was scared!"

"Ma'am, I won't say it was smart. It is best to lock up-especially for a woman living alone, with only a child for company. You should secure all windows and doors. It is important when there is a killer loose in town. Have you thought about installing a security system?" Bill explained.

"Sure, but I'm a nurse. Systems cost money. I hadn't heard any news about a killer, except the scuttlebutt that goes around at the hospital." She replied.

"Do you feel up to answering some questions?" Bill asked.

"Can you give me a description? Even small details are helpful. I'm sorry to make you go through this whole thing again but I don't know any other way. You're the only witness, is that right?"

"Yes, my daughter, Brittany, was asleep in the other room. I believe it happened between twelve and twelve-thirty. It was warm in my west bedroom, so I raised a window before I got into bed. That was around 10:30 p.m. I had trouble falling to sleep. We had a pretty busy day here at the hospital where I work. Sometimes it takes me a little while to unwind and get all that stuff out of my head . . . Anyway, I was about half asleep, when I thought I heard a noise outside the window. I raise my head just a little and listened. All was quiet at that point. I turned toward the window and waited. That was when I realized that it was really stupid of me to leave the window open. At times like this, I was hoping it was a dog, not some person, or, just my imagination. Well, in a few seconds, as I began to relax again, a black head with white eyes appeared in the open window. A small person crawled through the window, approached my bed and he had a big knife in his hand. I panicked, thinking '*he's going to kill me!*' Before he realized what was happening, I dove for his knees and knocked him to the floor. He was surprised and stunned for a few seconds, as if he couldn't believe what was happening. He still had the knife and started slashing at me. I grabbed his hand and we struggled."

She paused and added. "Thank God I took some karate lessons last summer with my daughter! Also, I run and exercise every day so I'm in pretty good shape."

"It helped that he was little and not very strong. Anyway, we wrestled around, then he heard the sirens and I imagine he decided it was time to make his exit. He rolled away from me but managed to stab me in the shoulder with his knife." She reached up to her right shoulder and rubbed it gently. "I grabbed for the facemask, but because of the pain I couldn't hold on. Then, he practically dove out the window. I was bleeding a lot by then. I heard a crash as he scrambled to get away before the police got there . . . I guess that is about all, Ranger."

Bill observed that she was breathing rapidly and he was sure that just talking about the incident made her realize how close to death she had come. He had made a few notes on a yellow legal pad while she talked. He patted her hand and told her she was going to be all right and to take some deep breaths. She did and then told him she was fine.

"Can you describe him? Did he wear rubber gloves?" he asked.

"Yes, I forgot about that but I remember feeling the gloves as we struggled."

"Oh, a girl came in right after I got to the emergency room and scraped my fingernails."

She said as she remembered her admittance to ER.

"While we fought, I may have scratched him or something," she added. "You know, I got the impression he was nearly as scared as me. He smelled dirty, like he never bathed or brushed his teeth, much less changed clothes. I couldn't see the color of his hair or eyes in the dark. The streetlight was enough light for me to see a shadowy figure."

Ranger, something seemed familiar about him, but, I can't put my finger on it."

The patient was remembering all that had taken place. Suddenly, a terrible thought came to her and she exclaimed, "Oh my gosh, what if he decides to come back to finish me off! I'm never going to feel safe in my own home again!"

Ranger Sullivan saw the tears pooling in her brown eyes and he decided it was time to leave and let her rest. He spoke gently, trying to console her, "Now, now, if that man was as scared as you seemed to think he was, he isn't coming back! You can bet he doesn't want another fight with you. You scared the daylights out of him, Ma'am!" Bill smiled that charming smile of his and remained until he was sure that she had calmed down. "Please, give us a call at the SO if you think of anything else, will you?" He wished her well and left.

As he drove away from the hospital, he was thinking about the incident and all the information that the victim had shared with him. *She is a brave woman. I'm mighty proud that she is alive to tell about it.*

Chapter 18

The next morning, the bold headlines of the paper read, "INTRUDER MEETS HIS MATCH." The man in the green Buick was angry as he read the article the reporter had written. *I'm a damn laughing stock! That bitch surprised me is all. She was a cow and built like a wrestler. Besides, the sexy, long-legged teenage girl was to be in that bed waiting for me. What went wrong?* He asked himself and made other excuses blaming the woman who attacked him.

Was I careless? Naw, it was that broad's fault. Next time—and there will be a next time very soon—I won't make that mistake twice, missy, he threatened. He jotted down the name of the woman and the hospital. He decided he might just pay her a visit. Nobody laughed at Butch Rafferty. He clinched his fists and shook it at the television set. "I'll get you, lady!" he shouted.

Later that afternoon, he drove to the hospital and parked around the side; his Buick not visible from the street. He entered the hospital and walked up to the nurses' station. Butch asked what room his cousin was in. He had cleaned up somewhat and his hair, though still dirty, was wet and slicked back, giving him a neater appearance. He smiled at the nurse, his rotten teeth calling attention to themselves. He saw the disgust in her eyes as he turned to go down the hallway. *Bitch!*

As he approached the room, he noticed the uniformed officer standing guard and quickly turned and darted into a nearby supply closet. He switched on the light and looked around. He could see green hospital scrubs neatly stacked on shelves. He grabbed a pair and slipped them on over his own clothing. He saw a nametag, Johnson, in a nearby box, pinned it on his shirt and walked out. A cleaning cart stood unattended. He pushed it to the door of the victim's room, hoping this would get him past the guard on duty. He started through the door, just as if he belonged there. The guard glanced at the man, assumed he was on staff and was there to clean up the victim's room, so he let him pass, without question.

This is just too easy! Butch watched the face of the woman in the bed. She was dozing. He took the mop and began to mop the floor, keeping his head down, drawing closer and closer to the bed.

Suddenly, the woman opened her eyes and spoke to him, "You're new here, aren't you? I work here and I've never seen you before." She glanced at the name tag and asked, "Are you kin to Rebecca Johnson?"

Butch felt nervous and decided he should hightail it out of that place before he got caught. "Nah, no relation." He tried to stay calm, kept his head low, as he quickly slung the mop here and there, grabbed the cart and took off out the door.

The guard was puzzled about the lack of time spent in the room. *You just can't get good help these days,* he speculated.

The patient lay there thinking that it was odd the janitor didn't empty the trash or put out a new box of tissues. *He was in a mighty big hurry. I wonder why?*

Suddenly, she had a horrifying thought, *My God! That was the man who tried to kill me. He came here to finish the job. Something scared him.* She yelled for the guard. *I should have realized that something was wrong when he seemed nervous.*

The guard rushed into the room and asked. "Ma'am, are you ok?"

The patient told him she thought the man who came in to clean might have been the intruder at her home. The officer immediately called for lookout for a man wearing green hospital scrubs. He gave a physical description the best he could. It was nearing the end of his shift and he was careless. He failed to get the name on the ID tag. The policeman reprimanded himself for being lax on duty. However, he remained firmly at his station, intently guarding the victim's room, as he scolded himself for being lax in his duty.

Butch left the hospital in a run, out through a side door, removing the scrubs as he hurried out to the Buick. He practically dove into the seat and cranked up the car and sped away. *The bitch was suspicious of me. My bad luck that she knew who worked at the hospital and who didn't. Dang it, I may have given myself away. I must be falling apart. Stay calm, Butch.* Those thoughts seem to calm him somewhat and he grinned, thinking that these were the very words old Al whispered to him in the dark when his rough hands caressed Butch and brought him such pleasure. *Damn the bitch!*

Chapter

Charlee was driving back from an incident on Gap Road, about ten miles out in the county, when she spotted a vehicle she believed to be the same mini van she had pursued which belonged to Jose Rodriguez. She turned on her lights and siren and pulled the vehicle over. Much to her surprise, a woman was at the wheel and wore a look of panic as she lowered the window on the driver's side. Charlee walked to the car door with caution. She dipped her head in greeting and asked to see the driver's license. An attractive brunette pulled the license from the visor and handed it to the deputy.

"Did I do something wrong, Officer?" she asked politely.

"No, Ma'am." She noted the driver's name and address on Texas Street and jotted the license number down on her note pad. As she handed the Texas driver's license back to Rita Guerra, she asked, "Are you acquainted with Jose Rodriguez?"

"Sure. Joe is my boyfriend. Is he in any kind of trouble?" Rita showed concern.

"I need to ask him a few questions, Ms Guerra. Do you know where I might find him?

"He works at Morton's, goes on at 3:00 p.m."

"Is he at your residence at the present time?" Charlee inquired.

"Yeah, I guess he is still asleep. He likes staying in bed late, while I get my two kids up and off to school. That's usually a hassle and Joe doesn't like being involved." She smiled. "The boys aren't his, you see. Their father took off three years ago. Me and Joe have been together about a year now. He is good to me and the boys, though. Takes care of us, you know? I can't complain."

After checking her insurance card, Charlee thanked Ms. Guerra and told her she could go. Charlee walked to her vehicle, making a note of the license plate number. The mini van drove slowly away.

Charlee drove to the Guerra's residence in search of Jose Rodriguez.

The small white-framed house on Texas Street stood out from the rest. The yard was neatly kept and there were various flowers blooming on each side of a small wooden porch. Charlee could see a child's swing in the back on the right side of the building. *At least they take a little pride in their home. It looks clean and the yard is recently mowed.* She breathed in a deep breath. *I can smell the new mown grass.* She grabbed her little notebook, walked up the narrow sidewalk and knocked on the front door. After a brief wait, a sleepy Hispanic male opened the door, blinked at the bright sunlight, and greeted Charlee politely, "What can I do for you?"

When he saw her badge, his demeanor changed and Jose appeared to be wide awake and very nervous.

"Are you Jose Rodriguez?"

"Last time I checked, I was." He smiled uncertainly.

"I'm Deputy Barnes, I would like to ask you some questions about a watch you pawned."

"I don't know nothing about no watch." Jose stated defensively.

"Do you sign your name Joe or Jose, Mr. Rodriguez?" Charlee asked.

"I don't guess that is any of your business . . . " he snapped.

Charlee was firm when she said, "I'm making it my business . . . The watch belonged to a lovely teen age girl who was murdered last month. I advise you to cooperate and give us any information you may have, Sir."

Jose Rodriguez backed away from the door, shaking his long black hair from side to side. "I don't know anything about no murder!" He seemed genuinely surprised to hear that one had occurred so recently. *Butch? Damn! Butch lied to me! I'll cut his heart out for sure.*

Anger spread across his tan face but Charlee felt it was not directed at her. *He knows something.* "Mr. Rodriguez, this man is dangerous and has made two attempts on two others since this murder. We need your help. If you know anything, tell us." She demanded, looking him straight in the eyes.

Jose downed his head and said, "You know, I'm still on parole. I don't need no trouble. I swear I didn't know the watch was any big deal. Butch said it belonged to his Mama and she asked him to sell it to buy some groceries. I swear I didn't know it was stolen, Deputy."

"Man, didn't you stop to think that if it was legit he could pawn the watch himself?"

Charlee stood right in his face—one hand on her hip and the other shaking a finger, up close and personal.

"Pretty dumb of me, eh? I never considered that." He raised both hands. She was getting a little too close to him.

"Please, tell me what you know, Joe. You need to do this for yourself. I'm not here to get you in trouble. I need your help."

"Well, this guy . . . we met in prison . . . he come to my house and asked if I would do him a favor. I asked him what it was and he told me this story about the watch being his Mama's and how they needed groceries, etc., and would I take the watch to the pawn shop for him 'cause his Mama was sick and he hated to leave her. I fell for his story—hook, line and sinker. I drove over to the pawnshop and got the cash and met Butch at Rosie's Coffee Shop that afternoon. He gave me $20 for my trouble and gas. I left and haven't seen him since."

"What was the man's full name?" She asked Jose, showing interest in getting a good lead for a change.

"His name is Butch Rafty or something like that." I don't rightly know about his last name. I expect the Butch part is just a nickname,too. Sorry. I don't know much else, Deputy."

"You have an address or his Mama's name, what kind of car he drove? Anything?"

"No, ma'am, I can't help you there. When he talks about her, he always calls her 'Mama'. I never found out where he lives but I suspect he lives with his Mama since he got out of prison. Let me think . . . yeah, he was driving an old green car, a Buick I believe."

"Tell me, Jose, did he tell you anything about his mother or father? Talk about his growing-up days?"

"Butch said his daddy beat him up and his Mama stood there and watched, just like she got all turned on about seeing her own flesh and blood beat to a pulp. It was weird, I tell you."

"What else did he tell you?"

"Well, Butch said that after a beating, he thought his mama and daddy got it on . . . you know, had sex. They left him lying in the floor, usually bleeding, and went to their bedroom and locked the door. They would came back out all lovey-dovey. That made Butch furious. He said they was sick, both of 'em." Jose paused and then added, "Butch was really a freak, too."

"What do you mean?"

"My cell was right next to Big Al's and Butch's cell. I heard things. They would knock one another around the cell for a time . . . real mean like . . . and then it would get all quiet and I could hear all the whispering going on and the moaning. I figured it out. They slapped one another around some and then had sex. Looked to me like the violence got them all worked up for it. Weird."

Charlee was jotting down comments as Jose talked. She closed her book and shook hands with him, saying, "Thank you so much for your cooperation."

"Am I going to get in trouble over this?"

"Since you have been so helpful and given me some information about this Butch person, I don't anticipate your getting into hot water over it. However, we may need you to testify at a later date. Right now we need to find the guy. I would appreciate your calling, if he makes contact with you or if you think of anything else important," she said as she handed him a business card with her name printed across it.

As she slowly drove back to the Sheriff's Office, Charlee went over all the information that Jose had supplied. *Not much to go on, so far, but more than we had. The perp is a freak! Seems his whole family are weirdoes.* She shivered. *We've got to get that murderer and soon!*

When Charlee entered the office, she found Jack and Bill in a serious discussion about the perpetrator. Both of them looked up and grinned.

"Where have you been?" Jack asked when he saw the look on Charlee's face, one of satisfaction laced with impatience.

"I ran across the black mini that I chased the other day. Rita Guerra was driving. She and Jose Rodriguez are living together. The car is registered to her. As it turns out, the two young boys are hers, too.

Anyway, she told me where she lived and that Joe would probably be at home, either asleep or watching television. He works at Mortons and goes on shift at three o'clock. I drove out to the house on Texas Street and saw a surprisingly neat little bungalow with the lawn mowed and well kept.

There were flowers growing along the front porch. Anyway, Jose answered the door and at first he told me he didn't know anything about a ladies watch. I could tell he was lying about that. I just kept questioning him. When he heard the word **murder,** he caved."

Charlee continued, glancing down at her notes, giving the two officers all the information she had jotted down. They seemed interested to learn more about the man, Butch, that they were dealing with in this murder investigation. It wouldn't solve any cases but they knew a little about what made him tick. She also gave them a name, Butch Rafty, which they ran through the computer but came up with nothing. They needed a legal full name. Could they get that information at the prison? It was worth a try.

Charlee said, "I'm calling the prison right now." She picked up the phone and dialed the number.

Chapter 20

Maxie felt stronger the next morning and Megan was ready to go back to school. They had a light breakfast and dressed for the day. Megan was still pale and listless. Maxie questioned her wisdom in letting her daughter return to school. However, Megan assured her mother that she would be fine. Because they were already late, they left the house in a hurry.

Maxie arrived at the office, looked at the stack of correspondence and messages and felt overwhelmed. Just being out a couple of days made her feel so far behind she would never get caught up again. *Couldn't be helped. I had to take care of my baby.* She looked through the mailed stacked high in her incoming box. *Oh, I knew it would be this way. May as well attack this stuff right now.* With determination Maxie tore into the mail and began sorting out the more important stuff. She could do the other junk mail later.

She was involved in this task when Bill arrived. He looked tired and worried.

He walked over to her and planted a light kiss on the top of her head and asked, "How are you feeling, Babe?"

"Like I was run over by an eighteen wheeler." She smiled up at him. "I do feel I'm going to live. For a while I wasn't real sure about that. I'm still very weak and shaky. It will take a little time to get my energy back after a bout of flu. Are you all right? You don't look so hot. I hope you aren't coming down with this junk. I feel guilty about letting you hang around and play nursemaid to Megan and me." She paused and added, "Again, thanks for being there." She took his big hand in her own and gently squeezed it.

"I'm not getting much rest. This case is eating at me, Max. Let me bring you up-to-date."

He told her the full details they had learned about the killer.

That's good news, Bill! Maybe we can get a name. The intruder is a creep, isn't he? Which means he is unpredictable as well." Maxie sighed and looked thoughtful for a moment.

"Did the results on the hair you found at the Meyers match up?"

"The DNA on the blood found on the window and the hair are apparently from the same person."

"That's a start." She said.

Maxie turned back to her desk saying, "I am going to wade through some of the correspondence this morning. See you later?"

"Sure thing. How can I help you, Max?" He spread his open hand across the clutter.

"Catch that killer." She said firmly and smiled that shy smile.

Bill walked out of her office feeling more energetic than in had felt in days. *I've got a pitiful case of lovesickness. That lady has me wrapped around her little finger and doesn't even know it. That's a good thing. I can't tell exactly where I stand with Max. I have to play these cards up close to my chest until I know how she feels. It could be that my heart is in danger of being broken. Be very careful, Ranger . . .* he cautioned.

Maxie worked the mail, stacking some aside to deal with later and taking action on others. She made numerous calls. There were other sheriff's offices calling about an inmate or status of the murder case. The lab in Waco called. When she dialed their number, Babe answered with a cheerful sound in her voice.

"Babe, this the Sheriff O'Bryan Have you gotten anything on the samples yet? I had a message that you called. Sorry, I have been out of the office a couple of days with flu and am just now getting back to you."

"Oh, hi. Let me think a minute . . . Here is your file. Oh, yes I ran the DNA through NCIC and got a match. Hold on a sec and I'll find it." Babe put the phone on hold and Maxie closed her eyes as she listened to a soothing melody that played as she waited.

"Max, the guy is Buford Rafferty, 1875 County Road. He has a record but nothing as serious as murder. He was released from prison about a year and half ago. Got a pen? I'll give you his ID number, etc." Babe called out several numbers to her. Maxie thanked Babe and then hung up.

Maybe we are finally getting somewhere with this case. Yippee! Maxie hurried down the hall to see if Jack or Bill were around the building. Both were gone. Well, she had plenty to do while she waited for their return.

Bill and Jack were driving away from the café when Bill exclaimed, "Damn! I remember something! The other day I was driving down a street and saw a man all slumped over the steering wheel. It just occurred to me that he was driving a green Buick. I wrote down the license plate, but he told me a story about how his friend lived in the house where he was parked and he was waiting for him to come home from work. Said he was napping a little while he waited. I noticed a partially filled can of beer and asked him about it. He said a friend of his left it in his car that morning. He willingly turned that over to me and I cautioned him and drove away. I had the murder on my mind and the murderer in my hands, Jack. I didn't run the license number through dispatch. Damn! I'll must be getting careless in my old age."

Jack smiled at his friend and said, "Now, Bill, don't be so hard on yourself. I would have probably done the same thing, if I had been wearing your boots. The guy wasn't breaking any law just sitting there parked, was he?"

"I suppose not and at the time I didn't know anything about a green Buick. At least, that makes me feel a little better. Generally, I am more thorough than that. Got too many things on my mind, Jack. I'm sorry."

Bill drove along silently for a few blocks and then he asked, "Jack, I'm sure you've noticed something is going on between Max and Me."

Jack looked innocent when he replied, "What do you mean, something is going on between you and Max? I hadn't noticed." He chuckled and added, "Of course, a blind hog would know something is going on. Hell, I can almost see the sparks flying when you two get near one another. It better be L O V E, old boy. I don't want to see that little lady hurt again . . . Bill, I'm not sure if the timing is right. She was pretty broken up when she lost Matt."

"Matt was a good man . . . "

"Jack, I never told you that I almost married many years ago, did I? I was madly in love with a girl that I grew up with. We attended high school and college together. We both assumed that we would one day get married and have a family. We were separated for a time after I got out of college. When I came home that summer, she had married my best friend. Just like that! My dream was shattered. I suppose I have been very cautious with women since then. Basically, I don't trust them and won't allow one to get close to me. In all these years, I have never found another to take the place of my first love, my childhood sweetheart. I didn't try to. Now, this little gal, Max, has my heart all tangled up with thoughts of settling down, buying a house of our own and having a family . . . Tell me, Jack, is this love?"

"Boy, sounds like the love bug bit you good. Hey, man, that is great! I love Max like a daughter and I have watched her suffer through the grief of losing a spouse. Then taking on this job as sheriff. It hasn't been easy. She was a fool about Matt. If it hadn't been for her job, I don't know if she could have made it." Jack turned towards his partner and inquired, "What does Max think about all this? You did tell her how you feel, didn't you, Bill."

"Well, not exactly. I've been going slow with that. I'm not sure she is ready to hear it. I guess I'm ready to tell her. You know it would about kill me if she refused me, Jack. I doubt this big ole heart could stand her rejection. At times, I just want to grab her up and shake her. She knows there is something between us but truthfully, I think she is in denial."

"What about that little girl of hers? How does she feel about all this?" Jack questioned.

"Meg likes me. She sometimes seem to maneuver our getting together to do stuff.

You know, she'll asked me to come over and watch a movie, or come eat supper with them. I really don't see any problems in that area."

"Bill, do you have any plans in approaching Max in the near future? Get off that butt and do it! What are you waiting for, Partner?" Jack sound a little peeved about the delay.

Bill smiled at his friend. That statement, pretty much, put his stamp of approval on the relationship. Bill was glad. Jack was a good officer and had the ability to see to the core of a person. Certainly it was evident, he was a true friend

After Bill pulled into the parking space at the SO, the two men sat silently in the vehicle for a few minutes, mulling over their conversation.

Jack opened the passenger door and stepped out; he turned to Bill and warned, "Don't wait too long, Bill." Then he closed the door and went inside.

Bill pondered the conversation; not really understanding the last statement, *don't wait too long. What did Jack mean by that?*

The truck was Bill's sanctuary at the moment. He began to seriously think about his feelings. He loved Max fiercely, protectively and possessively. Little Megan would just be a plus in their relationship.

Am I truly ready to make a commitment? My life would change. For 40 years I have only had myself to think about. Lately I feel something has been missing and maybe I have put my finger on it. I want and need a family and a home. Somebody to fill that void. Work keeps me busy and keeps me from thinking about my personal wants. I need Max and Meg, but, would Max be willing to change her life. It could mean giving up a job that has been her life for several years? I want her to work if she desires but, if not, I can support a family. The big question is does she love me?. I'm going to have to step up to her and ask, eh?

What will I do if she says she doesn't love me enough to marry me and change her whole life? I know we have some

chemistry and the sparks fly when we come together. Is that enough? Just thinking about the way her body responds to me. Makes me excited just remembering the other night. Even though she was sick, I wanted to take her to bed and make love to her all night long. Man, that's sick!

Bill was thoughtful as he drove away from the office. He wasn't ready to face Max right now. He needed a cooling off period. A time to think seriously about this relationship Look at the pros and cons of the situation.

Jack's warning came back to haunt him. "Don't wait too long."

Seated in her office, Maxie and Jack discussed the case. She asked him, "Do you want to go to the residence and bring Butch in for questioning?"

Jack said, "Sure, but I don't think you or I need to go to the house alone. We are dealing with a sick-o killer, Sheriff. He isn't exactly stupid. I'm sure he was aware that the city police tried to catch him when he left the hospital today. He will lay low but will be watching for any surveillance."

Maxie was thoughtful when she said, "You're right, Jack. We do have to be very careful . . . "

"Where is Bill? I thought the two of you were together."

"We were. I thought he would come in right behind me. He said he had a lead in the case." Jack said casually, looking a little guilty about what he had said to Bill only a few minutes earlier.

Maxie had worked around Jack long enough to realize that something was troubling him.

She wasn't sure if it was work related so she asked, "Jack, is something bothering you? You look worried"

"Yeah . . . I guess you could call me cupid or stupid." He ducked him head, not really wanting to see his boss' reaction to that statement.

Maxie's face was troubled when he finally raised his head and looked her in the eye. *Wow, that little gal is furious with me now! Why can't I just leave things alone? Oh no, I want to fix things—see progress—in this relationship. Dang, I'm not her father. So, why do I keep playing that roll?* He had interfered and had angered his boss lady.

"Listen, Max, you know my wife and I think the world of you. I'm not an idiot. I can see a longing in those green eyes for something that is missing in your life. I care about your happiness.

Bill Sullivan is a good man. He loves you, boss. I know this is none of my business but I guess I am making it my concern. You have to get on with life. Matt was a great officer, a good husband and father. Nothing will ever change that. Sweetheart, he isn't coming back. I know you will always have a part of him here, in your heart, and a constant reminder of him through Megan. Damn it! Matt would want you to move on and be happy. Meg is at a difficult age. She needs a daddy. Max, you're still young. Hell, you need a strong man in your life . . . Mind you, that's just my opinion."

Jack grinned at the little lady who looked so much like an innocent, confused little girl sitting there before him with tears glistening in her eyes. "Well, I guess I had to have my say, didn't I?"

"Jack, sometimes I get so mad at you! When I think about it, I know that you are concerned about Meggie and me. That certainly isn't a good reason to get angry with you, is it?" She smiled at Jack. "I guess I am just feeling a bit of pressure from you and Bill. I like him. I'm not sure I love him. I would never hurt him by marrying him because my daughter needs a father or because I need a man in my life. Sometimes I believe it is less complicated to plod along, day to day, just like we are. I have to admit that I still miss not having a man to love me. At times, I'm angry with Matt for leaving me. Then I feel so guilty . . . It was my fault he died, you know. I called for back up and that led to his death. I can never get over that, Jack! I live with that guilt everyday. It scares me sometimes." Big tears coursed down her pale cheeks. "Some days, I can't remember what Matt's face looked like! I never forget what it felt like to be loved by him. He was my life!"

Jack reached over and pulled his boss lady into his comforting arms and tried to console her, like she was a little girl. He could feel she was trying to let go of the past. As she boohooed her tears wet his shirt, but Jack didn't care. *She is being a woman for a change.* "Let it all out, little one."

Several minutes passed before her sobs ceased. She looked embarrassed when she pulled away from him and said, "I'm so sorry, Jack." She brushed her hand across the wet front of his shirt.

"I know you want the best for me. Right now I don't know what that is . . . I'm scared! I told myself a year ago that I would never marry another law enforcement officer. Here I stand, dreaming about a life with a Texas Ranger. Jack, I'm not sure that is what I want." Maxie said wistfully.

"Your problem, Maxie, is you're letting your head rule your heart. Anyone can see that you and Bill are drawn to each other in some mysterious way. Listen to your heart, girl. Life is full of chances. We take them every day, getting into our cars every morning. We have to step out and do it. It wouldn't be natural to stay at home because of what **might** happen to us, would it?" Jack said teasing Maxie.

She smiled up at him and patted his hand. "Jack, you're right as usual. Tell you what . . . I will seriously work on it."

Jack's expression was serious for a moment and he said, "Don't wait too long, Max. Your young man is impatient . . . Did you know he had his heart broken long ago?" Maxie nodded her head. "Well, he was hurt so badly, he hasn't ever wanted a deep commitment with anyone, until you."

"Jack, do you think he really and truly loves me, above all else? Or does he just want me to hop into bed with him?" She asked doubtfully, smiling up at his stern face.

"Hell, he wants to get you in his bed, woman, as his wife. You can take that to the bank."

Jack raised her chin so he could look right into those deep pools of green. "All I'm asking, Maxie, is that you give him a chance. He is afraid you will turn him down, I expect."

"Ok! Ok! I'll see if I can get to the true feelings of that big lug and my own as well. Maybe you're right. I don't know."

She was thoughtful for a moment. "Meggie has been playing cupid, you know? I know that she likes him but would she want Bill for a dad?"

"Why don't you ask her? Maxie, for heaven's sake, Meg isn't the one Bill wants to marry!" Jack blurted out in a loud voice.

Max threw her head back and laughed, "Sounds to me like you have all this settled in your mind, Deputy Jack Rankin."

"Sorry, Boss. You know patience isn't one of my virtues."

Jack downed his head, cut his eyes up to her and made a comment. "Max, friend to friend, I want to see you happy. That's all."

"So do I," she said wistfully. "So do I."

The Texas Ranger drove to a nearby lake and parked. He had a lot to think about. *What do I want from Max? I know she likes me and is physically attracted to me. I won't settle for less than her love and devotion. I know that my love for her will last forever. Shoot! We both have some baggage but can we leave it behind and have a future together? I don't want Max to forget her first love, anymore than I will. Surely she can find room in her heart for me. I love Megan and crave to be a part of her life as well. We need one another. Heck fire! I love them both and want them to be mine to cherish for the rest of my days.* Bill sat silently for a while with his head resting on the back of his seat, listening to the sounds of the water as the waves dashed against the rocks and slowly receded, only to repeat the procedure. A quiet peace invaded his being. He breathe a sigh.

Fifteen minutes later, Bill hurriedly drove back to town. He was starved to see Max, to confess his love for her. If he could get up the courage, he was going to ask her to marry him . . . if . . .

Chapter 21

The killer sat beside his mother's bed. She had been dead a while now. He guessed he would have to take a shovel and dig a hole to bury her body. It was beginning to stink up the place. *Sorry, old gal. You never was much mama to me, but I guess you did the best you knew how. Why, Mama, why did you let Daddy beat me? Why didn't you protect me from him? Afterwards, I knew you and Pa went in the bedroom to have violent sex. Was seeing me suffer and the blood a turn on? I guess I took after you and Pa after all. 'Cept, I like to do my job a little more thorough. I get hot watching them die. I love to see the fear and confusion, the watch the blood gushing out. Makes me feel like I'm a god. Afterwards, I can't wait to leave the victim so as I can satisfy my desires, Ma! It is a high . . . I forgive you, Ma.* The man looked at the corpse lying there, leaned forward, laid his head on the cold-skinned hand and sobbed. Then he raised his head and said, "Mama, I'm real sorry about sticking that knife in your throat while you was asleep. I just had to get all that stress out, you understand? I think I woulda exploded otherwise . . . That bitch in the hospital, screwed me! I nearly had her, Ma! She cheated me out of my relief that night. You understand, don't you, I had to do something or bust?"

Slowly, the man rose from the bedside and walked out of the house. In a nearby shed, he pulled out an old shovel, went around behind the house and began to dig a hole in the hard ground. As he shoveled, dip by dip, he softly sang, "Amazing Grace." He stopped, thought about what he was doing and then he laughed, an evil, sinister sound rang out in to the distance, traveling over hills and valleys, causing even Mother Earth to shiver in disgust.

As Bill entered the SO he met Charlee. After short greetings, he handed her a slip of paper with a license plate number on it and ask if she would run it for him. Then he walked down the hall to Maxie office. *While I still have the nerve, I'm confronting that little darling.*" Disappointment registered on his tan face when he found her office empty. He walked to the front office and spoke to Mary Bell, who told him that Max left a short time before but didn't say where she would be. She said to call her on the radio or her cell phone to get in touch with her

"Thanks, Mary. How are those grandchildren of yours?" he inquired.

"Just great! Bill, I'm having the time of my life with them. You are going to miss out on one of the most precious times of your life, if you don't hurry and hog tie that pretty little gal and start making babies." She winked up at Bill.

She saw his face turn a pretty shade of red and wondered what that was all about. *Don't suppose I embarrassed the ranger, do you?* She shook her head and continued with opening the mail stacked on her desk.

Bill went back to Charlee's office and asked her about the return on the license number.

"It came back to a woman named Bessie Hallmark. That's nothing like the name I was expecting." Charlee was thoughtful for a moment then added, "Which doesn't mean squat these days. She could have had any number of husbands for all we know. Right?"

"Exactly right, my friend." Bill replied. "Let me have the address and I will drive out and see what I can find out."

"Want me to come with you?" she asked Bill hopefully.

"That's not necessary. If the killer does live there I don't want him to know we are on to him. Since I am in plain clothes, I'll stick my badge in my pocket. That way I won't arouse suspicion. I can ask a few questions. I'll make up a nice story about being lost or something. You know the perp may not live with Bessie Hallmark anyway. Possibly neither of them live there. I don't want to jump the gun on this one."

"I agree, ranger. We want this guy brought in completely by the book, don't we? No loop holes!" Charlee said with determination.

Bill drove slowly to the address given on the DL return. He parked down the road about a quarter of a mile and watched the house. *Frankly, I can't believe someone is living in that little run-down shack. The yard is grown up. Some of the shingles are missing on the roof. The screens are MIA on most of the windows. There isn't a dog or cat anywhere around. My opinion is that this house is vacant.* He slowly drove down the dusty road, turned into what he thought was an abandoned driveway. There was no life stirring. The ranger crawled out of the truck and walked up into the yard, stepping over tall weeds and trash. He yelled, "Hello . . . is anybody at home?" There was no response. He stepped up to the door and rapped his knuckles loudly against the rotted wood. After a pause, he knocked harder and still got no response.

He turned to step off the portion of the porch still standing, picked up the sound of a rattler He quickly jerked his foot back. "You scared the living daylights out of me, big fellow," he said softly to the coiled snake, lying exactly in the path he was taking. "Sorry, I didn't know this was your place, buddy. I didn't mean to trespass. I don't want to hurt you." Bill stood perfectly still for a few moments until the snake slowly crawled away, his tail stuck in the air, rattling his warning.

Whew! I'm sure glad God made rattles on those boogers. I didn't see him when I came up on the porch. Probably stepped right over him." Bill walked cautiously back to the truck through the weeds and was glad to be safely out of there.

His old Indian grandfather taught him to respect all the wild creatures, especially the rattlesnake. *It is my humble opinion, Grandfather, that those fellows demand respect. They certainly do get mine!* He drove back into town thinking about his life as a wild child on the reservation, learning the Indian ways. *I miss not having a family. Maybe, just maybe, I can change that.*

Chapter 22

One more time, the man driving the green Buick cruised by the junior high school. Earlier, he had dumped the body of his dead mother into the shallow grave and covered her with dirt. He would miss her. Since she had gotten older, Mama had been nicer to her little boy. She slapped him around some but that was fine because he returned the favor at times. He needed a woman to cook for him and see to his needs, like Mama, or maybe he could fine a young man to take care of him in more ways than one. He laughed loudly at the thought. *I can be Big Al!*

He parked in the shadows of a big oak tree and watched the red head come out of the building, talking to a boy and smiling up at him. He followed them to the Malt Shop down the street. They were chummy. He didn't like that. He waited and watched. Five days since he had watched the blood spurting from the knife wound he had made when he cut his mama's throat.

It was funny. He never thought he would enjoy killing as much as he did. A thrill ran through his body with the picture of death in his evil mind. At first, killing was something he was curious about. In prison, Big Al talked about murdering his victims. Toward the end of his stay in jail, the excitement of the story telling was transferred to Butch. *The gory stuff was the best part.* Now, it was bigger than he had ever expected. The kill itself totally occupied his mind. At times, he felt the killer in him had taken over his body and he was no longer the weak Butch of years past. It was almost as though he had become addicted to killing. *Can that happen to people?*

He passed some time, while he waited, thinking about it. He could see in his mind this cute little red-haired babe, lying in a pool of dark red blood. Butch had selected his next victim. *Man, I can hardly wait!*

Megan sat inside the Malt Shop, laughing and talking with her friends. She glanced out the window, where she sat, and noticed a grungy looking man, wearing a worn red plaid shirt, watching the place. She shivered as she realized he was staring at her, with a cruel, evil expression on his unshaven face. His eyes were scarey. Quickly, she turned back to her friends. She couldn't shake the feeling that she was being watched. When the crowd broke up, she asked J.J. if he would mind walking her home.

She explained. "I saw a man watching me at the Malt Shop, J.J. He scared me. I'm pretty sure I've seen him a couple of times before. Do you think he could be stalking me or am I being paranoid?"

Her boyfriend turned to her in surprise and asked, "Meg, are you sure you aren't being overly cautious because your Mom is the sheriff and all? I didn't even see the guy. I'm not saying he wasn't there." He smiled that handsome smile of his and thought, *Megan is paranoid.*

"I guess you're right about that. Of course, I am more informed than most about what is going on . . . you know the murder and all. I know there is a killer out there and he goes after women and young girls. Mom has cautioned me about strangers." Placing her small hand in his, she said, "I always feel safe with you."

J.J. squeezed her hand and he grinned. They continued walking down the sidewalk towards her house, talking about school and other trivial matters. However, Megan kept looking behind her. The uneasy feeling remained. *Someone is watching me. I just know it!*

The lady sheriff had driven to the prison to find out more about the suspected killer, Butch Rafferty. She talked to the girl in the warden's office, asking to see files. Butch's files were pulled and handed to Maxie to examine. She took a seat in a nearby straight chair and began thumbing through the pages. Nothing spectacular jumped out at her. He was a model inmate during his stay. Although Butch was bullied by some, he mostly stayed out of trouble by doing what the leaders required. When he first come in the prison he was ordered counseling and drug rehab. Nothing indicated that he was a violent, dangerous man. Maxie jotted an address down that was listed as his mother's home. She thanked the clerk and left the prison in a thoughtful mood.

As she drove back to the office, she wondered, *why would a man like that turn to killing? Maybe he has so much anger built up inside him, that killing is a means of letting off steam. Hummmm, I wonder. What was his childhood like?*

Later Maxie arrived home and found her daughter doing homework at the kitchen table with her favorite music blaring in the background.

"Hey there, Meg!" Maxie yelled. "I'm afraid you'll ruin your hearing if you continue that noise?" She grinned at her daughter as walked over to the CD player and turned the volume down.

"Oh, hi, Mom. I didn't hear you come in. Sorry, I needed the noise today." Meg said and returned her mother's hug.

"What is bothering you, sweetie?" Maxie was concerned about the seriousness of Meg's expression. "Did you have a really bad day? Make a bad grade? Break up with J.J. What?"

Megan breathed a sigh. "No, my day at school was fine. I made 95 on my test, and J.J. and I am still together . . . " After a pause, Megan continued, "Mom, I got a weird feeling today at the Malt Shop. I was sitting there, laughing and joking with a few friends, when I glanced out the window and I noticed this creep. Mom, he was looking right at me! That gave me the willies." Megan shivered uncontrollably.

Maxie felt the fear in her daughter. "Did you see what kind of car he was driving or get a license number?" she asked.

Megan thought a moment before she answered, "The car was a greenish color but I couldn't see the license number."

A terrible feeling of panic rose in Maxie but she tried to appear calm. *This is the killer, stalking his next victim, my daughter! Oh, my God! Help me protect her.*

She turned to her only child and tried to reassure her, "Just some nut, I imagine, and maybe you thought he was looking at you. Perhaps he was meeting someone at the Malt Shop."

"Mom, I had the strangest feeling about him. So, I asked J. J. to walk me home."

"Good girl! For a while ask someone to be with you wherever you go, in case he is a stalker, will you Meggie?"

I can't tell her he might be the killer. Dang it! We have to catch that creep and soon.

"Oh, don't worry, I will, Mom." Megan hugged her mother. Maxie could feel a tremble of fear in her daughter's body.

"Mom, I'm going to my room for a while." Megan replied as she gathered her books and went to her room.

Immediately, Maxie called Bill on his cell phone. She was relieved when he answered on the first ring. "Bill, I just talked to Meggie and someone is stalking her or at least she thinks he is. This is the part that worries me; he drives a green car. I'm scared to death the killer has selected Meg as his next target. What am I going to do?"

Bill could hear the panic in her voice. He tried to reassure her and said he would be right over. Maxie heard his truck door slam in the background as he disconnected the line. She was relieved.

He really cares for us! Isn't that what Jack, and everyone else, has been telling me?

About ten minutes later, Bill came rushing through the front door. He was wearing his jeans and a tee shirt, looking more sexy than any man had a right to do. His hair was damp and disheveled, which only added to his masculinity.

He swept Maxie into his arms when he saw the relief on her face.

At last, she trusts me. I don't ever want to betray that feeling. They stood hugging one another while she shed a few tears.

When she could control her voice again, she looked up into those ocean blue eyes.

They are full of love and concern for me. She could feel the immediate response of his body as he held her close.

Maxie stepped away from him. He followed her to the kitchen where she got a couple of cokes our of the fridge and sat before each of them, Neither spoke until she handed him the glass and sat down across from the table from him, taking a sip. She looked troubled.

"Tell me about it, Max."

She went through the details as quickly as she could. "I don't like this whole situation, Bill. This has to be the killer!"

"I don't like it either, Max. I do need to talk to Meg later. First, let me tell you about my adventures to find this Butch Rafferty."

"Did you go out there alone, Bill? My gosh, you could have been killed!" Max exclaimed, her voice laced with concern for the ranger.

"Actually, I drove there to see if a vehicle or anyone was around the place. I can guarantee you that the place is vacant. A giant rattler has taken up residence, and I imagine some of his kin." He grinned at Max and continued. "That address isn't a good one. I suspect we are back to square one. Except for the vehicle, we don't have much, because it isn't registered in his name. Let's put out an APB on it and see what we come up with."

"Do we have enough evidence to do that?"

"Sure we do! Evidence of DNA is enough." Bill paused and reached over to take her small hand in his big one. A surge of protective spirit flooded his heart. *I won't let anything happen to you or Meg. I swear!*

"Is Meg around for me to ask her a few questions-if that is all right with you, Max?" Bill asked.

"I'll get her for you." She left the room, smiling to herself. *That man wants to be a part of our lives. Should I let him? It's tempting.*

Megan came into the kitchen. Her eyes were red and it was evident that she had been crying.

Bill opened his arms and held her in a loving embrace. "Did you have a rough day, kiddo?"

Megan nodded her head. Her bottom lip quivered as she placed her arms around him, leaned into him and sobbed. Bill petted her and let her cry.

She is scared to death! I won't have it! He muttered comforting phrases in her ear to reassure her that he would be there for her and he prayed that nothing would happen to her.

Finally, she raised her face, grinned shyly and moved out of his embrace. She was embarrassed about the way she had quickly turned to him for comfort. As she slid into a nearby chair, she asked the ranger, "What do you need to know?"

"First, start at the beginning and tell me what happened today?"

She began her story about the creepy-looking man who watched her at the Malt Shop. She had seen the green car a few times around the school. "I never really thought much about it, until today. You know, he could be somebody's dad."

"He could be." Bill tried to reassure her. Gently he warned, "Meg, don't take any chances. He could be dangerous."

"I had this awful feeling while he watched me. I saw evil . . . for the first time in my life." She shuddered. "He wants to hurt me!"

"It's very important that you get the license number if you see him again. Don't go anywhere alone for a while. Be observant! Make a note of anything unusual that you see."

Bill took her hand in his own, looking down at it he said softly, "I love you, Meg. You are like a daughter to me . . . it would about kill this cowboy if anything were to happen to you. Do you know that?" He grinned at her.

"I know. Thanks for caring about me. I wish you were my Dad." Meg ducked her head. She felt embarrassed by her own admission and his when she saw her mother standing in the doorway listening to every word,

There was a knock at the front door and Maxie quickly turned and went to see who was there. A ragged, umkept man stood on the step. He kept his head lowered when he asked if he could mow the yard. He said he needed money for food. Maxie agreed to a price and closed the door quietly.

She hurried back to the kitchen. "What are you up to?" She glanced at each of them.

"We're trying to figure out how to get you to marry this wonderful, incredibly handsome, very dependable man that we know and who is crazy about you. Right, Meg?" Bill asked.

"That's right, Mom." Megan replied, grinning at her mom.

"Sounds cool! Now, who could this wonderful, handsome, dependable man be?" Maxie said, playing along in a joking manner as if she didn't know whom they meant.

"Mom! He is sitting right here in our kitchen!"

Maxie laughed, making a happy sound ring throughout the house. "So, the two of you have figured it out, have you? Do I have anything to say about it?"

"Mom!"

Maxie smiled at her frustrated daughter, and walked up behind Bill, placing both arms around his neck. "Cowboy,

I don't want to break your heart. You are a good man. I'm not sure that what I feel for you is enough of a foundation on which to build a happy marriage. If I can't commit to you totally and completely, it would not be fair to you, Bill. I admire you, respect you and I do like you very much. But, love? Well, I need time to think about that. Ok?"

Bill turned and was serious when he looked into the eyes of the lady sheriff and said softly, "Don't take too long, Max."

He rose from his chair, picked up his Stetson and said, "Well, girls, I have to go. I have an appointment in about ten minutes. I'll see you tomorrow, Max." Without another word, he walked out the door, leaving Maxie feeling empty.

As Bill climbed into his truck, he could hear the buzzing sounds of the mower at the back of the house.

The killer continued to mow the yard. He was thinking, *my next victim sits inside, almost like she is waiting for me.* He could see in the house through a window, thanks to a small crack in the blinds. Anticipation ran rampant as he walked back and forth following the mower. *I can hardly wait.* He felt that familiar twinge in his groin just thinking about her death.

Chapter

Bill had mixed emotions as he returned to his rooming house for supper. *I'm not sure that I will be able to break down that wall that Max has build around her heart. I believe I have that sweet kid of hers wrapped up. She wants me to be her dad! My gosh, that makes me feel ten feet tall! I can't let her down. I have to protect her from that pervert. Her mother can be trying at times.* He told himself to be patient. Then he joined his landlady for a delicious fried chicken dinner. They passed the time as she chatted about her day working in her garden and gossiped about the stubborn neighbor across the street. The elderly lady called her neighbor, t*hat old fart!* Bill smiled as he listened, unable to get a word in edgewise.

Shortly after nine, Bill went upstairs to his room. He needed some time to think, and think, he did, most of the night, as he reviewed the case over and over trying to determine what he had overlooked. The remainder of his night was spend tossing, turning and dreaming about the two ladies that had recently turned his life upside down.

The grungy man came to the front door and knocked after the mowing was done. He waited and was surprised to see the lovely young girl come to the door. He quickly put his hand to his cap and pulled it low over his eyes and kept his head down as he said, "I've finished the lawn, Ma'am."

Megan turned, yelled for her mother and Maxie came and paid him their agreed price. He quickly turned away after a brief, "Thank you, Ma'am." He grinned to himself as he walked down the block where the old truck he had borrowed was parked.

Those dames don't have a clue! I'm good. I'm real good. He smugly thought. As he drove away, his evil laughter could be heard echoing down the street.

Megan was standing by the front window as the man walked away. *Something about him seems familiar.* She was positioned so that she could see a truck pull out about a quarter of a block away and she could tell that a lawn mower was being carried in the back.

At least, he isn't driving a green car. Wheww!

"Mom, who was that man?" Megan was curious.

"Honey, I didn't know him. He said he needed food, so I let him mow the yard for cash.

You know I have a tender heart for the down and out." Her tone was almost apologetic.

"Do you ever!" Megan turned to the remote control to turn on the television and sat down to watch a few minutes. Something about the man kept nagging at her. *Guess I'm running scared after that incident at the Malt Shop . . . I never want to see that man in the green car again!*

It was about ten minutes after two in the early morning hours, when Butch arrived back at neighborhood. He parked down the street about a block. The neighborhood was quiet as he pictured families peacefully sleeping all around him.

That was good! He checked for his knife. Then he quietly exited the green car and slowly walked down the sidewalk to the charming little house which was the scene of his next murder.

Suddenly, a huge German Shepherd bounded to the yard fence and began to loudly bark at him. "Shhhhhh! Big boy you will wake up the whole neighborhood." Butch pulled a doggy chew bone from his jacket pocket and tossed it over the fence to the giant animal. The barking stopped just as soon as the treat was spotted. He had heard the dog's master yelling, "Shut up, Bruno!" to silence his pet. Butch was a little concerned that the owner might come out of the house but that didn't happen. The treat did the trick. Butch felt smug. *I am always prepared.* He entered the freshly mowed yard. *Funny, there are no vehicles sitting in the drive. Come to think of it, there wasn't a vehicle parked here this afternoon. Probably put away safely in the garage. The big truck parked out front is no longer there either. Just a visitor,* he imagined.

There wasn't an outside light on but the street light at the end of the block made it possible for him to make his way around to the back of the house. He remembered the window that he had peeked into that afternoon. He was sure that this was the girl's room because of the girlie things he noticed sitting around. *Sleep, little angel, sleep forever.*

First, he slipped on his rubber gloves and ski mask. Slowly he removed the window screen. Quietly he pulled free his hunting knife from his belt and wedged it under the bottom of the window, slowly working it along the edge to loosen any tight spots. *Good thing the house is an old one. The windows seldom lock. Besides, folks around here trust everybody. They are fools!* Finally the window popped loose, making a small "snap." Butch stood still and listened for a few minutes to be sure he had not awakened his intended victim. There were no movements inside and he proceeded to carefully slide and push the window up, giving him enough space to crawl through. *I may be little but I'm big enough and strong enough to do this deed. You're dead, little girl!* He grabbed the windowsill and hoisted his lightweight body over the edge, half in and half out. He held tightly and didn't move for a moment, as he heard a soft moan from the sleeping party. Then he smiled to himself and carefully lifted both legs into the room. The room was dark except for the illuminated clock on the table beside the bed. The killer stood perfectly still until his eyes became adjusted to the darkness and he could see better. His heart was beating rapidly as he bent and picked up the long bladed knife and moved to the side of the bed. His eyes glazed over as he plunged the blade into the sleeping figure's neck, slicing the artery. He held the skinny little body down, placing his gloved hand over the mouth until the struggles ceased. As the excitement cruised through his body, his testosterone accelerated, and he felt his male member between his legs coming to life again. *What a high!*

The victim lay still and only a gurgle could be heard. He could feel the warm blood as it came oozing from the wound. The dark stain spread across the sheet. *Sleep, little baby, sleep!* He smeared the knife blade across the leg of his dirty jeans and holstered it. Butch grabbed some jewelry off the bedside table and he hurried left through the open window. *Probably a bunch of junk, but it is my trophy for now,* he was thinking as he ran back to the car.

Once safely inside his car, he released the piece of flesh that tormented him and with only a couple of jerks was spewing his juices bringing him the relief he longed for. *Damn, it gets better with every kill! I've found the ultimate high!* He laid his head back on the seat for a couple of minutes, closing his glazed eyes and reliving his moments of glory. As he fingered his trophy, the passions surfaced once again.

After he came to his senses, he zipped his blood-smeared jeans, started the green Buick and drove slowly down the street. He noted there were a few lights on in the neighborhood. *I guess some early birds have begun their day. My day just ended! I can sleep now.* He yawned as he parked outside a seedy looking house, which was in need of paint, and climbed out of the Buick. As he entered the house, a skinny yellow cat rubbed against his legs and meowed for food. He kicked the animal as hard as he could, slamming the body up against the wall where it thudded to the floor and lay lifeless. *Ma, I always hated that old cat of yours. Good riddance!*

Bill woke suddenly, feeling something was wrong. His watch told him it was only five o'clock. *Darn, I'm awake now so I may as well get up. Anyway, I have a lot to do today.* Bill Sullivan hefted his big frame off the lumpy bed, stretching his arms to the ceiling and he groaned. *I must be getting old! I hurt all over . . .* he smiled when he glanced toward the bed he had crawled from. He was thinking his and the bed's age might be pretty close to the same.

When Bill got into his truck, he drove by Maxie's place, just to check it and for his own peace of mind. Everything was quiet in the neighborhood. He drove slowly down the street. Suddenly, at the house next door which looked like Max's, the front door burst open and an elderly man hobbled out waving his arms and yelling for help.

Quickly, Bill pulled to the curb in front and asked as he got out of the truck, "Sir, I am a Texas Ranger, what is your problem? Calm down and try to tell me what happened. Okay?"

The emotional old man had tears streaming down his wrinkled cheeks. His faded blue eyes were filled with a sadness that touched Bill's heart when he said, "Somebody killed my wife!" He was wringing his hands and shaking his gray head in disbelief.

"Are you sure about that? Take me to her, please." The gentleman hobbled inside the house and down a hall to a bedroom. Lying on the bed was the body of a thin elderly woman surrounded by a pool of partially dried blood. Bill checked for a pulse but it wasn't there. The body was almost cold. He reached for his radio and called the local police station to report the incident. He tried, in his awkward way, to console the husband all the while thinking to himself, *what would I do if this were Max?*

While they waited for the police to arrive, the older gentleman tried to explain why he wasn't with his wife. He had arthritis pain that kept him up a lot at night. Lots of the time, he tried sleeping in his recliner to keep from disturbing his wife.

In ten minutes the place was swarming with police and reporters. Bill explained his presence there and backed off to let the police do their job. He said, "If you boys need me, here is where you can reach me." He handed them a card.

Suddenly, he found Max in his arms questioning him, "I just heard the news on the scanner, Bill. My God, what happened?" He explained that the elderly woman next door had been stabbed to death.

Maxie's eyes grew round with fear and disbelief. "Do you think this was our killer?"

"Now Max, don't jump to any conclusions." He attempted to console and comfort Maxie.

"Let's just stick to the facts." In his mind he was wondering the same thing that Maxie was, *did the killer mean his victim to be Megan or Max? Why would he want to kill an elderly lady? For that matter, why would he want to kill anybody? The house looks exactly like Max's place. In fact, all of them look the same on this whole block. I wonder . . .*

The morning of the murder was a long one. Police taped off the crime scene and continued the investigation. Finally, the undertaker took the lifeless form away, leaving an empty place in the heart of her husband, who walked around as if he was in a daze. He just couldn't grasp all that had happened. In a few short hours his life had been changed completely and he had lost his life companion.

Bill walked Maxie home, drank some coffee and devoured two pieces of toast, spread with strawberry jam. She was still very upset. After all, her neighbor of five years had been murdered. What nagged at her was the chance that the murderer had miscalculated and killed the lady that should have been her or Megan. After yesterday's incident at the Malt Shop, she couldn't help but feel that the killer had chosen Megan to be his next victim. Somehow, he got the houses confused. She felt guilty at the relief she experienced. So much so that she hardly had room for grief at the loss of a dear friend.

Bill told her that those feelings were normal. "I agree with you, though. I am convinced that he thought he was getting Meg, whom he had been stalking for several days." He paused and then continued, "He could try again, you know?"

"That worries me even more." Maxie replied. "What can I do to protect my daughter? I feel so helpless, Bill."

The tough ranger could see the tears glistening in those expressive green eyes as they shimmered there and then began to spill down the soft pale cheeks. His toughness melted into tenderness for this woman. As a man, he hardly knew what to say to make her feel better so he simply took her into his arms and held her as she poured out the emotions built up inside her.

Finally, she raised her head and said softly, "I seem to be making a habit of crying on your shoulder, Big Guy."

"Anytime, Max, anytime. You know I'm here for you, don't you?" Bill looked into the depths of green expressive eyes, searching for a sign that love might be hidden there. He only saw fear and some relief.

"Thanks, Bill. I do appreciate it and I want you to know that your presence is a comfort to both me and Meggie." She smiled sadly.

The killer slept soundly most of the day. When he finally woke up, he flipped on the television, wondering if he had made the evening news. He sat back in the lumpy lounge chair his mother had used and drank his coffee, only half listening. His thoughts were on early hour events. He was relaxed. Murder did that for him, along with the sex. In his mind they were both the same. He couldn't have one without the other.

I guess I'm hooked on violence and sex. For me, they go together. Big Al taught me that! Well, I 'spect Pa and Ma started it years ago. Pa beat me and then he and Ma 'got it on'. They never knew about the little peephole in the door. I watched as Pa screwed Ma violently. She groaned and moaned. At first, I thought he was hurting her but then I learned that she was enjoying it. I was in pain from the beating. Soon, I learned that watching Ma and Pa do sex made me feel good in a strange. I angrily fondled myself, feeling my wee—wee grow hard, and as Pa and Ma climaxed so did I! He laughed. *We did things together as a family. Weird things, I guess. But, that was the only thing we did together.*

Funny, I never outgrew that feeling of needing to be hurt or hurt someone else to get my pleasures. Strange isn't it? The only time I can enjoy sex is after violence to someone. He snickered.

They told me in prison that I was an excellent candidate for doctors to study . . . to find out what makes me tick. I'm too smart for that! It is nobody's damn business but mine!

Butch turned his attention to the television just in time to hear the newsman give a report of the murder of a female on the south side of town. "More details at 10 p.m." the reporter said. Butch Rafferty slammed his fist into the worn gold leather of the arm of the chair he occupied and swore loudly at the television, "You SOB, I wanted to hear all about it **now!**" Butch went into the kitchen to get something to eat. He saw the yellow cat lying still in the front room floor. He opened the screen door and roughly kicked the dead animal out into the back yard. "There you go kitty. Sleep with *Ma*. You wuz her cat, not mine! I reckon she liked you better than she did me anyways."

Bill Sullivan received a call from Waco headquarters. He was needed to take care of a matter of life and death. He argued with his supervisor to no avail. Bill called the Sheriff's Office and left a message with Mary Bell that he had to leave town to take care of some business. He called Jack and asked him to see about Maxie and Megan while he was out of town. He expected to be gone a day or two. He tried to talk to Maxie but wasn't able to get in touch with her by telephone and so he left a short message at her home.

Maxie was busy most of the day and it wasn't until she arrived home that she was reminded that she hadn't seen Bill since early morning. She played her messages as soon as she took off her gun and badge. Her mom had called again. Megan's friend, Allison, had called. Mrs. Patterson, Megan's teacher called Maxie about Megan, who appeared to be upset about something and preoccupied in class. This wasn't like Megan. She listened to Bill's short message, "Max, I am sorry but I have to get back to headquarters as quickly as possible. I tried to get out of this but apparently one of our officers is having emergency surgery. I should be back in a day or so. Be cautious and careful. Take good care of our girl. Sorry, I couldn't reach you. I'll try calling you later." There was a short pause and then he added softly, "I love you." The telephone dial tone sounded as the short message ended.

Maxie played his message again. *I know what he said . . . I just want to hear him say it again. Am I a romantic, sentimental fool or what?* Reluctantly, she turned from the phone and went in search of Meg who was in her room, sprawled across her bed, staring out the window.

"Hi, Squirt!" Maxie greeted with affection. "How was your day, Sweetie?"

"Terrible . . . Mom, I can't get over the feeling that I was the killer's target last night. I should be the one lying in the morgue. Do you know how that makes me feel?"

Megan laid her head on her arms and cried, her small shoulders shaking with emotion. Maxie walked to the bed and climbed up beside her frightened daughter. Putting her arm around her, she drew her close and let Megan cry.

Maxie softly uttered soothing words and phrases to comfort her only child. Apparently, comfort was the only thing she could give Megan right now.

No kid should have to deal with this. I hate this feeling of helplessness. What can I do to make Megan feel safe? I, too, am concerned that the killer was aiming for Meg, or me, and got the houses confused.

My gosh, I'm not sure about anything anymore! Law enforcement is important to me but family comes first. I have to protect Meggie. How can I do that and do my job? Maybe it is time for me to step down and let someone else do it . . . Maybe . . .

After a some discussion of the pros and cons of the murder, the two girls went to the kitchen together to fix a bite. They decided on a bologna sandwich, chips and a glass of milk. Both were mentally and physically exhausted from all that had transpired in the early hours of the day. They sat and talked quietly as they shared their mealtime.

Megan teased, "Where is your boyfriend tonight, Mom? You didn't scare him off did you?"

Maxie looked at her daughter and smiled, "He had to leave town for a couple of days. You know he does have a job to take care of and he has been with us longer than most cases he investigates. I expect that is because of a certain red head."

"Yeah, you!" Megan teased.

Maxie smiled, thinking of his phone message. *I love you,* he had said. He sounded sure of his feelings. Maxie wished that she could be that sure of her own. *He has been around so much lately that I miss him like crazy. I've grown accustomed to his face, his tenderness and those kisses that set my blood boiling. Can I live without him? Do I need to even try?*

215

So many doubts ran through the back roads of her mind. She thought of Matt. He was her man. He loved her and Megan. He protected her. She just couldn't protect him. She had failed her life partner. She wasn't there for him when he needed her the most. Now he was gone, leaving an empty hole in her heart. *Do I have the right to fill that spot with someone else's love?* She pondered . . .

The killer caught the ten o'clock news on Channel 12. Imagine his surprise when he learned he had killed the wrong one. *Damn!* The television newsman stated that an elderly woman had been murdered in her bed. "Did I make a mistake? I must be getting careless. Stupid! Stupid! Stupid!"

He shouted as he slapped himself on the side of he head several times.

The reporter continued, "The police have no suspects at this time. Entry was made through a bedroom window at the side of the home. She died from a knife wound to the neck. She is survived by her husband of sixty-two years. He was at home at the time of her murder." There was a plea to the public to report anything that was unusual in that neighborhood at two or three in the morning.

Butch swore and shouted to the television. "It was that stupid German Shepherd that got me confused about the location of the house. Dumb me! Stupid mutt! I'll take care of you next!"

He threatened, shaking a grimy finger at the reporter on the screen. "You wait, I'll kill that stupid dog!"

The killer stomped around the room, kicked at furniture, threw a flower vase that smashed against the wall and crashed his fist through a dingy windowpane. Glass scattered across the room. His own blood dripped onto the rustic wooden floor around his feet. He stared at it—almost experiencing the high of his murders. Then he licked the blood from his fist and wrapped a dirty dishtowel around it. *May have to go to the hospital for stitches. Son-of-a-bitch!*

"It's your fault, you stupid dog!" Butch screamed.

Maxie was unable to sleep that night. She was restless. *Admit it, you are scared silly!*

Her thoughts turned to the Texas Ranger pushing his way into her and Meggie's life. Just knowing that he was gone made her feel insecure. *What is wrong with me?* . . . Maxie pondered the question she had asked herself for a few minutes. *The handsome devil has wormed his way into my heart! Oh no! I'm not ready for that . . . Am I?*

She flipped to her side and finally got out of bed and walked to the window and looked out. The quarter-moon skimmed quietly across the heavens, and the stars twinkled down at her. She was unaware of them. As she hugged her body, her thoughts were of Bill, the man who made her heart pound and her body tingle when he kissed her.

Lordy, I get hot just thinking about him. I wonder what it would be like to make love with that handsome savage?

She scolded herself. *Stop it! I'm acting like a silly, lovesick, schoolgirl!*

Suddenly the neighbor's German Shepherd began barking loud enough to wake the whole neighborhood. *Hmmm, I remember Bruno barked last night about this time.* Maxie glanced at her clock to see the time. *One thirty. I wonder . . .*

Wrapping her robe around her, she reached for her weapon, quietly went down the hall and out the back door. She couldn't see much but Bruno rattled the chain-link fence as he fiercely barked at something or someone. She saw shadows moving. There was somebody near the back yard gate. She saw a shadow move away from the back fence. The big dog quit barking and the night was suddenly uncomfortably silent. Maxie made a dash to the front of the house. She saw an old car pull away from the curb. When it shot passed her drive, she could have sworn that the car was a green, or maybe black, a Buick?

Her heart leaped in her throat as she realized that this could have been the killer coming back to get Megan. The dog probably scared him off.

Lord, please protect my daughter! She prayerfully pleaded and hurried into the house to check on her daughter and double check the doors and windows. She breathed a sign when she found her beautiful little girl sleeping peacefully. *Thank God!* She leaned over to kiss the soft forehead. Megan turned slightly and nestled down to finish her night.

After a time Maxie grew numb. As she began to drift off to the land of nod, the alarm sounded and she almost jumped out of bed. She had been dozing about an hour and half.

While she lay on her back trying to bring life to her sleepy brain, the pierce ringing of the phone suddenly had her wide awake. Maxie quickly grabbed the receiver so the ringing wouldn't disturb her sleeping daughter.

She spoke softly into the phone, "This is the sheriff." Maxie sat up in the bed.

She listened as the owner of the German Shepherd said, "Maxie, this is Floyd, your neighbor down the street. My dog is dead! I think he has been poisoned. I wanted to call you to alert the neighborhood. The SOB that does things like this needs to be caught. I don't want a child or another animal to be poisoned. Bruno was family!"

"My sympathies to you and your wife. I know Bruno was like a member of your family. I'll spread the word. Leave the animal where he lies, Floyd. I'll call someone to come and pick his up to determine the cause of death. Thanks for reporting this to me. Again, let me say, I am sorry."

Floyd was upset but not nearly as much as Maxie was. To think that the killer had the gall to come back to the scene within twenty-four hours of the murder and kill an innocent animal. She just knew that he have been coming in search of Megan. *Bill Sullivan, I'm scared! I need you . . .*

The results of the test showed a beef steak loaded with a deadly strychnine poison, found in the dead animal's body.

That cinched it! Bruno died at the hands of the murderer! He had to be the killer . . . didn't he? A lump came up in Maxie's throat thinking that he came back to the same location two nights in a row. What would prevent him from returning once more? She prayed the murderer would not come back for Megan. She shivered at the thought. *I don't think I'll ever sleep again! Butch Rafferty, I'm going to get you . . . and soon,* she swore.

Maxie sent Charlee to warn the neighborhood about the killings. She didn't think the man would be back to destroy any dogs, but she had to put everyone on the alert. It was better to be cautious.

Megan went to school reluctantly that morning and at her mom's insistence.

"Megan, you have to go on with your daily activities. If you stay home, you could be playing into the killer's hands. You are safer with people around you, hon. Trust me."

219

Megan dressed hurriedly so that her Mom could drop her off at junior high on her way to the office. Her mother noticed the dark circles under her eyes. *Bless her, I'm afraid she isn't getting enough sleep either.*

Maxie drove to the office in a pensive mood. She made coffee and sat down to try and enjoy a cup. The phone rang just as she was about to take her first sip. She jumped, spilling the hot liquid on her brown pant's leg, burning her leg. "Damn it!" Maxie said as she swiped the spill and grabbed the receiver.

"Hello. This is the sheriff." She was curt.

"I know who killed the dog, Sheriff," the muffled voice said.

Butch figured he had a brilliant plan to get the sheriff out of the way so he could do his next deed.

"Who is this?" Maxie questioned.

"A friend."

"I need a name and a phone number."

"You can meet me outside of town. I don't want nobody to see me. There is an old shack in the woods off Valley Road 506. Come alone." The man hung up before she could get any more details.

Maxie had an eerie feeling about the caller. She reasoned that if he did know who killed the dog, then he might know who the killer was as well. She had to follow up on it. This could be the break they had been waiting for.

Neither Jack nor Charlee were on duty. Maxie decided to drive out and check with the caller. She left a brief note on her desk saying where she would be and quietly left the building.

It took about ten minutes to get to the narrow road, which was little more than a cow trail. The ruts were deep and hard. *Apparently, this road is traveled very little.*

She saw the shack up ahead, surrounded by trees. It could be easily overlooked because the unpainted walls blended into the brush and tall weeds.

The place looks unoccupied, no vehicle, no cats or dogs milling around. Surely, there isn't anyone living here. The front porch is barely standing. I wonder who owns this property? Maxie was thinking as she looked around the property. She saw a shadow cross the room, passing the filthy window. She very slowly put her right hand on the butt of her weapon.

"Anybody home? This is the sheriff. I'm here to follow up on a call you made," she yelled.

The killer was watching her closely. He stood very still, holding his sore glass-riddled hand up close to his chest and gripping a long-bladed knife with the other hand.

"My god! The sheriff is the lady whose lawn I mowed. Damn, it was her daughter I been following around. Hell! She messed me up! Butch scrunched up in a corner, not moving. His anger surfaced and his face turned beet red. The man was rattled.

Maybe she will go away. I can't believe I was going to kill the sheriff's kid. Stupid! Wait! Hey, that is brilliant! I'll take care of the mother first then my way will be clear to get the kid. Butch almost laughed out but quickly covered his mouth with his fist.

Maxie looked around the house for movement. She could detect a foul odor, either coming from the house or from behind. *Something dead, for sure.* She gagged.

Suddenly a horrible feeling of evil lurking nearby washed over her. She tended to pay close attention to her gut feelings. She would be back later with a deputy. As she turned to leave, she was sure somebody was watching her. She whirled around with gun in hand and saw nothing there. She holstered the weapon, climbed into her truck and drove away. Something was bothering her about the whole scene.

She parked at the courthouse and glanced at her watch. She wanted to check some tax records to learn the owner of the property she had just visited. *It's another hour until the courthouse opens.*

Maxie remembered the tax appraisal office, down the street, unlocked their door in five minutes. She drove to the County Tax Appraiser's office and sat quietly in her vehicle, thinking over last night's incident with the dog and the creepy feeling she had when she drove out to the little shack on Valley Road.

Her thoughts shifted to more pleasant things and she smiled to herself, *come home, Bill Sullivan, come home. I miss you . . . What would it be like to be his wife, to have Bill come home to me every day, like normal people? Nice,* was a good word to describe it. *Very nice!*

When Maxie entered the building, she was cordially greeted by employees of the tax office The sheriff was a frequent visitor.

The girl at the counter took the information Maxie gave her and turned to her computer. A map of the county came up on the screen. Maxie gave her a general location off Valley Road. It was a few minutes before the clerk came up with what Maxie supposed was the property the little shack stood on. Then the clerk took the survey name and pulled up the tax rolls.

"Maxie, this little plot of ground belongs to Bessie Hallmark. She hasn't paid her last year's taxes on the property. You may have to evict her, sooner or later."

"Does she have a family? More than likely she is an elderly woman. Right?" Maxie questioned the clerk. She had only limited personal information about the woman.

"I think I remember that she has a son. I do remember the rumor that his Pa beat on him a lot when he was a kid. He was a weird one. Quiet, though, he never said much. I think he went to prison for something or other. That is about all I know, Sheriff."

"Thanks for that tidbit of information. You have been very helpful."

The office door opened to two people coming in to check on some tax property. Maxie left after a brief greeting to the couple.

Is there a possible chance that the shack is the home of our killer? Why would he call my office? What was he up to? Maxie pondered all these questions as she drove back into town. She spoke, "What was that awful odor? Where was Bessie Hallmark? Was she in the house alone, perhaps dead? Who made the call to the SO?" Many unanswered question skimmed through her mind as she drove to the office.

Everything was in a tizzy for a few minutes after her arrival. There had been a robbery overnight and the police radios were going hot and heavy. Maxie flopped into her chair. A tired feeling washed over her body. She knew she needed some sleep.

What I need most of all is a man to take me into his arms and love my troubles away, she thought as she massaged the tense muscles in her neck. *Bill? Why do you keep coming into my thoughts? Am I becoming addicted to you?* Quickly, she shoved those thoughts away and dove into the paper work on her desk.

In the late afternoon, Jack came into the office. He looked worried as he sat in the chair beside the sheriff's desk and said, "Boss, you look tired. Didn't sleep, huh? Neither did I?"

He sipped a cup of hot, but stale, coffee. In a minute he glanced up into the sad eyes of a worried woman.

"Jack, I can't sleep or eat. I'm telling you the truth, this killer has me going in circles. My mother instincts tell me to get Meggie and leave the country, but, I know as the sheriff of this county, I have a job to do. My obligations to both have me torn to pieces."

"Now, Max, don't let this killer get the upper hand here. We will get him and soon." Jack stated and tried to reassure the lady sitting across from him. He was concerned about her . . . and her daughter.

His boss breathed a sigh and said, "Oh, by the way, Jack, I had a strange call today from a man who stated that he knew who had killed the German Shepherd. Can you beat that? It was weird. I got the address and drove to this old tumbled down shack on Valley Road. When I got out of my vehicle, I could swear I saw somebody walk by the window. It was dirty and maybe I just imagined it. Anyway, I called out that I was the sheriff and had received a call about the dog. Everything was quiet and still. I got **that** feeling. It washed over me—like a wave of evil. Then I noticed a strong smell of death and decay. It was so putrid, I thought I was going to be sick. My first instinct was to come back with some backup. I didn't see a vehicle of any kind and no pets roaming around. Someone was in there. I'm sure of that."

"You did the right thing, boss. Me and Charlee can go back out there and check it out. No reason you have to do it. You stay here and rest, you hear." Jack's concern for her was apparent.

"No way. I'll not send my two best deputies, and friends, out to a place from hell." she protested adamantly.

"Well, aren't you a stubborn lady!" Jack grinned as he continued, "What are we waiting for.? Let's do it!"

It was late afternoon when the two vehicles entered the rough drive at the house on Valley Road. Everything was eerily calm and quiet. The sun was just dipping below the treetops. Soon the darkness would blanket the area where the unknown lurked.

Maxie's adrenaline began to kick in as she got out of her vehicle and waited for her two best deputies, Jack and Charlee, to back her up. Maxie wasn't aware that her followers had their pistols in hand as they walked a step or so behind and on each side of her.

She approached the unpainted door, picking her way across the rotted porch floor and knocked loudly. The three of them were silent for a short time, listening closely for any sounds that might indicate a presence inside the house. Nothing. Maxie grabbed the doorknob and pushed. The door swung open. It startled her but she quickly recovered and looked into the sparsely furnished room.

"This is the sheriff! If you are in here, come out with your hands over your head," she ordered. *Better to be safe than sorry.*

"I'm here in response to a call you made this morning about the dog . . . Is there anyone at home?" Maxie's hand rested on her weapon and she realized it was shaking. She quickly stifled her feeling of uneasiness. *I'm in charge here!*

She listened for any sound coming from the house and decided that there wasn't anyone inside. Jack and Charlee entered the room, before she had time to push in ahead.

They searched for movement of any kind and finding none, they continued into the house.

"You know we don't have a warrant to enter this property, don't you, Jack?"

"Appears to be uninhabited to me?" Jack said avoiding her question.

They searched the three rooms quickly. Not able to find anything of importance, they decided to leave.

Jack, who had caught the decaying odor before they entered the house, now went to the back of the house to track it down. He found a lawn mower pushed up against the house. Hidden in the tall grass were car tracks and an oily spot that Jack assumed was from a leaking oil pan. The carcass of a lifeless yellow cat lay near a mound of earth.

"Hummm. I wonder what is buried there? The mound is too big for an animal. Besides, he didn't even bury the cat, which is small."

"Max, come out here for a second, please Ma'am." he yelled.

She stuck her head out the door, holding her nose with her thumb and forefinger. "What is it? My gosh, how can you stan' it! Smel' like sometin' dead."

Jack looked up at his boss and grinned, but it failed to meet his eyes. "Boss, this mound is big enough for human remains."

Maxie's mouth fell open. "You think there is a body buried on this property? Good Lord!"

Her hand dropped to her side. She frowned when she glanced around and saw the dead cat nearby.

"What kind of person would do that?" Charlee, standing in the back door, asked.

"Come on, Jack, let's get a warrant and do this legally. Do you think we may be lucky enough to have the murderer?"

"Sheriff, you are right. We need that warrant." Jack said as he took the elbow of his friend, and boss, ushering her to the front of the old house. She looked pale.

The sheriff was angry and Maxie refused to acknowledge the fear that she felt.

Maxie sat in her truck and waited for Jack and Charlee to back their vehicle out of the drive. As she watched the sun drop below the horizon, she felt a sense of urgency, *I have to get home to Meggie!*

As she drove away she made a call to the judge for a warrant that she serve early the next morning.

After reporting to Jack, she had to go home and check on Megan. She had a terrible feeling again that something was wrong. *Dear Lord, protect my child. Don't let anything happen to her.* This prayer was repeated over and over as she quickly sped to her residence.

She parked in the street rather than the driveway. The house was quiet. She didn't find any lights on as she tiptoed passed the bright blue planter to the front door. Placing her ear against the door, she listened. She thought she could hear words, softly spoken.

Something isn't right about this! She was alarmed. Her senses clicked on alert, as her hand automatically went to her weapon. She tried the doorknob and found it unlocked. As she pushed it open, she quietly stepped inside. Max stood still and listened.

Megan wouldn't leave the front door unlocked. Maxie heard the CD was playing softly in the background. She started down the hallway, her steps muffled by the soft beige carpeting. Megan's door was closed. Maxie listened for a moment. She didn't know whether to burst into the room or not. If Meggie was there alone, it would scare her to death for her Mom to enter the room with her weapon drawn.

"Megan, are you in there? It's Mom; I'm home."

Several seconds passed before Maxie heard the click of the lock and a frightened little girl fell into her mother's arms, sobbing her heart out. Maxie could see her daughter was scared.

"Mom, I though I heard a noise. So I just ran to my room and locked the door, hoping nobody bad was coming in. It was so quiet. Then I heard some other noise like someone walking down the hall. I kept telling myself it was you, but I didn't hear the garage door open or anything." "I'm so glad that you are home, Mom. It was creepy!"

Maxie hugged her little girl to her bosom, comforting her and rubbing a hand down Megan's long, silky red hair. Maxie was trying to soothe herself as well as her daughter.

"Honey, I was worried when I found the front door unlocked. Did you forget?" Maxie inquired.

"It was unlocked? Oh, Mom, I didn't know, I swear." Megan pulled away from her mother's embrace and looked into the concerned eyes, as clutched her chest visibly distressed. "Mom, I am so sorry. I would swear on a stack of Bibles that it was locked!"

"Wait here, Sweetie. Let me check around in the house to be sure its safe. You stay right here and lock your door." Maxie quietly left the room and crept down the dark hallway to her own room, glancing inside with her drawn gun in hand. She flipped the light switch and a comforting glow flooded the room. She hurried to the connecting bath and peeked inside.

*Nobody is here. A*s she entered the room, she was aware of the odor of body sweat and filth. *That smell! It smells exactly like the inside of that old house on Valley Road.*

Of God, he has been in my house! Her hand began to shake.

Stay calm, Max, she firmly told herself as she tiptoed to the closed shower curtain and jerked it aside, expecting to find the subject standing there. She breathed a sigh when it was vacant. Her heart was pounding so hard she felt sure that anyone close to her could hear it. However, she continued the search of the house, checking closets and finding nothing. The horrible smell still lingered throughout the house. *It makes me feel unclean. My space has been defiled! Will I ever feel safe again?*

As Maxie went from room to room, she was convinced someone had been inside but was gone. She found little comfort in that. After checking the hall closet, she returned to Megan's room and knocked gently on the door.

"Meg, its Mom. You can unlock the door now, honey."

"Did you find anything, Mom?" Megan tearfully asked.

"Not a thing. Lets go find something to eat and put this incident aside. With all the stuff going on, I guess we are running scared." Maxie attempted to reassure her child as they walked down the hall to the pleasant little kitchen.

"Mom, I'm old enough to know the truth and I recognized the odor as we came down the hall. Its a stinky body odor . . . Be honest with me. I need to know. This is my home, too." She had a worried expression on her pale face etched with fear.

"Well, I, too, smelled a foul odor. However, I couldn't see anything disturbed or out of place. Maybe some kid came in to steal something." Megan was not comforted by that statement . . . and.well, neither was Maxie.

Maxie walked around the kitchen, heated up a bowl of noodle soup. Megan made a sandwich and fixed a glass of iced peach tea for her mother. She poured a cool glass of milk for herself. Both of them were thoughtful as they sat down on the barstool and nibbled at the plate of food in front of them.

Suddenly, Maxie rose, went to the pantry, took out a can of flower scented air freshener and began deodorizing the rooms and baths throughout the house.

"Maybe that stuff will help get rid of the horrible smell, Meggie," she said as she stuffed the spray can back into its slot. She smiled as she added, "We may think we are eating flowers though. Either way, my appetite is gone."

"I know, Mom. It hard to believe a person can't afford a bar of soap and bathe once a day or so. It is totally disgusting. There are a few kids at school like that. How can they stand themselves?" Megan questioned. Maxie silently wondered about that herself.

"Megan, you must be extra cautious. Be sure you lock the door every time you come in and every time you leave the house. I'll double check the windows myself as well."

Maxie sat toying with her spoon. *I know someone came into our home. Maybe just a bum looking for food. Funny thing, nothing seems to have been disturbed. I didn't find anything missing either. It isn't like Meg to forget to lock the door.* Maxie wore the look of a worried mother.

Megan was quick to pick it up. She sat quietly studying her Mom's expression. *Mom is trying to hide it from me but I can tell she is really upset about this.*

"I can see you are upset, Mom, can we talk about what is bothering you?" Megan questioned her mother quietly.

"There are a lot of things going on at work . . . all right, its concerning the murder cases. Are you satisfied?" Maxie grinned at her inquisitive daughter.

She is growing up to fast.

"Thanks for sharing that, Mom." Megan picked up the spoon and began slowly eating the noodles from her bowl. "This is good but I'm not very hungry."

"Drink your milk. I'll put half the sandwich in a baggie. You may get hungry later." She bagged half of her own as well. "Would you eat some rocky road ice cream?"

"I don't think so right now, maybe later." Megan picked up her dishes, rinsed and placed them in the dishwasher.

She turned to her mother and said, "I think I'll go to my room and listen to my CD for a while." She left the room and looked as if she was carrying the whole world's burden on her thin shoulders.

Maxie busied herself around the kitchen, thinking about her day and about her daughter.

Bill, I wish you were here right this minute. I would let you love me all night long. I just need your strong arms to hold me . . . Darn! I have come to depend on that man too much, haven't I? Maxie questioned her judgement in doing so. As she placed dirty dishes in the dishwasher, added the liquid detergent and started the wash cycle, she was surprised to realize that she was thinking of Bill and not about Matt. *That's a first!*

The shrill ringing of the phone startled her. She hurried to answer and the man of her thoughts spoke softly in her ear, "Hi there, Sexy. Do you miss me?"

"Oh, Bill, of course I miss you. Its too quiet around here."

"Are you telling me that I am a loud mouth, woman?" He said, teasing the girl he loved.

"That's not what I meant," she protested.

"Now, just what do you mean?"

"All right, I miss you like crazy. There, are you satisfied?"

"Well, I guess that will have to do for now. Soon, lady sheriff, you will have to come up with a little stronger statement than that. Otherwise, this old Texas Ranger will be out of here!"

"Is that a threat, Bill?" She teased him.

"Nope, just the facts, Ma'am."

Maxie felt it was time to change the subject so they discussed a few general topics. She finally asked the question she had wanted to from the beginning, "When are you coming home?"

I like the sound of that. Home. Bill replied, "I may be here a week or longer. In fact, my boss is talking about pulling me off your case and sending someone else when needed. I'm trying to hold my own. I told Rick that I knew all the facts in your case there so I needed to be the one to return to finish it up. You know what he said? 'That Lady Sheriff has gotten to you, hasn't she?' I had to admit he was right on the money. Rick grinned that know-it-all grin, walked out of the room, shaking his shinny bald head and muttering under his breath.

Maxie giggled like a little girl, "Serves you right for wearing your heart on your sleeve, Cowboy." If she admitted it, she was thrilled that he cared enough about her to tell his co-workers.

"Bill, something happened today that scared me witless."

"What, Max? Tell me about it." His low voice was laced with concern.

"I am pretty sure someone broke into my house. I can't find anything out of place or missing but there was a very repugnant body odor lingering in the house. You know I had a feeling something was wrong before I came home. I got here quickly, parked in the street in case there was someone inside and found the front door **unlocked!** After all the stuff going on in this county, I know Meg would remember to lock the door when she got home."

"Of course, she would! Our Meg is a very responsible young lady, Max. Tell me, is she all right?" Bill wished he were there with Max and Meg.

"As fine as she can be, under the circumstances. Meggie said she was in her room when she heard a noise in the house. The garage door rattles enough to alert her when I'm driving in. That wasn't what she heard so Meggie locked her bedroom door and turned up the stereo. It wasn't long before I got here. As I said, I had a bad feeling and rushed home to check on her. When I saw the front door was unlocked, I proceeded with caution and even drew my weapon. I was that sure that someone was inside."

"Oh, Bill, I was so scared that something had happened to my little girl," Maxie was on the verge of a tearful outburst and was unable to continue.

"Honey, nothing happened. Let's be thankful for that . . . Max, I'm coming down tonight! I can't take not being there to protect you. Just tell me that you and Meg will be okay until I get there. Maybe you need to call Jack or Charlee to come and stay with you until I arrive. It will take me two to three hours, if I am lucky."

"That would be wonderful, Bill, but I can't ask you to put your job in jeopardy for me. I'll call Charlee and see if she can come over or maybe we can just go to her apartment and crash. Don't worry about us."

Maxie's last statement did nothing to reassure Bill. *It's my job to worry. It's even more my responsibility to protect you and Meg,* he thought.

"Max, I'm coming. Do you hear?" Bill was very firm and his words comforted her.

"Oh, Bill, I'm so glad . . . I'll see you soon?"

"I'll be there as soon as I can. You take care of yourself and our little girl now," he said softly. As he hung up the receiver, Bill was already rising from his office chair, getting ready to go to the woman he loved.

An hour later Maxie and Megan had thrown a few things together and were on their way to Charlee's apartment building. Both sat quietly with various thoughts running through their heads. Maxie drove up to the apartment and parked. She turned to Megan and gave her a little smile that failed to reach her serious green eyes.

"It will be okay, Mom. Our ranger will be here soon . . . I'm so glad. Bill makes me feel safe."

Maxie turned to her daughter and replied, "Yes, Sweetie, he makes me feel protected too."

Charlee was pleased to have unexpected overnight guests although she showed a real concern for the two after she heard the full story. She told them they were welcome to stay as long as they needed.

After they settled Megan on the small cot in Charlee's alcove, the two ladies sat at the bar, drinking warm cocoa and quietly discussing the murders and their visit to the old house on Valley Road. More than ever, Maxie was sure someone broke into her home. Charlee didn't want to believe that had happened. She realized the stress the boss and her daughter had been under.

Is there a connection between the intruder, the killer and that old house? Who is the damn murderer? Charlee pondered.

Chapter 24

The house Butch visited earlier in the day was now dark and quiet. *I have a surprise for you, little girl. Sorry, you ain't gonna like it much. I won't make the same mistake this time and get into the wrong house, or room. It was that damn dog's fault! He won't cause me no more trouble though. Took care of that one, I did. I know which house it yours, girlie, and where your room is located. You locked the door but I knew it was you in there, all scared and everything. I coulda had you then, if your Mammy hadn't showed up. It's all her fault! That damn woman sheriff! She searched around but didn't find me. I could smell her perfume when she stepped into the bathroom and looked behind the shower curtain. Yep, she thought she had me!*

Stupid bitch! While you two girls were in the kitchen, I crept out the back way. You didn't even think to look in the tiny dirty clothes closet right behind you. I was as quiet as a little mouse, sitting scrunched up there. While I waited, found a pair of silky panties. When I rubbed them across my face, I got your scent. Yum! You're sure to miss a pair of them sexy things, 'cause I got 'em. They feel nice rubbing lightly against my balls right now. He touched his crotch, massaged the evidence of his desire against the soft silky panty. It was time to go to work, do the deed and then he would welcome the relief when he spewed his seed inside the silk underwear. The killer got hot thinking about the warm blood dripping out, much like his own sexual body fluids would.

Butch Rafferty crept to the side of the house, where he took his knife out and worked the blade around the edge of the window. He prized and prodded. It was stuck! *Damn thing may be locked. Shit! What are you going to do now, Butch?* He asked himself. He quietly crept around to the rear of the house and tried the door. The screen door was latched but that wasn't a deterrent. Butch took his long bladed knife, slit an eight-inch hole and slipped his hand inside, lifting the latch. He tried the doorknob and found it locked, just as he had expected. It was darker in the back but an alley light down the way gave him enough light to work by. He pulled out a few small tools and began working at the lock. Before long the door swung wide.

He grinned. *People are so stupid. They think that a locked door or window will keep me out. I'm too smart for them. Now, down the hall on the right will be my pleasure spot. Here I come, red.*

As he started down the hall, he pulled on the rubber gloves and the ski mask. With the huge knife in his hand, he was ready. His sexual urges surfaced. They always did when he prepared to commit murder. It was a high like no other. The mere act of plunging the knife into his victim and feeling the warm sticky blood flow out of the body was a turn-on. He, Butch Rafferty, was once more in control. That was the way he liked it.

He stepped into the bedroom of the little red-haired female he had followed around for weeks now. A small amount of moonlight filtered through the shade. Suddenly, he realized the bed was empty!

Don't panic, man! He cautioned, *don't panic. Maybe she is sleeping with her maw. Maybe I can do both of them? That woman has a gun! Shit! I'll take the mama first and then the little girl. Yeah! I can do that. I am Butch, the man!*

The killer quietly tiptoed out of the room and made his way down the hall to the next bedroom. He walked stealthily over to the bed, finding it empty as well. Anger began to boil in his head as he ran his gloved hand across the center of the bed, unable to believe that he couldn't find a body, he swore loudly, "Damn!"

The man continued checking throughout the house. He was not able to comprehend the fact that there was no one at home. Then he lost control and began grinding his teeth, as he starting slashing the sofa and chairs. Slinging his arms back and forth, he continued stabbing into pillows in frustration. He groaned as he kicked over the television causing a loud crash

I gotta get out of here!

The crazed man in black ran out the back door and down the alley, removing his ski mask as he ran. He was angry with himself and the whole world at this point. He observed a porch light come on at the house next door and ducked behind the shrubs. His heart was beating furiously, his face was crimson as he hurried to the Buick.

You won't get away with this, you lousy broad! I'll get you for this. You can't continue to mess up my life. All this is your fault, bitch!

As he jumped into the car, he noticed that he still had his knife in his hand, sharp and ready to do its job. In anger and frustration, he plunged it into the fleshy part of his right thigh. Pain was overcome by the pleasure as the warm blood oozed from the wound. Removing the gloves, he pulled the knife free and hurriedly unzipped his soiled trousers. He rubbed lightly across the silk underwear feeling his erect manhood. Reaching inside, his hand found the release he sought. Time stood still for few minutes. Although his groaning could be heard, his emotions were more from the pleasure than pain.

When he became aware of the blood flowing from his leg, he grabbed a shop rag and tied it around his leg. *You bitch! Look what you made me do! Now I gotta go to the emergency room and get my damn leg stitched up. Damn that lady sheriff and her brat. It's their fault that I am in this shape. I'll get you yet!* He threatened as he drove away.

It was about 2:00 a.m. When Bill drove into the driveway at Maxie's house. There were no lights on. After checking the garage and finding it empty, he decided he would go to the All-Nite Café and get something to eat. If Maxie was at Charlee's, she was probably asleep. He drove by the apartment complex and saw her vehicle parked there. He noticed a light in a window.

I suppose the poor girl can't sleep after what happened. What the heck! I've got to see her so I can settle my mind that she is all right.

Bill parked across the street and found his way to the intercom. He buzzed in and a soft voice asked, "Who is it?"

"It's Bill Sullivan. Please, let me in." The voice he heard sounded like Max but it was so weak.

"It's Max, come on up, Bill," came a welcoming reply.

Bill climbed the stairs, taking two at a time, and softly knocked on the door of the apartment. His knuckle had barely made contact when the door opened up and the redhead flew into his arms, locking him in her embrace. She muttered endearments that he thought he would never hear and coming from the woman who had become the most important thing in his life. For a few minutes they just stood there embracing, savoring the physical contact and comfort of one another.

Bill pushed Maxie away from him long enough to kick the door shut. He gathered her slim body in his arms and he gave her the kiss she longed for. *Lordy, she feels so good in my arms. We fit together perfectly.* He pressed her back close to his heart and whispered words in the language of love.

Finally, Maxie stepped away. Bill saw that she was wearing that extra large, faded tee shirt that barely covered her cute rear end. *Sexy woman!*

"I missed you, Bill. You know you've shook up my life and now I am not sure that I can ever live without you!"

A serious expression crossed Bill's face, "Please, Darling, don't try! Let's get married and put an end to our suffering. I need you, Max. I need you today, tomorrow and forever. Will you consent to take me on as your equal partner in life? I love you, Honey, and you know I love Meg like my own daughter. Truly, I do. What do you say?"

Without hesitation, Maxie said, "Yes!" The weary look on her face disappeared for an instant. "We have a lot of things to discuss, Bill."

The remaining early hours were spent eating breakfast. They were wired after drinking a gallon of coffee. As Bill and Maxie discussed their future together, they managed to slip in a few kisses. Somehow, they put aside all the present anxieties and were able to think about their lives together.

Charlee roused and heard voices. She came to the end of the short hall to see what was going on. As she stuck her head around the corner, she saw the couple cuddled up on the sofa having a serious conversation. She shook her head, smiled and went back to bed.

Today is my day off! I'm taking it, Charlee thought as she snuggled down for a little more shut-eye.

The sun rose slowly and as it shone in the living area of a small apartment, a man and woman could be seen clutching one another on the sofa. Bill's head rested on the back while Maxie's lay on his broad chest. They were together and enjoying a short nap before their day began. Maxie opened her eyes slowly and looked up at Bill to see if he was awake. He grinned down at her.

"Good morning, Darling. Short night, huh?" Bill asked.

As Maxie rose to a sitting position she exclaimed, "I feel like I've been hit by a truck. What did you do to me, Cowboy?" She teased him, got up to stretch showing all her curves and that sexy, round bottom shrouded with a bright purple pair of undies. Her firm breasts stretched the knit fabric giving a good view to those brown nipples that were outlined behind the white cloth. Bill knew what they felt like in his hands—soft and pliable. He grew hot and hard watching this woman and remembering the smell and feel of her.

I can't believe she will soon be my wife! He smiled that sexy smile that said much more than words.

A look of surprise came across the woman's face. *I must look a fright but not so bad that I can't turn on the savage beast in him.* She gave him a smile that he would walk ten miles to see and with a flip of her long red hair, she marched down the hallway to the bath.

Bill sat and watched her swaying hips until they disappeared. *I've got it bad!*

Chapter 25

After Maxie had showered and dressed for the day, she suggested they drive by her house and pick up a few things. Megan was spending the day following Charlee around as she ran errands.

As soon as Bill and Maxie drove into her driveway, she felt that something was not right. They found the front door locked like she left it. However, when she unlocked and opened it wide, she could see all the damages that were apparent—broken television, slashed sofa and chairs.

"Oh, my Lord!" she exclaimed as her eyes traveled around the room, which was a destructive mess, to say the least. Maxie was heartsick.

Bill put his arm around Max, wanting desperately to make her feel better. There was no way he could do that at the moment. Her home had been invaded and defiled. About all he could do was to be there for her-a cushion for her to fall back on. She was going to need that. She was in shock right now, and, he realized, very angry. There was fire in those furious, green eyes.

"I'll get him! When I do, I may just shoot the bastard. How dare he come into my home and tear up my furniture and mess up my life! How dare he!" Maxie shouted angrily as she stomped her foot like a small, defiant child.

"Let's go, Bill. I'm picking up a warrant for Butch Rafferty's ass, also, a search warrant for his place this morning and I'm ready to serve it." She hurried out the front door. Bill lengthened his stride to catch up with her. He speculated that this was a woman with a purpose and he smiled. He rather liked that.

"Max, calm down. You're in no mood to confront the bastard. Leave your vehicle here and ride with me. I don't really want you out of my sight today. I agree that enough is enough," he said trying in a small way to reassure her that he was there for her. She needed to be clear-headed when, and, if she confronted the killer face to face.

They drove to the judge's house to pick up the warrants to be served and called Jack for backup at the Valley Road residence. It was barely daylight when they drove up to the house. There were no lights visible and they were greeted with total silence.

Hell, there is probably no electricity anyway! "What a dump! Max, are you sure somebody actually lives here?" Bill questioned.

"Well, we're sure that somebody stays here part of the time. There was a dead cat at the back. You know animals don't hang around without food. Although, there were no outward signs of injury, I have a gut feeling that this nut killed the cat. Doesn't that follow the pattern of our killer? First, they kill animals and then move on to bigger things. I swear there is a grave at the back of the house. We have people coming in to excavate today, so we will know soon. I suspect we will find a body." Maxie had gotten control of her anger but it was evident that it lay right below the surface of her business-like manner. She was all Sheriff and very much in control at the moment.

"Max, let me go in first." Bill begged.

"Hell, no! I'm the sheriff in this county and I'm going to serve a warrant on this bastard." She opened the door of the truck and jumped to the ground. With warrants in one hand and a drawn weapon in the other, she cautiously approached the house. The ranger was close behind her. His all-seeing eyes scanned the perimeter of the place. He noted no movement or sounds. The Indian in him made him extra sensitive to his surroundings. *I just don't like this!*

As they neared the house, they heard a vehicle pull in behind their own. Bill turned swiftly and noted it was a sheriff's unit. Maxie never took her eyes off the place. Bill whispered to her that her backup had arrived. She only nodded.

Deputy Jack Rankin hurried up to the couple and whispered that he was taking the rear of the house. Bill saw that Charlee was behind Jack. She walked quietly up beside her boss and told Max that Megan was at home with Mary Bell, the receptionist. Jack crept around one side of the house with his gun drawn, while Charlee eased around the opposite direction checking bushes and waving her Glock to and fro. There was a lot of tension in the air, which was normal in a situation like this. Nobody knew what to expect. Nerves were on edge. Maxie could almost hear her own heart pounding as her adrenaline pumped up.

The sheriff stepped up onto the dilapidated wooden front porch. She knocked loudly on the door and moved quickly to one side. The ranger planted himself on the other side of the doorway.

"This is the sheriff. I have a warrant for your arrest and a warrant to search your place. Put down your weapons and come out with your hands up." Maxie shouted with authority.

Inside, the shouting awoke Butch from a sound sleep. He hurriedly got to his feet, slipped on a pair of dirty shorts, and grabbed his weapon of choice, a five-inch bladed knife. He came fully awake when he realized who was there. *That damn sheriff! She is messing with me again! You're gonna be sorry, bitch! I'll get you! Just you wait and see. But . . . what am I goin' do now? Think! You son-of-a-bitch! You got yourself in a fix.* He hobbled over to peer out the front window.

He was aggravated at himself, "Damn idiot! You just had to stab yourself in the leg. It took five stitches in the emergency room. Now, look at you!"

He was mulling over his mistakes. *It's that bitch's fault, 'cause I needed that little girl's blood but got my own. She had the gall to leave her house. That lady sheriff is a damn nuisance and a coward. I can take her on, if that's what she wants. Come and get it, red!* Butch wanted to shout the words but struggled to remain silent.

He stood on his good leg beside the bedroom door and waited. The sheriff shouted again, "Lay down your weapons and come out with your hands behind your head . . . We're coming in on the count of three."

Damn, she has somebody with her! Maybe she's smarted than I thought.

Butch groaned as he crouched down behind the bedroom wall, peered around the doorway and waited. He raked his shaky hand through his tangled hair. His head hurt and his thigh ached.

His face grew crimson as his anger and fear kept building with each minute that passed. *I'm gonna kill that woman if it's the last damn thing I do!* This was his final thought before the front door crashed in and he heard what sounded to him like a dozen people running in from every direction.

There was a lot of yelling, "Put down your weapon, raise your hands and come out into the open. Now!"

Another female voice screamed, "Put your hands on your head."

Butch was outnumbered and he knew it. Could he fight his way out?

My knife is not a good weapon against ten guns. What have I got to loose? If they take me, I'll go back to the pen! Dying would be better than that, wouldn't it? He grabbed for the only hope he had, the lady sheriff, as she came through the bedroom doorway.

Before Maxie knew what was happening, a figure raised from a crouched position and her gun was spinning across the floor where it came to rest near a rickety table. She was aware she had a knife at her throat. Her back rested tightly against Butch's bare chest where he held Maxie against his smelly body. She recognized the odor. It was the same one that lingered in her house. His other arm held a knife against her throat. Quickly she assessed her situation. *No good.* She could taste the bile as it rose to the back of her throat. Maxie gagged.

This man has nothing to lose! He plans to take me down with him. Maxie knew she had to gain control of the situation and fast. Her eyes came to rest on the Texas Ranger. Bill was alert, but not able to control the anger that boiled within. She pled with her eyes for him to stand down.

Rafferty could see three guns pointed in his direction. The sheriff's gun lay across the room where it skidded after Butch had cracked down on her gun arm. One man had run to the doorway but stopped quickly when he saw the knife in Butch's hand and against the woman's throat. That was the Texas Ranger.

"You son-of-bitches, stay right where you are! One move and this little lady gets hers." Butch threatened.

Ranger Sullivan stood perfectly still, as did the two deputies, planning their next move.

"Drop your damn weapons. All of ya! Do it now!" screamed Butch.

The sheriff pled with Butch, "Mr. Rafferty, you don't want to do this. Put your weapon down and let me go. I can help you."

'Help me! Hell, you got me in this fix," he shouted in her ear, squeezing her so tight she could barely breath. When she could manage a short breath she was nauseated and wanted to pass out or throw up all over herself and him.

"I said put them guns down. Do it or I swear, I'll kill the bitch!"

The two deputies saw blood running slowly down Maxie's neck and they lay down their weapons. The ranger lowered his gun but he began to talk to Rafferty in a calm voice, trying to distract him.

"Butch, I know how you're feeling right now. I'm Texas Ranger Bill Sullivan and I have been in situations like this many times before. Put down the knife and let's talk. We can work this out."

Maxie knew Bill well enough to know that he was seething although he managed to cover his feeling pretty well. She was scared! No two ways about it, she was terrified this time.

Stay calm, she told herself, *and think of a way to get out of this. I don't want to get myself killed. I've got to get this situation in hand . . .* She took note of the fact that he continually shifted his weight. *I wonder if he is injured in some way? He keeps shifting his weight. That means most of the time he is putting his weight on his left leg. If I can throw him off balance, hurt him somehow, then I could get out of the way and let Bill take over.*

Maxie spoke to the defendant, "Why did you go into my house and tear everything apart? You did, didn't you? You know that I have never done anything to you." Her voice was soft and soothing.

Butch could feel her body beginning to relax against him. She felt good. His hand pressed tightly under her breast relaxed somewhat. One finger began to rub across her breast. He began to breath harder into her ear.

My god, the pervert is getting turned on by all of this! What kind of man is he? Maxie tried to remain calm. *Don't panic.* She repeated to herself several times. *That's what he is waiting for, a reason to kill me.* This was one of the hardest things she had ever done in her life. She felt the knife cut into her flesh and knew a trickled of blood followed. Right now she was more concerned with getting out of Rafferty's grasp.

She could see the fierce anger in the firey blue eyes of the savage only a few feet away from her. Bill was mad enough to kill the perp! Evidently, he had noticed the sexual tone of the defendant's embrace. Maxie knew she had to act fast! She couldn't stand seeing another person she loved killed in the line of duty. *Better do something now! Be damned if I am going to let him kill me!*

Bill saw the expression on Maxie's face—one of determination. Behind that, he recognized the redhead's temper pushing to the surface. *I almost feel sorry for the bastard!*

As Maxie began slowly rubbing her behind against the man, Butch was surprised and distracted momentarily.

He relaxed his hold on her even more. That's when Maxie poked him in the gut with her elbow and slammed her fist down on his right thigh. The man relaxed and groaned.

She twisted herself from Butch's grasp as he grabbed for his leg, writhing in pain. Maxie managed to get away with only a gash on her arm. Bill was on top of Butch like flies on a buffalo and knocked his weapon away. Jack was right behind him. They both had the killer disarmed and in custody within seconds.

Charlee ran to Maxie to stop the bleeding as she waited for an ambulance. Jack read the defendant his rights, roughly cuffed him and marched him to patrol unit.

Bill hovered over Maxie, holding her close and whispering soothing phrases to her. She was in shock and didn't even realize that she had been hurt. Suddenly, the pain became more evident as her arm burned like fire. Maxie needed to know that Bill was there and that he was all right. She needed him. She relaxed when she became aware that he was beside her.

As she looked into eyes the color of clear blue skies on a summer day, she whispered in a weak voice. "Don't you ever let me go, mister."

His eyes twinkled and some of the concern vanished. "Ma'am, is that a threat? So, what happens if I don't let you go."

"If you aren't careful, you will find yourself roped and hog-tied . . . shackled for life, my friend." Maxie smiled weakly up at him and mouthed the words he

Had waited to hear, "I love you."

At this moment, the ambulance arrived. Maxie grew faint from loss of blood. As she was wheeled out, it was almost as if this was happening to someone else.

Maxie was taken to the hospital for stitches. She had lost blood but the doctor said she would be good as new in a few days. He would keep her in the hospital for a day or so to be sure that she didn't develop an infection from the weapon used. Then she could go home.

Chapter 26

Butch Rafferty was checked over and pronounced healthy enough to go to jail. The emergency room nurse changed the dressing on his thigh. Apparently, it had bled a great deal after Maxie had slammed her fist into it.

Butch hung his head as he was ushered from the emergency room. He was ashamed that he had let a woman get the better of him. He cursed himself for his carelessness. As was usual, he shifted the blame for his circumstances to others, *That damn woman, it's all her fault that I'm here in this jail.*

Six months later.

Maxie sat on the side of the bed, nauseated. *When is the morning sickness going to pass? Damn that big Indian buck!* She slammed her fist into the bed and dashed for the commode, with which she now had a personal relationship. She had forgotten what it felt like to carry a child. The first three months certainly seemed like forever. She grimaced when she remembered being pregnant with Megan and how sick she was the whole nine months.

When she looked in the mirror, she couldn't find her shapely figure anymore. Her twenty-six inch waist was a thing of the past. She hoped that someday she could forget what morning sickness felt like. *Never again!* She weakly grinned as she thought, *wouldn't you know, I would get pregnant our first night together!*

She smiled as she remembered how sweet and gentle Bill had been on their wedding night. Their sex life had certainly stepped up since then. *Not so gentle anymore, eh, my savage hubby? We were so hungry for each other and couldn't get enough of coming together.* She smiled as she remembered the day she told him she was pregnant. Now he was more gentle with his loving. It was almost as if he thought she might break. Bill was certainly proud and happy about the news. Maxie knew that for a fact.

Megan was delighted about the new baby. She had spent several hours suggesting names for her brother or sister. Bill bought her a book of names and the meaning of each. Maxie was delighted that Megan and her stepfather got along so well. Whether this baby was a boy or girl, Maxie knew her family would be complete. Bill had threatened her with "many sons." He claimed it was the "savage way" to produce many warriors. Maxie replied that she thought it was Bill's means of having his way with her, as if he needed an excuse.

Their wedding had been a quiet one in a small country church, just outside the city limits. Their co-workers and a few close friends were the only people attending, other than Maxie's three brothers and her mother. The boys came to check out her choice of a mate, to determine if Bill was good enough for their sister. Fortunately, they got along very well. All were opinionated and strong-willed men so when they were together the conversation was forceful and loud. Each had an opinion, and wanted to his express his point of view. Discussions were heated at times, often to the point of anger. The tense moments were released through a joke or laughter as they teased one another. Bill seemed to fit right in with the boys who were so fond of their sister.

Maxie and her mother, Alice, sat in the kitchen after the wedding and listened to the loud bantering. They smiled at each other. It wasn't long before Megan had entered into one of the heated discussion.

Alice listened quietly for a moment and said, "Megan can hold her own with the boys, can't she? She is getting to be a very pretty young lady. They grow up so fast."

Her mother turned to Maxie and looked into her eyes and asked, "Honey, are you happy? You know, I have hoped and prayed someone special would come along. After Matt died, Max, you boxed up that heart of yours and tied it with a strong rope. I was afraid you couldn't find it in your heart to love someone else." She patted Maxie on the hand. "Matt was a good man. I know that you loved him with all your heart."

Alice paused as she thoughtfully fingered her coffee cup. "Sometimes, I wish I had opened my own heart to another man after your father died. At times, I get so lonely."

Maxie reached across the table and took her mother by the hand. "Mom, perhaps it isn't too late to do that. I didn't think I would let another person get close to me again. It hurt so much when Matt left . . . I've always felt guilty, Mom. I really thought it was my fault that Matt got shot. I called for backup and he came. It was all over so quickly. I was devastated . . . ." Maxie paused thoughtfully.

"Bill came into my life even before Matt was killed. He flirted with me when he was around. I could never see any man but my husband. Besides, Bill had to much respect for Matt to do anything more serious. Bill and I became friends a long time before our feelings became love for one another. I almost let him walk out of my life because I was afraid to make a commitment. Mom, I was scared of getting hurt again. You know when Matt died, I actually promised myself that I would never get involved with another law enforcement officer. Well, here I am. Involved up to my ears! Involved for the rest of my life, Mom. I'll always love Matt and never forget him. He's Meggie's daddy. Sometimes, I wonder if I have a right to feel this way about another man."

Maxie continued. "Mom, do you know the moment that I realized how short life is and I should grab happiness while I had a chance? It was when the killer had me under his power with a knife to my throat. That was my awakening. I looked across the room at Bill and I knew in that moment that he loved me more than his own life. Right then I admitted to myself that I loved him that much as well. I also knew, if I didn't think of something quick, he'd not hesitate to take the perp on and probably get himself killed in the process. That was the reason that I did what I did—to get away. I couldn't lose Bill. I'd rather die first."

Maxie smiled at her mother. "I guess this is the real thing, huh?"

"Could be, daughter. Could be."

After hours of interrogation, the man admitted that his mama was the one in the grave. When he started talking, he couldn't stop. He confessed to the murders of the young teenage girl, the elderly lady next door to Maxie, and other break-in and attempts at murder. He finally admitted that he had stabbed his own mother. As Butch Rafferty put it,

"Mama deserved what she got, after all she put me through as a kid. She wasn't fit to live!"

Butch Rafferty was placed in jail where he awaited trial. The results of the forensics, DNA, on the body in the grave behind the little shack matched Butch's DNA. The officers found other evidence, which was enough to get a guilty verdict.

Butch sat in his prison cell thinking about his future. *Maybe it won't be so bad. I survived prison before and I can do it again. In fact, I bet I could find my own bitch to satisfy my appetites.* His evil laughter could be heard all the way down the hall, causing hair to rise on the back of the necks of cell inmates—a sound that echoed of evil.

After a guilty verdict, his court appointed attorney filed an appeal, to no avail. A year and half later, Butch experienced his ultimate high. He died alone, strapped down on a table in the death chamber, as his veins filled and the lethal fluid which took his life away. At last, his evil appetites were appeased and his tormented soul at rest.